# THE MAN I NEED

**SHANORA WILLIAMS**

**Copyright © 2019 Shanora Williams**

All rights reserved. This paperback is licensed for your personal enjoyment only. This paperback is copyright material and must not be copied, reproduced, transferred, distributed, leased, licensed or publicly performed or used in any form without prior written permission of the publisher, as allowed under the terms and conditions under which it was purchased or as strictly permitted by applicable copyright law. Any unauthorized distribution, circulation or use of this text may be a direct infringement of the author's rights, and those responsible may be liable in law accordingly.

Thank you for respecting the work of this author.

Cover Design by Cover It Designs

Editing By Librum Artis

Cover Image: Wong Sim

Cover Model: Mitchell Wick

Trademarks: This book identifies product names and services known to be trademarks, registered trademarks, or service marks of their respective holders. The author acknowledges the trademarked status in this work of fiction. The publication and use of these trademarks is not authorized, associated with, or sponsored by the trademark owners.

## DUET NOTE

Hey hey! Just a heads up - this is book two of a two-part duet and cannot be read as a standalone. To start from the beginning and to officially meet Mr. Ward, you must start with The Man I Can't have, which can be found on Amazon or my website www.shanorawilliams.com

Reading Order

THE MAN I CAN'T HAVE
THE MAN I NEED

## AUTHOR NOTE

Hey there,

So, if you read *The Man I Can't* have and got to the end, you'll know this duet involves domestic abuse. As many readers stated, it was easy to look over the signs of abuse in book 1, but in book 2 it is not.

This book is a bit grittier, and includes violence, assault, and even rape. It is not as easy of a read as book 1 is, so I do encourage you to proceed with caution, especially if you are or have been a victim of domestic assault, and reading things like this triggers something inside you. I am not a soft writer. I write very raw, real things, and what I've written in this book may be a little too heavy for some people to bare. If you are going through a situation as sensitive as this and need help but don't know where to start, please contact the Domestic Violence Hotline at 1-800-799-SAFE(7233).

If you decide to give this book a go, I really hope you enjoy the rest of this story, and as much as I love Marcel, I

## AUTHOR NOTE

must admit this is most definitely Gabby's story and how she pushes through to fight for her freedom.

Sending love,

Shanora

# PROLOGUE

Will Lewis flips his wrist, checking the time on his watch before focusing on the door of Kyle Moore's office. An impatient sigh falls through his parted lips as he studies the black door.

*What is taking so long?*

Pushing to a stand, Will trots toward the secretary's desk across from him and grabs another Hershey's Kiss from the glass bowl on top of it. The secretary isn't here, but that doesn't surprise him, considering it's a Saturday night. It was the only time slot Kyle Moore had available within the next three months, and Will booked it without question.

As Will stands by the secretary's desk, peeling the aluminum wrapper off the chocolate, he can help overhearing the conversation happening in Kyle's office.

"You need to make something happen soon, Kyle. We have given you more than enough time to prepare for this. If you aren't willing to date, marry, and have children anytime soon, then we will have to turn the company over to Taylor. He has been working for the company just as long as you have, and he already has a child. Your father has gone through a lot lately. The last thing I want him worrying about is his successor. You should be his automatic choice, but you won't be if you don't get your personal life in order. It's always strange to men in this field when a fellow businessman is in his thirties and isn't married. We must continue this family's legacy."

"Why would he give it to Taylor, of all people? That guy doesn't know a damn thing," Kyle snaps.

"Dan wants to keep this company above water. You not being settled, with a family, will make us look bad to other investors, whether you see it that way or not. They won't trust you, but if you marry and have a child soon, who can grow up to take all of this on, things will go a lot smoother for you. Why do you think so many companies have been turning us away? It's not because we aren't making them good offers. No, it's because they don't trust you. You're new to this business and young, and oddly enough, when a man is married, he appears a whole lot wiser."

"That is ridiculous. I can still keep this company running without being married, Mum."

"No, you can't. You have to be trusted, and I don't want this company in the hands of an idiot like Taylor when you are perfectly capable. You must put your pride aside for once and make this happen, Kyle. I can find a potential bride for you, if you want. If not, find a lady you at least like, get to know her, and then move forward." Will notices the woman's voice is closer to the door. Realizing she's likely about to exit, he walks back to his seat. He doesn't hear what they speak about after that, but less than a minute later, the door opens, and an Asian woman walks out. She's dressed elegantly in a black dress with a fur coat. Pearls are in her ears and draped around her neck, her hair pinned up, and not a single strand out of place.

Kyle's mother, Sophon Moore, gives Will a nod of her head as she trots toward the elevator. When she's gone, Kyle calls for Mr. Lewis from his office, and Mr. Lewis hops up, collecting the folder he'd placed on the chair next to him.

"How are you, Mr. Lewis?" Kyle greets Will as he enters the office, walking around his desk and shaking Will's hand.

"Never better. I hope you're doing well."

"Never better. Please sit," Kyle insists, taking the chair behind his desk. "How can I help you?"

Will fumbles with the folder in hand as he lowers in the chair. "Well, as I mentioned in my email to you, I wanted to possibly go over having an investment in my docking business. I am making steady income right now, and with spring coming, the sales will most likely increase. I know that with an investment I can remodel the docks, buy more boats, and open more slots for tourists to dock, which could lead to an easy return of investment if more tourists are attracted to the area. My son is also very good with social media and the SEO thing kids do these days." Will huffs a laugh.

"Where is this docking business located again?" Kyle asks, narrowing his eyes. Will can already tell he hates the idea of it.

"In Fredericksburg, Virginia. Very close to Lake Anna, which gets a lot of visitors during the spring and summer."

"Well, to be frank, I have never invested in a *docking* business before. How would this even be worth my time?"

Will hesitates a second before sliding a sheet of paper

across the desk. "This is the income I made last year from docking and renting boats. It was a good year for—"

"That doesn't answer my question, Mr. Lewis. This business of yours is not what I usually invest in or even buy. I'm usually into corporate things, not self-made, small businesses such as these. Who's to say that I won't lose money doing this? How will I know for sure that remodeling and buying boats won't just put a dent in my pocket? Boats aren't cheap. You do realize that?" Kyle asks, leaning back in his chair as he studies the sheet of paper.

"Well, I can't assure you that it will, but I will do everything in my power to bring in business. Most people spend hours on boats. Some even book hotels so they can enjoy the scenery of Lake Anna. My son and I have come up with a marketing plan and—"

"Okay. I'm going to stop you right there." Kyle holds a firm hand in the air. "I appreciate you taking the time to come and see me, but at the moment, I don't think an investment in your company would be wise for me. I have never done it before, and I'm not up for the risk of losing money at this time. Perhaps if your numbers pick up, then we can chat a little more about it."

Kyle slides the paper back across the desk and Will takes it, disappointed. He stands up and walks to the door but, along the way, he can't help thinking about all of the debt that has piled up for him.

Unexpected expenses and bad weather have caused him to take several loans to keep things afloat. He may end up losing the house if he doesn't act quickly.

"What if I make a deal with you?" Will asks before he walks out the door.

Kyle looks up with a quirked brow. "What kind of deal?"

Will turns back around, clutching the papers in hand. "I couldn't help overhearing your mother earlier. She said you need to get married soon? Well, I have a daughter, and she's a very lovely girl. A few years younger than you, but very nice." Will tucks the papers under his arm quickly and pulls his cell phone out of his back pocket while walking toward the desk. "Look, this is her right here."

Kyle studies the image Will shows him, stunned by what he sees. It's an image of Will's daughter, Gabrielle Lewis, posing in front of Will's house. "She's gorgeous," Kyle admits as Will sits again.

"Yes, and she doesn't date much. She hasn't had a real boyfriend since eleventh grade."

"Is she still a virgin?" Kyle asks, and his face is dead serious.

"I wouldn't know," Will states firmly. "I don't ask her those kinds of things. She's in college, though, so I'm not sure if she's experimented with others."

"I won't bother with her if she isn't a virgin. I want a woman who is pure—one that I can say is mine without a doubt."

Will looks uncomfortable. He lowers the phone and straightens his back. He doesn't like Kyle's tone at all, but he knows to tread carefully with him, seeing as he'd still like the opportunity to have an investment.

"She is not an object, Mr. Moore."

"She's a woman. Aren't they all?" Kyle laughs, mocking him.

Will pushes to a stand, clearly fed up. "You know what?

Never mind. This is a clear sign to me that I shouldn't sell my company to a man like you. I'll take my rejection and be on my way." Will walks back to the door, his steps much heavier. "Have a good day, Mr. Moore."

Will takes off, marching out the door, his blood slightly boiling. When he reaches the elevator, Kyle calls after him.

Will looks back with a grimace.

Kyle is standing in the middle of the hallway, a few steps shy of the secretary's desk. "I was only kidding, Mr. Lewis. Your daughter is quite beautiful."

Will simply shakes his head. He doesn't know whether to believe him or not.

"You are right about me needing a wife soon. She seems like a great person who could possibly fill that void. When can I meet her?"

"She deserves better than you," Will snaps.

"Well, perhaps, if I like her, I'll change my mind about investing in your company. As long as she's nice, I don't see the harm. My parents expect me to be married within two years, or they'll hand everything over to some prick who doesn't even know how to deliver a presentation. If I like her, everything will work out."

Will looks away from Kyle, focusing on the tips of his dress shoes. Deep down, by the sudden booming of his heart, he knows this is wrong, but he also knows he has a nice daughter and that Kyle isn't a bad looking man. Gabrielle has been struggling for months with paying off student loans, and he's at a point now where he can no longer help her because he's paying off his own debts.

She needs help, and all of them could get it from Kyle. For all he knows, they may not even last. Gabby has always focused more on her art and books than boys, but even if she does, what's the harm? She'd be happy. Debt-free. His whole family would be.

All he needs is for Kyle to like who she is as a person—which Will has no doubt that he will—and he can have that contract in his hands.

They could split up later, but even so, his worries would be over, because the contract would be signed and filed for at least a year.

But little does Will know that he's about to make one huge mistake—a mistake that will change his daughter's life forever.

"She works at Nuni's by Colegate College," Will informs Kyle. "She's there part-time and works every other night."

Kyle puts on a smug grin. "If I like her, I'll consider the deal, Mr. Lewis." He starts to turn for his office. "You'll know my answer if you receive a phone call from me. If you don't, well, I guess it means that I didn't see her as a great fit."

Kyle shuts his office door, and Will sighs, boarding the elevator after pressing the button.

For the rest of the week, Will tosses and turns in his sleep. There hasn't been a single phone call from Kyle, and he assumes that Kyle must not have liked his daughter much.

He can't understand how he wouldn't, though. Gabrielle is a sweet girl. She's friendly and smart and gorgeous, courtesy of her mother.

But then Sunday night arrives. Will's phone rings around ten o' clock that night, and it's a familiar number he has called dozens of times before, in hopes to schedule a meeting.

Will takes the call in his backyard, while his wife watches a soap opera on the television in the living room.

"Your daughter is a catch, Mr. Lewis. I like her a lot," Kyle murmurs into the phone. "Meet me Tuesday at three. We'll talk about that investment."

# CHAPTER ONE

**GABBY**

**PRESENT**

Sunlight.

It's the first thing I see, spilling through the sheer white curtains.

With a gasp, I shoot up in bed, looking all around me as I press my back to the headboard. My heart races when I realize where I am.

At first I think it was all a bad dream—that maybe I had imagined all of it. I take a look around the bedroom, panicking, but there is no sign of him.

My face burns, and when I touch it, it's unbelievably sore.

"No," I whimper. Climbing out of bed, I rush to the bathroom, closing the door behind me as quietly as I can and flipping on the light switch to look into the mirror.

The reflection staring back at me is horrifying.

There is a reddish-blue bruise on the left side of my face, surrounding my nose and upper lip. My upper lip is busted and slightly swollen. I'm surprised I don't need stitches for it.

I lightly graze the pads of fingers over the tear on my lip while hot tears pool in my eyes.

"No." I sob this time. *How could he do this to me?* Out of all the times he's grabbed and hit me, he made sure I would be able to hide it, but my face? He's never hit my *face*.

I look down, and it's now I realize my clothes have been changed. I even smell like soap. With a loud gasp, I back away from the mirror with wide eyes, studying the gown I'm wearing. It's the same one I wore the first night Kyle hit me—a silky green one I picked up from Victoria's Secret.

*He changed my clothes. How long was I unconscious?*

I hear footsteps coming up the stairs and I leave the bathroom, scrambling back into the bed.

The bedroom door is wide open, and Kyle strolls toward it seconds later. My stomach churns when he smiles at me from the door. He has a tray in his hands with food and orange juice on top of it.

"Finally awake?" He's still smiling, like this is just another morning. *What the fuck?* "You were asleep for nearly fourteen hours. Figured you'd be up soon so I went out to get you some breakfast." He places the tray on my lap, and I look down at the meal. French toast and scrambled eggs, with syrup in a little jar on the side.

He sits on the edge of the bed near me, and I flinch as he lifts a hand. His hand pauses midair when he realizes my defenses are up, but as if he doesn't care, he continues, leaning forward and stroking my hair back with a sigh.

"I can't believe our lives have gotten so out of hand."

I work hard to swallow and clear the dryness in my throat while avoiding his eyes.

"Anyway, I have to go to lunch with a few colleagues who are in the area." He stands and looks me over, mostly at my face. I almost expect him to apologize. I want him to beg for my forgiveness like he did the first time, tell me he won't do it again.

But he doesn't.

Instead, his forehead creases and he takes a step away. "Don't leave the house until your face heals. I've been icing it, and you should probably continue doing the same. I've decided to work here for the rest of this week, so if you need something, tell me and I'll get it for you."

I work hard to swallow again, but my throat is so dry that it's painful. I simply shake my head and draw my lips in to smash them together.

"Okay, then." He kisses my forehead. I focus on my lap, hiding my shaky hands. I'm tempted to grab the knife that's on the tray and stab him with it, but that's not who I am. I'm not *evil* like he is. There are other ways to get out of this.

Kyle finally walks out of the bedroom, and I close my eyes when I hear the garage gate opening. When it closes, I know he's gone. Or at least, I hope he is.

I study the meal in front of me again, hating everything about it. Is this supposed to be his form of an apology?

*Fuck that!*

I get up and take the tray to the dresser, slamming it down on top of it and causing some of the orange juice to slosh over the rim of the cup.

I go to the bathroom and turn the faucet on, but then I

catch myself in the mirror again. I swear I look worse than I did a few minutes ago.

"Oh, God," I cry, and my eyes are on fire. The tears stream rapidly, but I avoid looking at myself any more than necessary, rinsing my face and letting the cool water soothe me. It doesn't help much.

I shower quickly, unsure what Kyle may have done to me while I was unconscious, and then toss on a robe.

I hear yelping as I slide into slippers.

My heart drops.

"Callie?" I call. She sounds sad—hurt, even. I rush to the room down the hall where she sleeps. The door is closed. I try opening it but it's locked.

"Callie!" I scream, yanking on the doorknob. She whines even louder. "That *motherfucker*!" I run to my bathroom, snatching one of the drawers open and digging through it for a bobby pin. When I come across one, I go back to the door and pick at the lock. It clicks and pops open and I rush inside, thankful that Ricky taught me how to pick a lock when I was ten.

Callie is in a black cage that I didn't buy. I hurry toward it but there's a silver padlock on it as well. I yank on it. She whines again, scratching at the cage.

"It's okay, girl. It's okay." I feel like I'm telling myself that more than anything. I yank on it another time, but it's no use.

Why is he doing this? It's one thing to punish me, but to mess with an innocent puppy is cruel.

Anger brews in my veins.

I hate him.

I hate him so much!

My anger always morphs into tears, so I drop to my knees with a hand on the cage, and sob while Callie whines, telling her that I'm *so sorry*.

Honestly, I'm apologizing to myself. I never should have forgiven him that day at Teagan's. Maybe if I hadn't, I wouldn't be in this situation. I wouldn't have this bruise on my face, or an innocent puppy locked in a cage.

Has she even eaten? She probably has to pee too. It's been over fourteen hours. There's no telling how long she's been in this cage.

Fuck this. I need to help her.

I swipe my tears away and get up, shoving my frustrations aside and trundling downstairs to the garage where Kyle's toolbox is. I find the wire cutters and rush back in, taking the stairs by twos.

"Don't worry, girl. I'm going to get you out." I cut the first piece of metal, and then move to the next, until I've created a hole large enough to take Callie out. When she's free, I hug her to my chest. "I'm so sorry I dragged you into this, sweet girl!" She's shaking and whimpering. When she licks my cheek, I say, "I'm going to get us out of here, I promise."

I have no idea where I'm going to go, but I move quickly, going to my room to pack a light bag and then going downstairs to pack up some things for Callie.

But as I head toward the garage door and check the key hook, I swear my heart almost stops.

My keys aren't there. *That bastard took my keys!* I rush out to the garage to see if my wallet is inside the car, but my car isn't even here. What in the hell did he do to my car?

I jog inside and open the front door to check the driveway. The car isn't there either.

"No!" I scream, slamming the door behind me, and Callie yelps, running away from me.

I break down in the living room, my knees on the floor once again. I drop my face in my palms, and the sob that cracks through my chest hurts so damn much that it's almost unbearable.

How the hell am I supposed to get anywhere now? I can't walk. I don't even know where the nearest bus station is, and even if I did, I can't pay for it without my wallet, which is in my damn car.

I pull myself together enough to sit on the sofa. I could always call Marcel, have him pick me up. He would take me and Callie in, I know it. I could explain to him what happened, and he wouldn't think twice about it…but it's then I realize I have no idea where my cell phone is, either.

Pushing off the couch, I go upstairs to check the bedroom. It's not there. I check my studio, not there either, and neither is my laptop. Is he serious? He's taken *everything* from me—any means of communication or running away, he took it or locked it away. He knew I'd reach out to Marcel, or even my family. He was one step ahead—has been several steps ahead for who knows how long now.

I could always go to Meredith's house, but she seems like the kind of person who would report what's happened to me, and I can't allow that right now. Not with so much on the line.

Kyle has a hold on me.

My mother.

And if my father sold his company to Kyle, then he has

a hold on him too. Is that what he meant when he said I would regret it? That my family would regret it, too?

Defeated, I trudge upstairs with Callie in my arms. I cuddle with her on the guest bed after locking the door. I don't know what to do. I could always run away, take my chances and figure out a way to get to Marcel, but a part of me is too afraid to.

I can't drag anybody else into my mess. I created it and now I have to find a way out that won't ruin everyone else's lives.

The saddest part of all this is the only person I can blame for the mess I'm in is myself. I decided to put myself through this again the moment I took Kyle back, even going so low as to believe the promises he made that he'd never hurt me again.

What was I thinking?

Once a monster, always a monster.

# CHAPTER TWO

### GABBY

### PAST

"I'm so glad you two are finally married!" Mrs. Moore chimes over her glass of red wine.

She's smiling wide at me, with almond shaped eyes that are thick with black mascara and round, brown irises, similar to Kyle's.

We're seated in a restaurant that I never would have chosen to dine at, our legs beneath tables that are swathed with white tablecloths. Soft classical music trickles out of the speakers, and waiters and waitresses walk around with gloved fingers and black suits, almost like trained soldiers.

It's honestly a bit creepy, but they all must be on their toes, because it seems the only people who dine here are the rich.

I personally don't feel like I belong, but I play it cool.

This is my life now, having fancy dinners and sipping champagne and wine. Faking smiles and pretending to be a charming young lady.

I don't mind doing it. It's for Kyle.

I return a smile to Mrs. Moore and say, "I'm glad too!"

"So, how was the honeymoon?" she asks, and I glance over at Kyle, who is chatting away with Mr. Moore.

Mr. Moore has chestnut hair, but is slowly balding at the crown of his head. He has a long, bird-like nose, and his skin is pale, unlike Mrs. Moore's, whose skin is a shade darker than Kyle's. I don't see much of Mr. Moore in Kyle at all, but Kyle does carry some of his father's habits.

"Oh, the honeymoon was amazing," I sigh. "I never thought I would be able to take a trip to Thailand—let alone any place outside of the country—but we did! It was lovely, and I got a great tan, too."

"Yes, the honeymoon was incredible," Kyle declares. "Thank you for that recommendation, Mum."

"I am glad to hear that." Mrs. Moore smiles appreciatively and then sips her wine. "So, Gabrielle, what are your plans now that you two have tied the knot?"

I laugh a little, unsure by what she means. "Um…well, we plan on moving to the house Kyle bought in Hilton Head Island and growing from there."

"Yes, yes, but I mean, with yourself?"

"Myself?"

"Yes. Do you plan on having children anytime soon?"

My eyebrows shift up to my forehead, and I look at Kyle, who is studying his mother. "I do want children one day, yes."

"And when do you think that day will be?"

I avoid a frown and as if my silence confuses her, her thinly arched brows dip. "You two haven't discussed this?" she asks when Kyle and I look at each other.

I study Kyle warily, and notice he grips his fork a little tighter. "We have talked about wanting them, which we both do, but I'd like to wait and spend time with Kyle as my husband first, before bringing kids into the picture."

I force a smile, and his mother locks eyes on Mr. Moore before removing her elbows from the table and placing her wine glass down. She clears her throat before saying, "I see."

She says nothing more, and I pick my fork up to move the ingredients of my salad around, avoiding her face.

Mr. Moore changes the subject to talk about some new building that's being built in New York City, and I run a hand over Kyle's thigh beneath the table, making sure he's okay.

He reaches down, and I think he's going to hold my hand and squeeze it to silently reassure me that what I said was fine, but he doesn't. Instead, he shoves it away, but carries on the conversation with his father with a nod and a smile, as if everything is perfectly fine.

My heart drops as I look down at my hand and then his. When I swing my gaze up, I notice Mrs. Moore is looking right at me with narrowed eyes as she sips her wine again.

I'm beyond relieved when dinner is over. The valet brings Kyle's BMW after we say our goodbyes to his parents, and when we're in the car, I finally take a moment to collect my composure and breathe.

Dinner with his parents was intense—then again, it's always tense around them. They're such serious people. His mother can be intimidating at times, but I've learned not to let Mrs. Moore's stares get to me.

"That could have gone better," Kyle mutters.

"Really? I thought it was fine," I say back.

"Why would you tell her that?" Kyle demands when we pull away from the restaurant. He looks at the rearview mirror as if his parents will hear him, then glances sideways at me.

"Tell her what? That I'm not ready to have kids yet?"

"You can't say things like that to my mother, Gabs. She's very old school. She expects us to be thinking about kids right away."

I frown. "Well, this isn't her time anymore, Kyle, and I'm not old school. If I'm not ready to have kids yet, then she should respect that."

"But what if I am?" he snips.

"Then…that is something we can discuss privately, not in front of your parents."

"You know what? There has been something bothering me awhile. You shouldn't even be on birth control. You are my wife now, so if you end up pregnant, then it is meant to happen, is it not?"

I scoff, so shocked by this attitude of his. "Wow? Are you serious right now?"

He stops at a stoplight, giving me a solid stare. He's dead serious.

"Kyle, this is *my* body, okay? If I don't want a baby to stretch me out right now, then that means I'm not ready yet. If I want to take birth control, then it's my right to take it unless we decide down the road that we are *both* ready for that responsibility."

His nostrils flare, and he grips the steering wheel tighter. I expect him to retort, but he pulls off when the light flashes green. He's quiet the rest of the way home. I honestly don't give a shit.

When we pull up to his condo, I shove my way out of the car, trotting inside in my too-high heels. I hate these heels, and I'll most likely return them sometime this week.

Heat envelopes me when I enter the building, and I shake off the cold. I jam my finger on the elevator button.

Kyle is beside me when the doors draw apart, and we step inside it, riding up to floor four. He's stewing and I'm pissed all the way off.

When we make it into the condo, Kyle tosses his keys on the counter, and I go to the room to kick my heels off and strip out of my skirt and blouse to put on something more comfortable, a silky green gown I bought from Victoria's Secret.

Ice rattles in a glass a short distance away, and I'm certain he's making himself a drink.

I don't want to see him right now, so I grab the book I was reading and climb into bed. I believe an hour passes before I hear something crash.

"What the hell?" I jump out of bed and leave the room barefoot. Kyle is in the living room, in front of the teal vase I'd painted for him when we first met. It's in shards on the marble floor, and he's staring down at it.

"Kyle? What did you do?"

He looks up then steps around the mess to get to me. "What if I want a baby *now*, Gabs?"

I frown up at him as he comes closer to me. "What is wrong with you? How much have you had to drink?"

He grabs my wrist and squeezes it tight. I cry out as he drags me to the bedroom and tosses me on the bed.

"Kyle! What the hell is wrong with you! Stop!"

He ignores me, climbing on top of me and pushing his way between my legs.

"Kyle!" I yell again. He's kissing my neck now, reeking of alcohol. He's never been this way with me before, and I don't know how to take it, so of course I panic. I try to relax my body and voice, even though my heart is pounding dangerously hard in my chest.

"Kyle, I'm really not in the mood tonight, babe. Please," I plead.

He sits up, and I expect him to understand and move away, recognize his mistake, but instead he shoves the hem of my gown up and then snatches my panties down.

"Kyle! Get off of me!" I start to sit up, but he forces me back down with a solid hand on my chest. The pulse of my rapidly beating heart is in my ears now as he unbuckles his belt and drops his pants and briefs with his other hand.

He roughly thrusts his way inside me, curling a hand under the back of my neck and gripping it tight. I cry out again.

"You are mine, Gabby. All *mine*. Do you understand that?"

A feeble noise catches in my throat, a tear sliding down the side of my face as he thrusts again, so roughly it hurts.

"If I want *my wife* to have my fucking baby, then she will have *my fucking baby*." There's venom in his voice—I've never heard it until now.

More tears roll from the corners of my eyes when he squeezes the back of my neck even harder.

"Kyle! Stop it!" I wail, but he ignores it and moves faster, grunting and huffing. His weight crushes me as he sucks on the crook of my neck, making sure to leave marks. He brings his head up and uses his other hand to grip my face between his fingers, kissing my mouth roughly.

This is all wrong. I should be fighting it but...he's my *husband*. Shouldn't I want to give him everything? Shouldn't I do whatever he wants, whenever he wants?

*He's drunk...he doesn't know what he's doing.* That's what I tell myself, but it doesn't stop the tears from falling.

Kyle gives one final thrust and then groans loudly, coming hard. He pants raggedly as he sucks on my neck again, and then he pulls away, walking around the bed and collapsing with his head on the pillow.

I swallow hard and swipe at my face as I sit up, then scoot toward the edge of the mattress, yanking my gown down in the process. It's now that I notice my hands are shaking uncontrollably.

I step out of the panties he didn't even have the decency to take off completely and walk to the closet to grab new clothes—yoga pants and my baggiest T-shirt.

Sobbing, I go to the shower, and once inside, I scrub so hard it hurts. I cry as I wash away the horrors of tonight, and when I'm finished, I get dressed quickly.

When I leave the bathroom, Kyle's back is to me as he rests on the bed, and I assume he's asleep, so I walk back to the closet to pack a bag.

I have to get out of here. I don't know what to think right now, but I can't be around him.

When I've packed enough clothes to last me at least a week and leave the closet, my heart plummets when I realize Kyle is no longer on the bed.

With a booming heart, I tip-toe out of the bedroom and look around the corner. Kyle is standing right in front of the door, my only way out.

"Where are you going, Gabs?" he asks, and his voice is one I've never heard before. His British accent is thicker. There's twice the venom there was before.

"I—I don't know, I just need to go," I murmur, trying to keep my voice steady. Fortunately, I do.

Kyle frowns and walks toward me. He looks me over when he's closer, and I hold my breath, like I'm being preyed on by a vicious beast.

Why is he doing this? I have never been scared of him until now.

"You're going to leave me." It's a statement, one filled with fury.

In an instant, his hand shoots up to my throat, and I gasp as he grips it tight. He turns me around with his grip still tight around my throat and shoves my back against the front door.

"You're going to leave me! Is that it?" His voice booms, and I scratch at his hand, needing oxygen. "You are so fucking pathetic, Gabby! I swear you are! I do so much for you—*marry you*—and you want to leave because I want *one* little thing?"

"Kyle—please!" I choke out, blinded by tears.

"What part of *you belong to me* did you not understand? You are *my wife*, therefore you are mine! If you ever try to leave me or betray me, I will make sure you pay for it, so that you will know better than to *ever* try it again! Betray me, and I will fucking kill you, Gabby. I mean it!"

I can't breathe at all.

Can't see behind the thick layer of tears.

*I need air.*

Before, I never wanted to hurt him. I loved him so much that I never thought I could, but this night changes *everything*. I almost start to wonder if I'm having a nightmare, but this pain is real. Everything I feel is real.

I thought surely Kyle was a good, loving man. He's not the kind of man who would hurt anyone. That's what I thought. Now I know he's anything but. This monster in front of me is an entirely different beast. He isn't the man I married.

Did he wait until our status was solidified, just to reveal this side of himself? I think about all the times he was drunk before. If he got drunk, he fell asleep shortly after or left the room altogether. When we were on our honeymoon and he'd drank a little too much, he simply passed out. I assumed it was because he was tired.

Anger spikes my bloodstream, and I lift one of my legs, kneeing him right in the balls with all the strength I possess.

With a loud grunt, Kyle pulls away and collapses, landing on his back. I grab my keys off the hook by the door and rush out, all while sucking in a breath.

I run down the hallway and don't bother taking the elevator. Shoving the door open for the stairs, I go down all four flights, dashing through the parking deck for my car as I tug the handle of my bag over my shoulder.

When I'm inside Lady Monster, I waste no time bringing the engine to life and driving away. My eyes are thick with hot tears, but I don't stop. I have this fear that he'll be in his car and chasing right after me, so I keep going, checking my rearview mirror. No one is following me. *He's not following me.*

For a while, it's hard to drive, because the tears are so thick and blinding, so I pull over on the side of the road when I feel like I've gotten far enough away, and then rest my forehead on the steering wheel, letting it all out.

I'm not even sure how long I cry.

I don't know what just happened or why. Why would he do that to me? Why would he hurt me that way? He practically *raped* me on that bed!

The Kyle I love would have *never* done this…but maybe that Kyle never existed. Maybe he was just putting on a show up until this point.

I finally pull my shit together, wipe my face, and drive four and a half hours straight to get to Virginia.

I find the familiar, colorful apartments and pull up to building 2002. Grabbing my bag, I rush up the steps, knocking hard on door 6A.

It swings open after my third knock, and my best friend stands on the other side of it with a deep scowl before she realizes that it's me.

Teagan is in pajamas, and her eyes are really squinty, like she's just woken up.

"Gabby? What the hell?" she croaks.

"I'm sorry to wake you, T. C-can I come in, please?"

Her eyes widen then, most likely sensing the panic in my voice. With a concerned frown she steps forward and grabs my hand, towing me inside.

"What the hell is going on? What happened to you?" she

asks, looking me all over. I drop my bag by the door and walk to the couch.

As soon as I sit, I drop my face into my palms and cry. I cry harder than I did in the car. Sob after sob wracks through my body, and it doesn't take long for a hand to start rubbing my back.

"Gabby? What in the hell happened?" Teagan demands.

"I—I don't know!" I cry.

"What do you mean you don't know? Tell me why you're crying!"

I can't even do it. I hate having to put Kyle in a bad light, but he did this. He's the reason I'm here at four in the morning, interrupting her night.

"What happened to your neck?" she asks, running a hand over the side of it. When she does, I can still feel the prints of his fingers there, like he's still holding me. "And your wrist—Gabby! What is going on!"

"Kyle," I sob, and I can't even look at her, so I keep my face buried in my hands.

"Kyle what?" Her voice is clipped.

"We got into an argument about having kids and he—he came onto me a little too roughly. Grabbed me too hard. When I tried to go, he choked me."

"*Choked* you? Oh my God." Teagan sounds worried too, and I'm so glad she believes me because to anyone else, this would sound completely made up.

Kyle is the one who's known not to get a temper. He's the guy who is sweet and kind and charming and would never hurt a fly. How can he be so *different* now? How didn't I see this coming?

"I knew that fucker was putting on a show! I knew it! I

told you there was something about him I didn't trust but this solidifies it!"

I peer up at her, and she's just a blob behind my tears. "I know, but I didn't see *this* coming! He has never put his hands on me before!"

"Are you sure he never has?"

"I'm positive, T. I would remember. He has never hurt me. He was drinking a lot tonight and—"

"Nuh-uh! Fuck that! There is no excuse for what he did, so don't try and make one up for him!"

I clamp my mouth shut, swiping my tears away. "Do you think I can stay here for a few days? Until I figure out what to do?"

"Yes. Of course, stay here for as long as you want, Gabby. That's what I'm here for."

"Thank you."

I can feel her staring at me. I'm so embarrassed right now, but I know she would never tell a soul or judge me for it. Not only that, but she's all I really have at the moment. I can't tell my parents. They'd go overboard and blow things way out of proportion.

"Let me get you some blankets and a pillow." Teagan walks off, and I drop my head again, staring down at the floor.

She returns a moment later with thick blankets and a pillow. I stand so she can pull out the sofa bed and spread the blankets.

When she's done, she walks to the kitchen, pulling down two white mugs and grabbing her kettle. "I'll make you some tea."

"Sure. Thanks." I sit at the four-top dining table.

When she's done with the tea, she brings it to me and I thank her, blowing it before sipping carefully.

"How did you get away?" she asks, holding the mug in both hands.

"Kneed him in the balls."

She smirks. "That's my girl."

I focus on the gold liquid in my cup.

"You know you can't go back to him, right?"

My eyes slide up to hers. "What do you mean?"

"I mean he *hit* you, Gabby. A man is never supposed to hit a woman!"

"I get that, Teagan, but he is my *husband*. The paperwork has been finalized. I can't just leave for good over this one thing."

"He'll do it again, and you know it."

I shake my head, looking away. "He won't—he can't. What he did was unlike him."

"In my book, that's unforgivable. You can't trust that he won't do it again, even if he promises that he won't."

"He was drunk, T. He wasn't thinking straight, and we were already upset with each other—"

"So that's what you're going to do? Make excuses for that piece of shit? Your case is that he was drunk and just *being a man*, even though he tore you down in the process? Gabby—I mean, look at you! I saw your eyes and heard the way you spoke when you got here! You were terrified! Why stay with this guy when he made you feel that way? Something tells me he's always been this way. He was a spoiled, rich kid who grew up to be a spoiled, rich man. He's entitled and thinks he owns whatever he touches, including you." She pushes from the table, leaving her mug there.

"I'm not trying to make you feel like shit but just…think about what you're doing. I have to work in a few hours, so I'm going to try and get some rest. You should try and do the same."

Teagan walks off, clearly disappointed. When her bedroom door shuts behind her, I sigh, and leave my tea on the table too. I curl up on the couch, and my phone rings in my pocket several seconds later.

Kyle is calling.

I ignore it.

I spend four days on Teagan's couch, wallowing in my own sadness. She doesn't say much to me—really, what can she say? She does give me food and makes me feel comfortable, for which I'm eternally grateful.

Kyle calls repeatedly on every single one of those days, but I don't answer. On the fifth day, there are no calls from my husband, but there is a knock on the door that evening.

Teagan looks at me warily before going to it. She swings it open and I sit up straight, my pulse thundering in my ears when I hear Kyle talking.

For a moment, I think he's going to push past her and snatch me up, just to tear me down again.

"I know she's here, Teagan. Please let me speak to her." I'm surprised his voice is so calm.

"Screw that. You put your hands on her. I refuse to let a *woman beater* into my apartment, now fuck off!"

She slams the door in his face, and I stand from the sofa, twisting my fingers.

Teagan looks me over, her eyes screaming *are you serious?* "Gabby, don't go to him. He doesn't deserve you."

"He's my husband, Teagan. We'll have to talk about this

eventually." I go to her, holding her shoulders. "And I can't stay here with you forever. You know it."

She shakes her head and begins to protest, but clamps her mouth shut within a second. I can tell she's thinking that I'm partially correct.

What kind of marriage would this be if we don't at least talk about what happened? Despite how low I feel, or how terrified I was, I need to know why he did it. I need to know if he will always be like this or if it was a one-time thing because he was drunk and angry.

I walk to the door and pull it open. Kyle is still standing near it, like he was thinking of another way to get to me.

"Gabs," he breathes when he spots me, and his brown eyes light up, like he's so glad to see me. He seems almost boyish, and for a split second, I regret being away from him and having him worry for so long, but then I remember his hand around my throat, the way he forced himself inside of me, and I drop that regret instantly, rubbing my neck at the reminder.

I close the door behind me. "How did you know I was here?"

"Your father called me and didn't mention you were with him." He looks at the hand I have on my neck, eyes full of guilt.

I drop my hand then swallow hard, wrapping my thick cardigan sweater around me. "I'm not coming home."

"I get that. I don't expect you to, so just listen for a second." He squeezes his eyes shut, holding up a hand. "Gabby, *I am so, so sorry*. What I did was wrong, and I understand your anger and your fear. I have a bad habit of drinking and getting out of control. It's happened to me for years—to the point I've had to go to therapy for it."

I almost start to lower my guard. He never told me he went to therapy for anything.

"I never should have put my hands on you that way, and I swear to you I will never, *ever* do it again," Kyle murmurs.

My throat feels dry. The wind bristles by, making my face feel colder. "I don't know if I can trust that, Kyle. You hurt me that night. You *choked* me."

He winces, like he remembers well, and the thought of it pains him. "I am so sorry, babe. I swear."

I shake my head and look away.

"Gabby, please. I was drunk and stupid and—and I let my frustrations get the best of me!" He steps forward, cupping my face in his hands. I hate that I wince, almost like I'm preparing to get hit by him again. With his eyes locked on mine, he says, "Gabs, I swear to you it will never happen again. We've just gotten married, babe. Don't forget about the house we are about to move into and the life we will get to build together."

A tear escapes me. He strokes it away with the pad of his thumb.

"We don't even have to worry about kids. We can talk about that much later. Right now, my wife is the most important thing to me in this world, and I can't lose her. I need her so damn much. I haven't been able to sleep—I was worried sick." He holds my face tighter and kisses my forehead. "I love you so much. Please, come back to me."

My heart is racing, along with my thoughts.

I don't know what to do.

And I don't know why I still feel so weak for him after

what he did to me. I still love him, that's the only answer I can come up with, and I love him even more when he kisses me deeply on the mouth. After the kiss, he collects me into a hug, cupping a hand around the back of my head and holding me to his chest.

"Come home," he murmurs. "We can work this out, I promise."

I shake my head and pull away. My vision is blurry with tears. I'm so torn. So confused.

"I'm sorry but…I—I can't." I spin around and go back into Teagan's apartment, closing the door in his face before he can react, and then curling up on the couch again.

Teagan is relieved when she sees I've returned, but of course, Kyle is persistent. He shows the following day as well, this time with white roses and another speech about how he needs me more than anything. He even drops to his knees and *cries*, begging me to come back.

I'm such a fool to fall for it. I think I fall for it more so because Teagan isn't around, and no one can tell me not to do it.

Like a fool, I write a note to Teagan, pack my bag, and go back home with Kyle.

I wish I'd realized that going back was going to be the biggest mistake of my life.

I believed his promises, knowing damn well that my best friend was right. He did it once, and he'd do it again, but his words were so sincere that I refused to believe he would.

I considered what he'd done a drunken mistake, not even realizing that it would happen again, and again, and again, but in so many different, horrible ways.

# CHAPTER THREE

**MARCEL**

I'VE BEEN TRYING to get a hold of Gabby for two days now.

I've emailed her repeatedly, sent her text messages, and I've even called. I've left voicemails, some a little more desperate than others, but she hasn't responded to any of those either.

I know she didn't want what we had going on for long, but to flat-out ignore me is pretty fucked up. Not only that, but I still have her wedding band. You'd think she'd have called to ask me about it, considering the fact that she'd told me she never took the rings off.

I don't understand her at all.

I sit at my work desk, rolling the platinum band between my fingers. I have the urge to toss it in the trash bin, but that would be pointless. That stupid husband of hers would just replace it with a newer, better one anyway.

I don't know what it is, but deep in my bones, it feels like something isn't right. I know her well enough to know that no matter how upset she is, she'd at least respond. Doesn't matter if it's a negative response, she always does.

I push out of my chair, grabbing my keys off the desk and heading out of my office to get to my truck.

I don't think too much as I drive up the highway and veer off the ramp that leads to Venice Heights.

I pull into the neighborhood, spotting a few people jogging and others working on their yards. I don't stop until I'm parked along the curb in front of Gabby's house.

I waste no time pushing out of the truck and walking down the driveway, hoping her shithead husband isn't around. I don't see his car, so that's a good sign.

I give the door a quick knock and for several seconds, there's no answer, so I knock again.

Still no answer.

I frown, looking through the sidelight windows. I don't see a sign of anyone, so I walk down the stoop.

I'm tempted to go back to my truck and leave, call this whole thing an act of desperation, but honestly and truly, something does *not* feel right about this situation.

It's a weekday, and she isn't home. She was always home during the week when I worked on the yard. What would change now? And so soon? She didn't tell me about any vacations or leaving town while we were together—not that she had to, but I'm sure she would have at least mentioned going somewhere.

I make my way to the backyard, going around the hot tub to look up at Gabby's studio window. No one's there.

I peer through one of the windows of the double doors

next and that's when I spot a silhouette by one of the sofas, just past the kitchen.

I try getting a closer look, but it's useless at this angle. Someone's there though, and judging by the feminine silhouette, I'm pretty sure it's her.

I jog to the front of the house again, knocking harder this time.

"Gabby, open up!" I yell, pounding on the door. I hear a small bark after I knock again. "I can hear Callie barkin'! I know you're in there! Open up, Gabby!"

All I get is silence in return.

I press a hand to the door, dropping my head. "Please. I'm askin' you nicely."

"Just go away, Marcel. It's over. Okay?" Her voice catches me off guard. I pull away from the door, noticing the shakiness in her tone.

"I have your wedding band," I tell her. "You left it on the nightstand."

She's quiet again.

"Open up and I can give it to you."

"Just leave it in front of the door and go."

"I'm not doin' that."

"Well, keep it. I don't care."

"Oh, now you don't care?"

Quiet, yet again.

I sigh. "Gabby, I want to see you. I fuckin' miss you, all right? Is that what you wanna hear?"

"No," she responds, her voice lower. Thicker.

"What's goin' on with you? Is everything okay?"

"Everything's fine," she says, but her voice is even thicker with emotion. "Just go away."

"Gabby," I call. "Open the door. Let me see you."

It's quiet for so long I assume she's no longer there. But then, several seconds later, I hear the lock clink and the door slowly cracks open.

All I see is the right side of her face and one of her bright green eyes. Still, it's a relief.

She holds a hand through the crack of the door, extending her arm. "Give me the ring."

"You gonna open the door all the way?"

"No."

"Why not?"

"Just give me the ring, Marcel, and hurry," she demands.

"What's the rush?"

Her eye shifts up to meet mine. "Kyle is in town. He'll be back soon."

I scoff. "So? Fuck him."

"Marcel, seriously! Just give me the ring and stop joking around!"

"What in the hell is wrong with you, Gabby?" I give the door a little tap, which clearly catches her off guard because she gasps, then pushes it back in place just as quickly. "What the fu—" I push it harder and it swings back again, revealing her whole face. It's a quick reveal, but I see it.

I knew my eyes weren't playing tricks on me. There's a mark on the other side of her face, but she rushes to push the door back where it was again.

My frown grows even deeper, my chest tightening as I ask, "What the hell happened to *your face*, Gabby?"

She looks up at me with that one eye, and it's full of tears now. I notice her chin is trembling. She drops her hand, and I push the door open a little bit more.

This time she doesn't put up a fight.

What I see shocks the hell out of me. At first, I don't even know how to take it. There's a bruise on the left half of her face, discoloring that whole side of it. Her upper lip is busted, her cheek swollen.

My eyes widen as I stare at her, almost too shocked for words.

"Did he...did he do this to you?" I ask, clasping her chin between my fingers.

She looks away, taking her chin with her.

"Gabby, answer me!"

She flinches. "It's nothing!"

"Nothin'? Are you fuckin' kiddin' me? You have a fuckin' bruise on your face, Gabby! You were hidin' behind the goddamn door! How is that nothin'?"

"We're over, Marcel! Okay?" she shouts back.

I push the door open completely, ignoring her.

"When will he be back?" I snap as she leaps away. "Tell me! I swear to God I'm going to rip that spoiled bitch in half!"

I'm seething now, only seeing red. If there's one thing I hate in this world, it's when a man puts his hands on a woman.

My father? He wasn't perfect, not by a long shot. He hit my mother several times when he was drunk or couldn't get a hold of his anger, but he got help, and I respected him for doing that because most men feel like getting help is beneath them.

I hated seeing my mother hide her bruises and scars every morning before sending Shay and me off to school.

Now I get it. Now I see why Gabby wore what she wore

sometimes—long-sleeved shirts and jeans on some of the hottest days. It wasn't because those were the only clothes she had, but because she was hiding what her husband was doing to her.

Seeing the bruise on Gabby's face brings me back to the days when I had to fight for my mother and even myself.

"I don't know when he'll be back, but you can't be here when he does, okay? I'm going to take care of it! I'm going to make a plan to leave so I can deal with this myself!"

"Has he hit you before now?" I demand, and she clamps her mouth shut. Her eyes water even more, which is all the answer I need. I figured he had, but the confirmation kills me.

How could I not have seen this? Why didn't I put two-and-two together? I feel like such a fucking idiot.

The way she freaked out when she left the villa was a clear sign. I asked her what he had on her, and she got this look in her eyes, like she was *afraid* of something…little did I know it was *someone*.

I cup her face in my hands as delicately as I can. "Why are you still with that motherfucker, Gabby? *Why?*" I look her in the eyes, but she squeezes them shut so she can't see me. "Leave with me right now. We can get the fuck out of here before he comes back. You won't have to deal with his shit anymore, I swear to you."

"I can't do that," she sobs.

"Why the hell not?"

"Because…I just can't, Marcel! Kyle has done a lot for my family—for *me*. He'll end it all if I go! He'll kill me if I try to leave!"

"Then let him fuckin' end whatever he has on your

family, Gabby! Who gives a shit? This is your life, and he's threatening it!"

She breaks down into a heavier sob, bringing her face to my chest. I'm still pissed the fuck off, but I don't know what else to do besides hold her.

I hope he comes soon. I swear I'm going to beat the shit out of him.

"Come to my place," I murmur. "Right now. You and Callie."

"He'll find me. He knows about us…what we did behind his back."

I'm surprised to hear this. I grip her shoulders and hold her back so that I can see her face clearly. "Wait…is that why he hit you?"

She nods and her throat bobs as she swallows some of the emotion. "He knew I was with you on that trip. Threatened that if I didn't end whatever this is that we have, I would regret it."

I pull away.

"He's known since the day after we first did it, Marcel. In the kitchen, when the table broke. He found one of your business cards there. I don't know if it fell out of your pocket or what, but it was there, and I guess he put it all together when I went with you a few days ago."

Shit. "This is my fault then. I should have checked—I should have made sure to pick up after myself—"

"No—it is not your fault. It's not. Don't say that! You have no control over his actions."

I look at the table. The leg has been fixed.

We're both quiet for so long. She looks at me with questions in her eyes. She and I both know she's doomed here. I can't let her stay, and I'll be damned if he hurts her again.

"Go get some clothes," I tell her, pointing at the staircase. "You don't need a lot. Just enough for a few days, until you can get situated. You're comin' with me."

"I can't leave with you, Marcel!"

"Yes, you can!" I grip her shoulders again. "Listen to me, your family will understand if shit goes south, Gabby! That's what family is for, but being around him has clearly made you forget about that! Now fuckin' go!"

She blinks her tears away, and like my words finally make some kind of sense to her, she rushes around me and jogs up the stairs.

I head for the kitchen, grabbing Callie's dog food and bowls. I snatch up a few of her toys as well and go to my truck. I put it all in the bed of the truck and jog back to the house.

Gabby is rushing down the stairs with a suitcase when I walk back in, Callie hot on her heels.

I grab her suitcase, locking the handle in my hand. She scoops Callie up and follows me out the door, closing it behind her.

"He'll find me, Marcel. He'll kill me," she says, panicking.

"He won't find you without me around. And if he even tries to lay a finger on you, I'll fuck him up." I march out of the house, walking down the stoop, but as soon as we hit the cobblestone, a car rolls down the driveway.

Through my peripheral vision I see Gabby freeze at my side, and out of instinct, I stop walking as the black BMW rolls right up to us, parking only a few steps away.

Kyle steps out of the car with a pair of sunglasses on, then he lowers them, focusing right on the suitcase in my hand. His eyes then shift up to Gabby, before locking on me.

"Well," Kyle says with a smug smile. "This is interesting."

# CHAPTER FOUR

## MARCEL

I ignore Kyle, grabbing Gabby's hand and walking around the passenger side of his car.

"You know if you leave, this changes everything, right, Gabs?" Kyle calls after her, his voice way too calm as he closes his car door.

She starts to look back. I squeeze her hand, and she looks at me again. "Fuck him," I mutter. "Don't look back."

She obeys, dropping her head and walking with me again up the driveway.

"I mean, think about your mother—how much I paid just for her to get an immigration lawyer so she could *stay* here! She was almost deported because her visitation period had been over for two years! Don't you remember that? I came to your rescue when you needed me! I helped her when she got into that silly fight and had the cops called on her! I'm the reason she's still here, Gabs!"

Gabby stops walking immediately, pulling her hand out of mine.

"No—Gabby, let's go!" I tell her. "Don't listen to anything he's sayin'. He's just tryin' to get to you."

"And Ricky? Remember when he asked if I could invest in his tech business, help him get started, but instead I gave him money out of *my* pocket, that I worked my ass off for, to do that? And your father, Gabs. Oh, man. Your father. He will be *very* disappointed when he finds out that the contract we currently have will be terminated soon. Null and void, all because of the reckless adultery of his daughter. Knowing your father, he doesn't have a backup plan. If he doesn't have any money stashed somewhere, he'll lose everything, Gabs. His house, his cars. Hell, he may even lose his wife if I decide to give ICE a call. Those documents for her to stay are still processing. Wouldn't be hard to put a word in and have that all go down the drain, considering she's just like *you*."

Fed up, Gabby spins around, placing Callie down. "You're a fucking bastard!" she screams at him.

He shrugs. "You know I would do it."

Gabby turns to me with a hopelessness in her eyes that makes my heart ache. "I'm sorry." Her head shakes fast. "I can't go, Marcel. I can't take the risk right now."

"Yes, you can, Gabby! This is a risk you'll have to take to get away! You can't let him have this kind of power over you!"

"Would you listen to this guy? Gabs, you hardly even know him! What can a landscape architect do for you? He won't be able to do half the things I can do! I make way more money in one day than he does in a month! Why sell yourself short?"

Fire floods through my veins. I drop the suitcase and charge toward him, not giving a damn about the consequences.

When I'm closer, Kyle holds up his hands and says, "If you even think about laying a finger on me, I will have you arrested so quickly, you won't even see it coming."

I keep walking.

"June 14th, 2010. Marcellus Ward was charged with four counts of assault! One of the men barely survived the brutal beating but was kind enough to let the assault charges go because you'd recently lost your sister, so you only spent five days in jail."

I stop dead in my tracks, looking him straight in the eyes with a frown. How the fuck does he know that? Did he really do research on me? Find my record? Twisted fuck!

As if he can hear the questions I ask myself, he smirks and says, "The man that let you off was very kind, but I am *nothing* like him. If you so much as touch me, I will not let you get away with it. With another charge like that, I'm certain you'd spend several months in jail, considering the kind of man I am. I know people. My father knows people. You touch me, and your career—your *life*—is over."

I steel my jaw and flare my nostrils. I swear I want to hit him square in the fucking mouth.

Instead, I take a few steps closer, pointing a finger at him. "She's not staying here with you."

"Oh yes she is." He looks over my shoulder and I look, too. Gabby has her suitcase and is walking back to the stoop.

"Gabby, what the hell are you doing?" I call, chasing after her.

"Just let me come up with my own plan, okay?" Her eyes glisten as I approach. "I'm sorry for dragging you into this. I really am."

"Just walk away with me. I don't have to hurt him, but you can walk. You have that right."

"He won't let this go."

I hear footsteps, and Kyle is walking around me to go up the stoop.

"Get inside, Gabby." He's standing by the door now, waiting for her with impatient eyes and folded arms.

With wet lashes she looks from him to me, then shakes her head, walking up the rest of the stairs and going past him.

"Gabby!" I yell. I rush up the steps, but Kyle raises a brow and blocks the entrance of the house. I'm face-to-face with him, seething like a fucking bull now.

I want to strangle this motherfucker so bad. The last time I was this mad was right before I got tossed in jail for the same assault he brought up.

"You touch her again, and I won't give a damn about the fuckin' assault charges. You got that?" I snarl. "I'm gonna come by here again, and if I see so much as a *scratch* on her body that I haven't seen before, I will rip your pussy-ass to shreds. And trust me, I will know if there's a scratch or bruise that hasn't been there before because I explored her body in more ways than you can count several days ago."

He straightens his spine after that remark, that stupid smirk of his rapidly fading.

"I don't give a fuck if I'm in jail for the rest of my life," I rasp. "Destroyin' you and settin' her free will be well worth it. Trust me when I say that as soon as she reaches out to me and is ready to leave your sorry ass, I'll be right fuckin' here." I shove a finger into his chest.

Kyle tries to stare me down, but I don't let him win. I stare back with a glare that's twice as intense.

When he's fed up, he takes a step back, shaking his head and giving me his back.

"Get off my property before I call the cops," he snaps then walks inside.

Before he can shut the door, I notice Gabby staring right at me, and I don't know what it is about the look in her eyes, but it tells me everything I need to know.

When she's figured this out, she will run. She knows this isn't just her battle anymore. It's ours. I don't care if I have to camp out in front of her fucking house, I'll do it, because my word is all I have and I mean everything I say.

The door closes and I stand there a moment with a hand at my hip.

I hear a bark behind me and peer over my shoulder. Callie is standing beside the BMW, looking right at me. I glance at the door before walking down the stoop, then scoop Callie up in my hands and head for my truck.

Gabby would never leave Callie out on her own, no matter how distressed she is. I'm taking it as a sign that she wants me to take her, protect her.

I'm going to do just that.

## CHAPTER FIVE

**GABBY**

WHERE DOES a person like me go from here?

I don't have much to my name. When I met Kyle and we ended up getting serious, it was a relief to not have to work anymore.

He told me to quit my job, promising he'd take care of me. He claimed he wanted me to focus on school and to live my life without the stress of paying a late bill or working overtime to cover some of my school loans.

He swore he had my back and, for the most part, he did. He always came through with a hefty deposit in my bank account every week.

I was lucky to get a partial academic scholarship, but working wasn't enough to cover everything, so to any person who has struggled, someone like Kyle would have felt like a godsend. Kyle lifted the burdens and washed most of my stress away.

It wasn't just about the money; I really liked him. He

was unique, dedicated, and charming. I thought he really loved me, but I realize now that someone who loves me would *never* hurt me.

I know one thing for a fact now: I fell for a madman. He dove in, learned everything about me, and used it against me.

I thought, at the time, he really wanted to help me, but it turns out he was only using it as leverage. I'm nothing more to him than a pawn.

He wanted to have something to hold over my head from the moment we met, that way if he revealed his true self, I couldn't just run away or back out.

I hate that I just handed my worries over to him. I'd much rather deal with the stress of paying off student loans than this, being tormented and abused every day.

I'm sitting at the kitchen table Kyle demanded I sit at, while he attempts to prepare dinner.

I feel like a child, and I'm so humiliated that Marcel saw me like that. I never wanted him to see me in that position, beaten and emotionally weak.

Would he really come again, or was he just saying that out of anger and spite? Deep down, I hope he does. Seeing him, if only for a moment, made me realize that I can be cared about in a saner way.

"Do you want cheese?" Kyle asks, snapping a finger in my face.

I look up at him as he stands in front of me with a container of parmesan cheese in hand. I look down at the bowl of whole wheat spaghetti topped with red sauce. It's the only dinner he knows how to make.

I peer up at him again, shaking my head. "No."

"Whatever." Kyle sits in the chair beside me—something he never does—and tops his pasta off with cheese. He normally takes the seat across from me, at the opposite end of the table. Having him this close causes me to stiffen in my chair. "Eat," he orders.

I pick up my fork and shift the noodles around with it, but I don't eat. He, on the other hand, digs right in, as if he has no worries in the world.

"He took Callie, you know," Kyle mutters after taking a sip of water.

I don't respond.

"I don't believe a word you said about finding her now. He gave her to you, didn't he? Why would he do that?" I lower my gaze to my spaghetti and Kyle slams a palm on the table, causing the silverware to rattle and the glasses of water to almost tip over.

I gasp and flinch.

"I'm asking you a fucking question, Gabby!"

"I—I don't know," I murmur. "He found her, and she was hurt. I offered to keep her when he brought her with him one day. He said he wouldn't have time to watch her and he didn't want to put her in a shelter."

Kyle scoffs and rolls his eyes, picking up his fork again. He takes a bite of noodles then points his fork at me. "You were probably walking around in those dresses and shorts. You *made* him want you. Now he thinks what you did with him means something. *Pathetic*."

I don't even say anything to that. Kyle has no idea that what Marcel and I have done does mean something—to both of us.

"You know what? I'm curious how you did things with

him," he says, dropping his fork. "Did *he* fuck *you*? Or did *you* fuck *him*? After all, that makes a huge difference, doesn't it?"

I blink through my tears, staring at him. He stares right back, like he's waiting for an answer. "Are you serious?"

"Do I look like I'm kidding? Answer it."

I work hard to swallow, but my throat is dry now. I pick up my water and take a small sip, but Kyle reaches forward rapidly and snatches the glass away from me, causing some of the water to spill on my lap.

I drop my hands with another flinch, tucking them between my thighs.

"Tell. Me." He's looking right into my eyes.

"I—I don't know, Kyle! Okay?" My voice breaks. "God, why are you doing this?"

"You do know!" he barks back while pushing out of his chair. He steps beside me and grabs my arm, snatching me up to stand and bringing me around to his side of the table.

He shoves the bowls of spaghetti and glasses of water away. The dishes crash to the floor, and I suck in a breath as he reaches for my shorts and shoves them and my panties down enough to reveal my ass.

"Kyle! Stop it!" I scream as he grips the back of my neck, slamming my face on the table.

"Oh, you want me to stop? Did you tell him to stop when he fucked you on *my* table?" I lift my arm, but he pins me down by the wrist, keeping both of my hands on the table.

"Get off of me!" I scream but he doesn't listen. I hear his belt buckle jingle as his grip tightens on my wrist, then he forces my hips up even more and shoves himself into me.

The pain is excruciating.

My body had no time to prepare for this, but he doesn't stop. He acts as if he doesn't even feel that I'm in pain. He grabs both of my hands, planting them on top of the table and slamming his hips forward.

"You think he scares me?" he grumbles. He slams again, but the thrust is so dry, that my tears tip over and I cry out. "You let another man fuck what was *mine*. I told you that if you ever betrayed me, you would be punished!" Another dry thrust. "You better hope he doesn't come around tomorrow, or I guarantee you, I'll do this again. I'll have the doors locked and the curtains drawn, so he can see what I'm doing to you and not be able to do a damn thing about it."

I cry louder as he shoves into me again. The legs of the table scrape the floor with every single one of his thrusts and he grunts as he pulls the hand that's at my neck away and pushes hard on the back of my head, keeping me pressed to the table.

I hate him.

I really, really hate him.

I have no love for Kyle anymore. The more damage he causes, and the more vicious he becomes, I know that I hate him with every fiber of my being.

I let him finish, no longer putting up a fight. When he's done, he makes sure to come inside me, groaning loudly as if he has an audience. Then he pulls back, running his fingers between my folds and sticking them inside my vagina.

It's only natural that I clench, and I'm pissed at my body for reacting to his touch. I hate that he knows just what to do to make me feel *something*.

Hovering over me, he works his fingers in and out while I squirm.

"Get off of me, Kyle!" I yell, trying to move my hips. He keeps my upper body pinned down.

He doesn't let up, and my body is only my body, not at all connected to the raging thoughts running through my mind.

I hate that he knows what I like, because he's using it all against me. He plays with me until I cry out in a mixed web of agony and disoriented pleasure, and I feel his hardness on the back of my thigh, anxious for more.

He pulls away, and I'm relieved, thinking maybe he's done. I wait for him to leave the kitchen before making a move, but he doesn't leave.

The legs of a chair scrapes across the floor and he grabs my waist hard, bringing me down and forcing my vagina around his penis.

"How did you fuck him, Gabs? Hmm? Show me."

I don't move.

I'm absolutely still but he forces my hips forward and backward again.

"Show me!" He shouts, grabbing a fistful of my hair and yanking on it, his face near the side of mine.

I still don't move.

I don't care what he does to me, he's not getting me to ride him, and as if he knows it, he yanks again, this time causing some of the hair to rip at the scalp.

"You're a terrible fucking wife!" he yells when I shriek, then he releases my hair and shoves me off of him completely.

He stands and then grabs me by the hair with one hand,

gripping my face between his fingers with the other, and looking me in the eyes, his now a shade darker.

"This," he pants. "It's not over. You better pray he doesn't show up tomorrow, Gabs. And I mean it. Pray hard, otherwise you'll get what you deserve."

He shoves my face away and I groan as I hit the ground. He then reaches down to pull his pants up before stalking out of the kitchen.

"Clean that mess up!" he yells before he's up the staircase.

When I hear a door slam upstairs, I weakly push up to a stand. I sniffle loudly as I clean up the broken shards from the glass, careful not to cut myself with any of it. I wipe up the water and spaghetti next, leaving the stained red rag in the sink.

Turning toward the double doors, I draw in a shaky breath and push them open. I walk out, crossing the patio to get to the gate that leads to the beach.

I don't know why, but I feel numb now. My mind is reeling, but my body moves, doing its own thing.

Wrapping my arms around myself as soon as my feet hit the sand, I walk close to the shoreline and finally, my mind syncs with my body.

I break down, knees hitting the gravelly sand as my face lands in my hands.

I'm not sure how long I cry, sob after sob taking over me, but when I stop, the sunset that was just ahead of me is barely visible now.

I have to get away from him. I don't care if I have to drag other people into this anymore. I'm leaving.

That monster in there isn't the man I married. He's

doesn't even come remotely close to the Kyle I thought I knew.

He's degrading and rude and abusive. He's controlling and manipulative and fucking insane.

I thought I could be strong enough to withstand him, but I thought wrong. Instead, I'll be strong enough to fucking *leave* him. Forget his threats, or the fact that I will be living in fear and paranoia, at least I won't be around him while it happens.

"Gabby!" Kyle's voice startles me, interrupting my thoughts.

I shoot to a stand with a gasp and look back. Kyle is standing by the gate of our house with a frown on his face.

"What the hell are you doing? Get back inside!"

I turn quickly, going to the gate. He opens it, allowing me to walk past him.

He watches me rinse my feet off at the small sprinkler by the gate, and I'm surprised he doesn't hurt me when we're back in the house again.

Instead, after looking me up and down with disgust, he says, "Go take a shower. You smell like him."

I go, but only because I'd like to be anywhere that isn't near him.

As I walk up the stairs, I recall the times when I've heard stories about how women never leave their abusers until it's too late. They either end up injured really badly, or worse, *killed*.

Now, I understand why those women waited. You give the abuser many chances, hoping they'll change, but instead they shatter your trust—not just once, but many, many times.

You don't want to give up on that person, whom you loved unconditionally, hoping there's a chance to make things right again. But that's the thing about abusers.

They *never* change.

They just space it out, waiting for the abused to forgive them, and for another opportunity to strike.

## CHAPTER SIX

**GABBY**

SHORTLY AFTER MIDNIGHT, Kyle has fallen asleep. He made me lay in the bed with him after my shower, though I really didn't want to.

I cringed when he wrapped an arm over my midsection, a stray tear sliding over the bridge of my nose when I squeezed my eyes shut, waiting for him to drift off and for this nightmare to end.

Now, I'm struggling to peel his arm away. I do so carefully, though, while inching my body sideways to get off the bed.

When I've successfully removed his arm from around me and am standing, I place it down on the bed as gently as possible. He stirs a bit and I freeze, but then he rolls over with his back to me.

I rush out of the bedroom when he starts up a light snore, making sure to keep my steps light. I don't bother packing any clothes because the suitcase I'd packed earlier, when Marcel was here, is still downstairs in the living room.

After snatching off the stupid engagement ring and tossing it on the floor, the silver metal lightly clinking behind me, I grab the suitcase by the handle and pick it up, then hurry to the double doors in the kitchen.

Those doors are the quietest, and closest to the alarm system. I plug the code in, thankful that he hasn't gone so far as to change it. I'm sure he would have gotten to that eventually.

I leave the house in a frenzy, rushing past the hot tub and patio furniture, toward the path that leads to the cobblestone driveway. I'm surprised I don't trip over anything.

Warily, I peer over my shoulder, hoping none of the lights turn on, or that the door doesn't open. Maybe some other alarm will go off for him, and he'll know I'm trying to get away. Sounds crazy, but I wouldn't put an idea like that past someone like him.

I'm sure he thinks that I'll stick around because I have to—because, at the moment, I need him—so he isn't taking action to keep me locked in.

He's wrong this time.

When I've made it far enough and don't see any signs that he may be awake, I jog across the street with my suitcase lifted in the air, going straight to Meredith's house.

I jam a thumb into her doorbell, peering over my shoulder every other second, anxious for her to answer.

There isn't a response for a while, so I ring it again.

I spot a light turn on from the window and then I hear footsteps. The lock clinks, the door cracks open, and Meredith is looking through it with bleary, tired eyes.

"Gabby?" Her voice is thick with sleep. "What's going on? Are you—oh my goodness!" she shrieks, her eyes widening. She opens the door completely, then flips on the porch light. "What happened to you?" she screeches, and tears instantly pool in my eyes.

"It's a long story. I'm so sorry for interrupting your night, but can I come in, please?"

Her eyes drop to my suitcase and then back up to my eyes. As if she can sense all that I've been through within the last seventy-two hours, she immediately nods and lets me into her home.

I expected to feel fully relieved when I had planned to come here, but being across the street from Kyle is just as terrifying. He knows I'm friends with Meredith, and that I can't be too far away this late at night. He'd probably check here first before going to find Marcel.

The stairs creak, and I look up, spotting Bill walking down. He has on a white T-shirt and blue pajama pants. He looks at me with sleepy, confused eyes as Meredith stands in the middle of the living room.

"Sit, sweetie," Meredith insists, focused on me. "Tell me what happened."

I place my suitcase in the corner and take a seat on the sofa.

"Is everything all right?" Bill asks, concern laced in his voice, and I don't know what it is about his voice, but it guts me. Perhaps because they care to ask? Immediately, I start to cry.

"I'm sorry," I sob, embarrassment and shame taking hold of me.

"No, don't be sorry. It's okay, sweetie," Meredith coos, and I feel her hand on the middle of my back, rubbing in full, gentle circles.

"Do I need to call the cops?" Bill asks.

I shake my head, brushing off the emotion and swiping the tears away. "No, it's okay. I, um…I'm so sorry for interrupting your night like this. I just…I didn't know where else to go this late. I don't have many friends in Hilton."

"Stop it, Gabby. You are more than welcome here at any time," Meredith assures me, still rubbing my back.

"That's right." Bill sits in the recliner to my right.

"But I need to know what you're running away from." My eyes connect with Meredith's. "You can tell me."

"It's Kyle," I say blatantly. I don't even care that they know it. I'm no longer making him out as the good, dutiful husband they once thought he was.

Through my peripheral I can see Meredith and Bill looking at each other before focusing on me again.

"Kyle?" Meredith asks, confused.

"Yes. He's…not as nice as he seems. He found out some things about me and he *hurt* me for it."

Meredith gasps.

Bill clears his throat, and then says, "I really think we should call the police."

"The police won't help. He has a lot of money. He wouldn't spend more than one night in jail—if that. The charges would most likely get swept under the rug."

"He left this bruise on your face?" Meredith asks, still stunned.

I nod.

"Wow." Her head moves from side to side, and I spot tears lining the rims of her eyes. She pulls her hand away from me, staring at the floor. "I didn't take him as *that* kind of person. It's always the people we least expect."

Her statement confuses me. I glance at Bill, who presses his lips and focuses on his wife.

"You won't be going back to that house," Meredith announces, standing. "I'm going to make you some tea, and you're going to stay here until you can make arrangements to get as far away from him as you possibly can. We'll get you a restraining order first thing in the morning and—"

"No—Meredith, really. I don't want to intrude like this. I came here because you're my friend, yes, but I also just want to use your phone, give someone a quick call. I can't stay here for long. He'll know where I am."

"I'll be damned if he sets foot in my house," Bill objects, then he grunts as he pushes to a stand. "Meredith is right. If you need to stay, you can. You'll be safe here. My brother is a certified bodyguard. I can have him watch the house, keep an eye on things if you'd like."

"Oh, God, no, Bill." I wave my hands. "It's okay. I don't want to drag more people into my mess."

Meredith sighs and walks to the short table in the corner. She picks up her cellphone and hands it to me. "Make your calls, sweetheart. Do what you need to do. But I'm not kidding about staying far away from him." I've never seen Meredith so serious, or her eyes so intense. I almost start to ask her what's wrong, but she walks away after I accept the phone and trots into the kitchen.

Bill follows after her, so I stand, walking to the patio door and stepping on the cool stones.

I'm glad that I've memorized Marcel's number. After I took a shower, Kyle took one, and while he did, I quickly went to his office, logged onto his laptop, and found the emails he'd sent to Marcel weeks ago, when we first hired him.

Marcel always left his number beneath the signature in his emails. I repeated his number in my head until it was seared in my brained.

I type his number into the keypad of the phone then press it to my ear, impatiently waiting for the ringing to stop.

Then he answers. "Yeah?" His voice is gruff. It sounds like he just woke up.

"Marcel?" I breathe a sigh of relief.

I hear rustling on his end and then he says, "Gabby?"

"Yes, yes, it's me." I close my eyes, fighting the sudden burn I feel in them. I can't believe I'm so happy to hear his voice.

"Where you callin' from?" he asks.

"It's Meredith's phone. My neighbor."

I hear him breathe a sigh of relief into the phone. "You're with the neighbors. Good. What's goin' on? You need me?"

"Well, I thought about everything, and I'd really like it if you could come and get me."

"Say no more. I'm on my way—"

"Not right now," I tell him, though I'm glad to hear he'd drop everything to come to me. "Meredith has questions, I'm sure. I don't want to be rude and just leave after interrupting their night."

"Are you sure? I'm positive she'd understand."

"She will, but I'd like to talk to her for just a

moment. I'm sure you're tired anyway. I can wait a few more hours. I just wanted to call and let you know that I'm not in that house anymore, in case you were worried."

"Has he hurt you again?"

I breathe in through my nostrils, and this time my throat feels raw. I recall the pain of his thrusts on the table, his angry words.

"I'm okay," I whisper, my eyes sealing.

"You don't sound okay. I'd rather come get you now, Gabby. You're right across the street from that bastard."

"Yeah, but he's not an idiot. He knows he can't barge into their home."

Marcel sighs. "I'll be comin' first thing in the mornin'. 'Round six or seven. Understand?"

"Seven is good."

"Good."

"I'll see you then."

"All right, Gabby." He pauses. "Goodnight."

"Goodnight."

I end the call then go back inside. I walk into the kitchen, placing the phone on the island counter.

Meredith and Bill are sitting at a four-top table with mugs of tea in hand. I see a third mug, and Meredith smiles, patting the chair to her left.

I sit with them and sip my drink as I take a look around. Meredith's kitchen is just as stunning as her living room. White counters and a peach backsplash.

I look down, focusing on my cup.

"I'm so ashamed right now," I blurt out, stirring honey into my tea.

"Don't be. Seriously." Meredith places her purple mug down.

Bill sighs and pushes out of his chair. "I'm going to let you girls chit-chat. Give my name a shout if you need me."

"Okay, honey." Meredith smiles up at Bill. He kisses her on the way out, and I love how icky-sweet the gesture is.

"How long have you and Bill been married?" I ask when he's up the stairs.

"Fourteen years."

"Wow. That's a long time."

"Yeah." She smiles dreamily. "I met him when I was about your age—twenty-four. He used to work at a car dealership, and I had saved up enough money to finally get my first car. I was going to community college on top of a part-time job that felt like a full-time one. Hardly ever slept. He offered to help me out by cutting the price, if and *only if*, I went out to lunch with him the same day."

I grin. "And you took him up on it?"

"Of course not!" she laughs. "He was so much older than me, and I felt way out of his league. But I told him I would so that I could get a good price cut. But as soon as he handed me those keys, I told him I had to work. Me, being the silly person I am, had completely forgotten that I'd mentioned where I worked, so color me surprised when he showed up at my job the following day and reminded me that I owed him. He told me he wouldn't stop coming to the job until I went out with him. It wasn't too forward though. More like the movies, where the guy really wants to take the girl on a date. I thought it was cute that he remembered where I worked." She sighs and continues a smile. "So, I agreed, of course, but I really didn't want to. I'd just gotten out of a bad relationship and another relationship was the last thing on my mind. He came at the right time, though."

"I get that."

Meredith sweeps her eyes all over me. "It's good you got out of there, Gabby. The man I was with before Bill was just like Kyle, in a sense. He was abusive. He hurt me in so many ways. Some days I'd have to miss work if he hit me in the face, or wear my hair down because a bruise was on the back of my neck." She looks off absently then releases a ragged breath, as if she's reliving the horrors of that time.

"I'm so sorry to hear that, Meredith."

She waves a dismissive hand. "It was years ago. I guess I realized I deserved better than him. It's hard to see it that way at first, especially for us women. We think we don't deserve more, or that we have to put ourselves last. Being with men like them either makes you open your eyes or makes you turn a blind eye. I'm glad you opened yours."

I nod then sip my tea.

"What made him break?" she asks, and I look up to meet her eyes. "With guys like them, there is always something that sets them off. They're like ticking bombs, you know? Pull the wrong move and they explode."

"Oh." I take another sip of tea. "Well, I'm not exactly innocent when it comes to him doing what he did."

"There's *never* any reason for a man to put his hands on a woman that way, even if she isn't innocent. Doesn't matter what she does, there's no reason. Walk away, yell about it, break it off or get drunk and break something, but there's no reason for a man to hit a woman. *Ever*."

A tear skids down my cheek as I tuck my hands between my thighs. I'm almost ashamed to confess, but I was even more ashamed to come here with this bruise on my face, yet I did it. Why stop now?

"It was…well…I had an affair…with Marcel."

Her eyebrows nearly stitch together. "From Ward Landscaping?"

"Yeah."

Her eyes expand as she asks, "You *slept* with him?" Then she grins. "Oh my goodness! I knew it!" She claps her hands together and tosses her head back, like she's just solved the world's hardest question. "I knew I wasn't crazy! That man was looking at you all night during the housewarming! I kept thinking the only explanation for a man looking at a woman that way is if he really wants her!"

"Seriously?" I fight a smile. "My best friend said something similar."

"It's true. I kept thinking it, but I figured maybe I was just assuming things." She fights a grin. "How was he, anyway?"

"Meredith!" I laugh. "That is so inappropriate right now."

"What? I'm just wondering!" she shrugs. "I see that man, and he makes parts of me tingle that shouldn't be tingling for other men, girl. Don't tell my husband that, though, or he'll never hire him again."

I giggle as she winks at me.

"Listen, I don't judge you at all for what you did, honey. If Kyle has hit you before now, which I'm assuming he has, then I can understand why this sort of thing happened with Marcel. Not saying this is justification for cheating—cheating is still wrong—but… well, I suppose if I were in a situation like yours, where you've just gotten married and a new house and all, I'd feel a bit confused too." She looks me over, but I drop my eyes, focusing on the rim of my mug instead. "You stopped loving Kyle when you met Marcel." It's a statement. A solid one that punches me right in the gut as I think about it.

I have to mull it over for a while. "I wouldn't say I stopped loving him…but I definitely noticed how different he was compared to Marcel. I noticed way too many differences. Marcel would never hurt a woman, I'm sure, but Kyle does it so ruthlessly that I started to feel like it was *normal*. I found comfort in Marcel. He was kind, and respectful, and honest, even when it was hard to hear."

Meredith nods, like she completely understands.

"You're right, though. I fell out of love with him the moment he laid his hands on me…and that was nearly six months ago. Right after we got married."

"He is ridiculous." Meredith pushes out of her chair, taking her mug to the sink and dumping the rest of her tea out. "Is he the one you called out there? Marcel?"

"Yeah." Just the thought of him makes my heart beat faster. "He's coming to get me soon."

"Good. At least you know you'll be safer with him."

"Yeah." I lower my gaze. "I actually think I'm going to text him, tell him to get me now before Kyle notices. I don't want him giving you guys too much trouble later."

"Sure, sweetie. Go right ahead."

I stand up and grab her phone off the counter again. When she tells me the passcode, I send Marcel a text, and there's a reply in seconds.

**Marcel: Already in the neighborhood**

"What?" I place the phone down and walk to the window in the living room, peering out. Sure enough, Marcel's black Ford rolls up to the curb of Meredith's house, his headlights shutting off.

"He's here that fast?" Meredith asks behind me.

"He was already on the way." I go for my suitcase as Meredith opens the door.

"Man, he wasn't kidding," she laughs.

Marcel is already making his way up the driveway. I walk out to meet him, and he collects me into his arms without warning.

I sigh as he holds me tightly, then close my eyes for just a second, relishing in the comfort of his hug. He smells so good—fresh, like he's showered recently.

"There was no way in hell I was goin' back to sleep after you called. Would've parked in front of this house all night and waited for you if I had to."

"I'm glad you came now." I look toward the driveway of my house across the street. "We should go before he notices I'm gone."

"Yeah." Marcel grabs my suitcase and takes it to his truck.

As he tosses it in the bed of the truck, I turn toward Meredith and give her a hug.

"Thank you," I sigh over her shoulder.

"Always, sweetheart. Even if you don't come back to this neighborhood, I'd still like us to keep in touch."

"As soon as I get another phone, I'll have Marcel give me your number so I can text you." I pull back, gripping her shoulder caps.

"That sounds good. You be safe, okay?"

"I will." I turn away, walking across the grass to meet Marcel at his truck. He opens the passenger door for me, and I climb inside, but as I do, I hear someone yelling my name.

And the person sounds *pissed*.

## CHAPTER SEVEN

### GABBY

"Gabby!" Kyle roars.

I gasp as I look toward my house. Kyle is standing in front of the driveway, eyes wide and jaw clenched.

"Close the door and buckle up," Marcel demands hurriedly. He shuts my door, but before he can get to the other side of the truck, Kyle has already crossed the street.

"What the hell do you think you're doing?" Kyle barks in Marcel's face.

Marcel folds his arms. "What the hell does it look like? I'm takin' Gabby with me."

Kyle looks past Marcel and right at me. "Gabby, you can't be serious. Did I not tell you what would happen if you tried to leave?"

My heart thunders in my chest. I look away, spotting Meredith on her porch with her phone in hand. She'll probably call the cops if this gets crazy. Good. I want her to, so she can back me up on this. Two witnesses are better than one.

"You will lose everything! Do you not get that?" Kyle takes another step forward. "Your family will have absolutely nothing!"

"Just back the hell up, all right?" Marcel warns. "It's over. She's comin' with me."

"Like hell she is!" Kyle spits at him, and he shoves Marcel against the chest. Marcel stumbles backward a bit, caught off guard by the shove, which gives Kyle enough leeway to rush around him and get to the passenger door.

I scream as he snatches my door open and seizes my arm, wrenching me out of the truck.

"Get your ass back in the house and stop being a *dumb cunt*!" Kyle shouts.

"Let me go!" I scream. I try snatching my arm away, but he won't let up.

Marcel appears with a growl and shoves Kyle twice as hard as Kyle shoved him, which causes both me and Kyle to hit the pavement.

He then grabs Kyle by the collar of his shirt, panting like a bull, as he picks him up and tosses him right on Meredith's lawn. Kyle hits the ground with a loud thud and a groan.

"Touch her like that again, and I will fuckin' kill you!" Marcel roars. I can tell he wants to rip Kyle apart. He even takes a step toward him, but I hop up and rush for him.

"No—Marcel, let's go! He's not worth going to jail over!"

He's still seething. I tug on his hand, pleading, and he finally looks down at me.

"It's okay. Let's go," I whisper.

Backing away, Marcel turns to help me get in the truck again, and I'm so glad he listens. After shutting my door, he turns back to Kyle.

Kyle is pushing to a stand now, but he doesn't attack. He knows just as well as anyone that Marcel would beat him to a pulp. Marcel has more mass. Anyone can see that.

"Stay the fuck away from her, or I swear I'll fuck you up," Marcel snarls at him.

"You're making a huge mistake, Gabs!" Kyle yells. Marcel walks around the truck, opens his door, and then climbs behind the wheel.

He starts the ignition, but before he can put it in drive, Kyle appears at the passenger window, slamming his palms into the glass just inches from my face. I let out another yelp, and Marcel presses his foot on the gas, peeling off.

I'm shaking like a leaf, my pulse thundering in my ears. I take a look over my shoulder, through the rear window.

Kyle is standing in the middle of the street with his fists clenched. Meredith has gone back into her house and has shut her porch lights off.

When he's out of sight, I turn back around, slouching in my seat and closing my eyes. That doesn't stop my tears from falling.

"You okay?" Marcel asks as we speed out of the neighborhood.

I shake my head. It's all I can do.

He grabs my hand and squeezes it. "He won't hurt you like that again. I promise you."

Yeah.

I wish I could believe that.

# CHAPTER EIGHT

**MARCEL**

SHE DOESN'T SAY much during the ride, not that I expect her to after all that just happened.

I steal glances of her as I drive, while she stares blankly out of the window. Every time a street light flashes across her face, it's a clear reminder of what her husband's done to her. That bruise will take at least two weeks to heal.

I still can't believe he did it. I will never understand how any man can lay his hands on a woman like that. How do they live with themselves? When I saw him grab her and yell in her face, I almost lost it.

I was about to beat his ass, but I had to remember where I was and what I was doing. I wouldn't have been any help to Gabby if I was sitting in jail. Plus, he hit me first. Shoving him back and tossing his ass was self-defense. There are witnesses around to prove he touched me first, too.

I finally pull into the driveway of my house and Gabby

sits up higher in her seat. She looks all around, almost like she's surprised by her surroundings.

"This is your place?" she asks with a quiet voice.

"Yeah."

"Wow." She looks around again. "It's nice."

"It's a quiet neighborhood. Don't have much to look at inside, but hopefully it's comfortable enough for you." I unlock the doors and push out of my truck.

Gabby steps out as I get to the passenger side. She slides out of the way so I can grab her suitcase from the back, then follows me to the front door.

As soon as I unlock and open the door, there's barking, and Callie is right there waiting.

"Oh my gosh! My sweet girl!" Gabby squeals and bends down to pick Callie up, hugging her to her chest as she enters the house.

I shut the door behind her, putting on a small smile as I place her suitcase down.

"I missed you so much, even if it was only for a few hours," Gabby murmurs, nuzzling her nose on the top of Callie's head. Her eyes pop open again, and as if she realizes she's in a place she's never been before, she places Callie back on the floor and takes a hard look around.

"Like I said, not much to look at," I mumble with a shrug.

"No, stop it. I like your house. It's cozy." She gives me a faint smile.

I shrug, looking from the brown leather sofa and matching recliner to the four-top dining table behind her. It's a simple home. A two-bedroom house with a moderate kitchen and two bathrooms.

"I always assumed you lived in an apartment or something like that." She smiles, but it doesn't reach her eyes.

When she tucks her hair behind her ears, I ask, "How did you get away from him after all that?" It's clear she's trying to avoid the topic right now. I won't have it.

She shifts on her feet. "He fell asleep and I snuck out. Went to Meredith's and called you first thing."

"But what about all that talk with your family? You're not worried about that? The things he'll do?"

"I am…but if I can get to them first, then perhaps they can work something out before things get too bad." She shrugs, her eyes becoming misty. "I'll figure something out for them. I put them in this mess, and I'll get them out. I don't care if I have to work two or three jobs, I'll do it as long as it means I don't have to go back to him." She drops her eyes, and I notice her step sideways, almost stumbling.

I rush her way, hooking an arm around her waist and bringing her to the sofa. "You're *never* goin' back to him. That's not even an option." I sit her on the couch then take the spot next to her. Lifting a hand, I tip her chin, forcing her damp green eyes on mine. "We'll work it out, Gabby. I promise you. It may seem like all hope is lost, but it isn't. I'm here to help you however I can." I pull my hand away to scratch the back of my head. "Still can't help thinkin' this is my fault. Had I not met you, I'm sure you'd be fine—"

"No, Marcel. I told you, had I not met you, I would have been *stuck* with him. I never would have left him, no matter how bad things had gotten."

"But maybe things wouldn't have gotten so bad at all if it weren't for me."

"Stop," she demands softly, closing her eyes. "Just stop,

okay? It happened for a reason, and I'm here now for a reason."

I sigh, then nod.

She sits back, running her hands over her face and making an exasperated sound. "I never thought I'd be in a situation like this. I mean, I thought I could handle the shit Kyle put me through. Him going away to work helped some, but not much."

"It's better that you walked away, Gabby. Don't feel embarrassed or guilty about any of that. What he was doin' to you was wrong, and you can't let it happen again, no matter how tough shit gets, or how much he claims to have against you."

She meets my eyes. "I won't go back."

"Promise me."

"I promise."

"Good." I grab her hand, stroking the soft flesh on the back of it with the pad of my thumb. "You can stay here for as long as you want, but if you think you'll feel comfortable elsewhere, I completely understand."

"No." She looks around again then focuses on Callie who is laying on her dog bed by the kitchen. "I think I'll stay here for a while."

"Well if that's the case, let's try and get some sleep, then." I help her to a stand, and she goes right for her suitcase, unzipping it and taking out some shorts and a cropped top. She asks where the bathroom is, and I lead her there.

She starts up the shower when I shut the door behind me, and after several minutes have passed, I hear her crying. I can tell she's trying to do it quietly, but it's not working.

As badly as I want to go in there to comfort her, I

change clothes instead, giving her time to let whatever she's feeling out.

I know it's hard. I hate that it's even happening, and I still can't help blaming myself for it.

When she's out of the bathroom, I'm already in bed with the lights off, and she's holding her pre-shower clothes close to her chest, like she needs their protection.

I guess I can't blame her. This is all very new. This isn't like the villa, where it was our form of escape and we could say and do whatever the hell we wanted without boundaries. This is my home, where we've both been thrust back into reality and are dealing with the consequences of what happens afterward.

I've never had a woman sleep in my bed for longer than a few hours, but Gabby will be here all night. Something about that makes me completely aware of everything that's happening right now, even if it is nearing three in the morning.

"Don't act shy now," I murmur as she places her clothes down in a corner. "Come here."

And she does. She climbs into bed as I open my arms, sliding between them. I wrap them tight around her.

A slow sigh escapes her, and a long silence passes by. Then, before I know it, she sucks in a breath, and her body shudders with a loud sob.

"Shh." I stroke her damp hair back with one hand, using the other to hold onto her tighter. "It's over, Gabby. You're with me now." I stare up at the ceiling as her sobs become heavier. I let her cry again for a moment then I sit up, which causes her to shift a little.

"Gabby, look at me."

"I can't," she says through a loud sniffle. "I'm sorry. I'm trying to stop, but it's just—it's too much to take in. I feel like an idiot, and my face is—"

"No, Gabby. *Look. At. Me.*"

She finally peers up, eyes shimmering from the slits of moonlight above. My heart aches just looking at her, realizing the pain she's in.

"You will *never* be hurt like that again, do you understand?" I murmur. "You have my word. You won't be hurt by him, and you *definitely* won't be hurt by me, or anyone else, for that matter."

She blinks most of her tears away with a nod. "I'm sorry," she whispers brokenly.

"You have nothin' to be sorry for." I close my arms around her again. "I've got you, little thing. You're safe with me."

As if my words are the balm she needs, she shudders one last breath and then wipes her face. I hold her the entire time, even when I realize she's fallen asleep.

As I start to doze off, she makes a small noise and cries out a little, her body twitching. I don't want to wake her, so I stroke her hair, hoping it'll soothe her.

Fortunately, it does. She's sleeping soundlessly again.

Damn.

Kyle really messed her up. I'm certain she's been traumatized, and I can't help wondering what he did after I left their house. I'm certain if it caused her not to care about the consequences for good, it had to be something that broke her even more than she already was.

And now, here I am, left with a woman's fractured soul —a fractured soul that I pray I can help heal.

## CHAPTER NINE

**GABBY**

WHEN I WAKE UP, I smell something salty.

I sit up in Marcel's bed, scanning the room with tired eyes.

I didn't get the chance last night to take in the view of Marcel's bedroom. From where I am, there isn't much to look at, but again, it's cozy and homey. It seems he's lived here for years, despite not having much to look at.

There's a dresser across from me with a TV mounted above it. A nightstand is on the right side of the bed and there's a black and white poster on the wall to my left that says **Wake Up Every Day And Be Grateful**. The name *Shayla W* is written in thick, black ink on the bottom corner of the poster. Above my head is a square window, the sun beaming through dark-green curtains.

I roll out of bed, planting my feet on the carpet. I brush my teeth and then wash my face in the bathroom, taking note of the bruise. It's gotten even darker, healing in the ugliest way. I squash the thought, refusing to let that dampen my mood. I cried enough last night. I'm safe for now.

When I'm out of the bathroom, a picture frame on top of the dresser catches my eyes. It's a small, sepia-colored picture with three people in it—a teenage boy, a younger girl, and a woman with glasses and curly brown hair.

It takes me a while to realize who the boy is. It's Marcel, only a much thinner, happier version. He's smiling in the picture, with teeth that are too big for his face. They're the same teeth he has now, and I'm glad to see he's grown into them. I laugh at the thought. His eyes are full of joy in this picture.

The girl is several years younger, also with dark hair. She has freckles and round, friendly eyes. The mom looks a little more serious than the kids, but she's wearing a faint Mona Lisa-like smile, almost like she's proud of where she is and wouldn't trade her life for anything in the world.

I smile as I run the tips of my fingers over the silver frame.

"You're awake." Marcel's deep voice catches me off guard and I gasp, snatching my hand away from the picture.

I take several steps back, looking away. "I'm sorry—I didn't mean to snoop."

"Not exactly snoopin' when it's out in the open."

He's smiling. Good. I'm glad this doesn't bother him.

"You look so happy in this picture."

"What are you sayin'? That I don't look happy now?" He's teasing.

I laugh. "You look fine now. I'm glad to see you grew into your teeth, though."

He belts out a laugh, coming closer to me. "You know I

used to get picked on for my teeth? I was glad when the day came where I actually looked okay with them."

I giggle. "They're nice teeth. The people picking on you were probably just jealous."

He caps my shoulders with both hands. "How you feelin'?"

"Better." I shrug.

"Good." He points outside of the bedroom with a thumb. "Made breakfast. Bacon and eggs. It's all I had. Want some?"

"Sure."

I follow him out of the bedroom, looking at the picture one last time.

He pulls a chair out for me when we meet at the table, and I sit, then he brings two plates and forks, placing one of the plates in front of me. He hands me a fork and I grin, digging right into my food.

Surprisingly, I have a fierce appetite this morning. I guess I shouldn't be surprised, since I didn't eat the food Kyle cooked and didn't eat much before the incident with Marcel or after he made the spaghetti.

I'm halfway finished with my food when Marcel returns to the table with two glasses of orange juice. "Damn. Someone's hungry," he chuckles, sitting and digging into his food too.

"Sorry," I garble out, covering my full mouth. "Didn't eat much yesterday."

"Well, there's more in there if you want it. Don't apologize." He smiles warmly. I return a smile that's just as warm.

We eat in silence for a while, forks scraping across porcelain, and I lower my fork, thinking about everything I had planned last night.

I need to get in touch with my parents, let them know what's going on. The sad thing is that I'm a millennial at heart, and since we can save contacts in our phones without writing the number down, I don't remember either of my parents' numbers. Trust me, I know it's terrible.

They also changed their numbers several months ago, when they got new phones. They were marked in the phone Kyle gave me as Mamá and Dad.

As if Marcel senses that my mind is elsewhere, he asks. "What's going on up there?" He points at my forehead with his fork.

"Oh—uh, nothing." I wave it off.

"Gotta be somethin'. You're frownin'."

*I am?* I rub my forehead, as if the gesture will smooth out the wrinkles. "It's just…well, I'd hate to even ask you this, but I don't think there's anyone else to ask at the moment."

"You can ask me anything. You know that."

"I know, but this is a pretty big favor."

"What is it?" He straightens his back, waiting for me to spill it.

"I need to catch a ride to Virginia. It's where my parents live, and I don't remember their numbers, but I do know their address."

"You don't remember their numbers?" Marcel asks, slightly confused. "How do you forget your parents' numbers?"

"I don't know. I have their number in my old phone, but Kyle has that phone now. They used to have another number for years, and I remember that one, but they got new phones and new numbers a few months ago, and I can't recall either one." I smile sheepishly. "I do remember Teagan's though, but I don't think she has my parents' new numbers either."

Marcel can't fight his laugh. "That's gotta be the funniest thing I've heard in a long time. Even if I can't remember, I write all my numbers down. What if you lose your phone and need to have a backup source? Then you're shit out of luck."

"Well, that's what they have iCloud for! You're older than me, okay? To me, a phone can be replaced. You probably hold onto the same phone for years," I tease.

"Nah, I ain't *that* old," he chuckles.

I shrug, still smiling.

"Well, about the ride, that can be arranged, no problem."

I sigh, relieved. "Really?"

"Yeah. When do you want to go?"

"Maybe tomorrow? I bet they have a few rental cars up for grabs somewhere. Or…if you want, you could come with me," I offer.

He quirks a brow. "You sure that's a good idea?"

"Maybe not, but at this point I don't really care what anyone thinks."

He nods and smiles, as if pleased to hear me say that. "If I go with you, we can just drive my truck up there. That way we can take Callie with us. I'd hate to leave her here."

I look over at Callie, who is eating the dog food Marcel must've poured for her before I woke up. "You'd be willing to do that?"

"I'll do whatever you want me to do, Gabby."

My eyes are getting hot, burning with emotion. I blink it all away, focusing on my plate.

"You're too nice to me. I'm not used to it."

"That's because all you were used to was *him*." I look up, and he's scanning me with curious blue eyes. "He was your first, wasn't he? That's why you stuck around for as long as you did, even after gettin' married?"

My head bobs with a press of my lips.

"It's hard adjustin' to what's right after dealin' with somethin' so wrong. Give it time. You did the right thing by walkin' away, trust me."

"It just feels so wrong. I mean, we *just* got married. Everything was supposed to get better, not worse." He's quiet, probably unsure what to say to that. I don't blame him, so I decide to switch the subject after taking another bite of egg. "Shayla was very pretty. You two looked a lot alike."

He pauses on his next bite, avoiding my eyes. "We got that a lot."

"Your mom, too. She looks like she used to keep you in check."

He smirks, taking another bite. "That she did."

"Why isn't your dad in the picture? If you don't mind me asking…"

His blue eyes finally lift up to mine. "He'd just been diagnosed with cancer around that time."

"Oh."

"He's the one who took the picture. Believe it or not, he was a great cameraman. Had a good eye."

"Really?" I can't help smiling. "That's cool."

"There are a lot of pictures of us. Most of them are in

my shed out back, though. I kept the one in my bedroom out because it was one of the last pictures he'd taken before his health started deteriorating."

"I'm sorry to hear that, Marcel."

He doesn't say anything to that. Instead he finishes up his food and then stands, grabbing his plate. He grabs mine as well and carries both to the kitchen.

I go with him, bumping him out of the way with my hip and turning the faucet on.

"Take Callie out. I'll clean up."

He smirks. "Look at you, demandin' things under my roof already."

I fight a smile. "I guess some things never change."

"I guess not."

Before he can get out of the kitchen, I shut the water off and catch his hand. I reel him back my way and push up on my toes, throwing my arms around the back of his neck and gluing my lips to his.

He catches my waist in his large hands, his touch soft and warm, and kisses me right back, groaning at the surprise.

We kiss slowly, carefully. It still lights me up inside, which proves that maybe I didn't just want him because I couldn't have him. I have him now, and I still feel that fire—I feel it times ten. It travels down my throat and blooms between my legs.

But the thought of having sex right now completely turns me off. I look hideous with this busted lip and bruise, not to mention I feel sore from what Kyle did to me last night. I blink hard, biting back tears.

I pull my lips away, and step back, locking eyes with him. "Thank you for letting me stay here for now."

"Yeah," he breathes, putting on a smirk. "More than welcome."

He leaves the kitchen and immediately starts playing with Callie, patting his upper thigh and telling her to go out the back door with him. I wash the dishes and place them on the drying rack.

As I dry my hands off, I step in front of the door, watching Marcel as he stands in the middle of the backyard with his fingertips tucked in his front pockets while Callie trots around and sniffs.

I'm not sure if I'm supposed to be with this man. Maybe he's only here for now, as a means to rescue me, but nothing more. I'm not sure, and I don't want to think too hard about it.

What I do know is he's a good man.

Kind.

Giving.

Protective.

He's everything I never knew I wanted, mainly because I'd been blinded by abuse, neglect, and demands for months.

Marcel is different though. I just can't help wondering if maybe he has other secrets that I don't know about. Secrets that could possibly destroy everything between us.

There was the fight he had where he was charged with assault.

Is there more to him like that I should know?

Marcel takes me to the police station so I can file a report shortly after bringing Callie inside. After I file it, one of the officers, Officer Reynolds, snaps photos of my face, and then informs me to go to the courthouse, where I wait several hours to file a report and request a restraining order. Marcel waits with me, and I feel guilty—like I'm wasting his time. He assures me it's fine—that he doesn't want to be anywhere else but here.

I grow increasingly impatient, and am more than relieved when my case number is called and I am seen by a judge, who grants the order of protection without hesitation.

It's around six in the evening by the time we leave the courthouse. Marcel picks up dinner, and we head home.

His phone rings on the table and he stands up from the couch to grab it and answer.

"Really?" I hear Marcel say. He blows a sigh of relief. "Well that's good. At least something happened. Thanks, Officer Reynolds."

I turn to look back, sitting up on the couch. "That was Officer Reynolds?" I ask. "What did he say?"

Marcel places the phone back down, returning to the couch. "They brought Kyle in. He's in jail for now, but Reynolds believes he'll make bail by morning. I told him to call me if he could, once they arrested him."

I huff. "Yeah, I'm not surprised to hear that. He has plenty of money to bail himself out."

He strokes a thumb over my cheek. "We'll be gone by then and he won't be able to bother you for a few days, so don't stress, all right?"

I nod. He sits beside me again, sighing.

We watch TV a moment, both of us quiet.

"Marcel?"

"Yeah?" His voice is lower.

"Thank you for everything. Seriously. I know you could be doing something ten times better than dealing with my shit."

He reaches down to tip my chin. "It's all good. I'm here for you. Don't forget that."

His words bring me comfort, and I can't help smiling as he brings me closer to his chest and rests his chin on my head, like he never wants to let me go.

# CHAPTER TEN

## GABBY

AROUND 4:45 in the morning, Marcel is placing his suitcase on the back seat of his pickup truck. Callie's dog bed, food, and a few toys and treats are packed up, and my suitcase is in the back already.

I climb into the passenger seat with Callie in my arms, and Marcel shuts the door for me. When he's behind the wheel, he looks my way. "Sure you want me taggin' along?"

"Yes." I give him a reassuring smile. "It'll be fine." I have no idea if my parents will understand. I'm driving hours to see them, all with *another* man. They've only met Marcel once, and that was at our housewarming.

They'll be confused on sight, not only from seeing Marcel at my side, but by the bruise on my face too.

∼

The drive isn't all that pleasant. Callie clearly doesn't like being confined to the truck, so we have to stop several times so she can use the bathroom, eat, and so on.

Our seven hour and forty-five-minute drive turns into an eight and a half hour drive. Marcel swears he's okay, even when I offer to drive for him so he can rest, but men will be men.

When we're about an hour away from Fredericksburg, I look over at him. "Can I use your phone really quick?"

I don't know if it's me, but I notice he hesitates before saying, "Yeah, go ahead."

I shrug it off and grab his phone from the cupholder, and after he tells me his passcode, I plug Teagan's number into the keypad.

She answers. "Hello?"

"Hey, T, it's Gabby."

"Hey, girl! Did you get a new number?"

"No—I uh…" I glance at Marcel, "I'm calling from Marcel's phone."

"Oh." That's all she says, and I'm sure that's all she can really say to that. "What's going on? You okay?"

"Not really. Marcel is driving me up to see my parents, but I was thinking we could come see you first since you're along the way, before heading to see them?"

"You know you can! Where are you right now?"

"About thirty minutes out."

"Well, I'm home and not working tonight. It's perfect timing."

"Okay, good."

"Did something happen?" she asks in a lower voice. "With Kyle, I mean?"

I sigh, stroking Callie's back. She's resting on my lap, but her eyes are wide open. "Everything happened with Kyle. Tell you more when we get there."

"Okay," she says, more seriously. "See you soon."

I end the call and then type in Teagan's address in the GPS of Marcel's phone. I have no idea how I remember her address, but considering how often I stayed at Teagan's apartment during my college breaks, it's not shocking that it never left my memory.

Teagan went to a college in Virginia and had her own apartment by the time she turned twenty. She lives about forty-five minutes away from my parents in Fredericksburg now. One thing I can say is I do remember my parents' home address. I won't ever forget that.

"You and Teagan are complete opposites," Marcel says. "How'd you two meet?"

"Oh, I met her in middle school. We had science class together and partnered up for a project. We got in trouble because we couldn't stop complimenting each other's clothes and shoes."

"Really?" he laughs.

"Yeah," I laugh. "She used to live a neighborhood over from me, so we got closer that way. Had sleepovers all the time, rode the bus to school together every morning. She used to have a huge crush on Ricky."

"Really? Well, I guess I could see that. That's cool how you two met, though. Can't say I had many friends back then. Due to my big teeth, I was a bit of a lone wolf. I did get good grades though."

I giggle. "I would have been happy to be your friend back then."

"Well, back when I was in middle school, you were most likely a toddler. Not sure that would've worked out."

I bump his shoulder playfully. "You know what I mean."

"So, we're headed to Teagan's?" he asks.

I nod, handing the phone back to him after plugging the address into the GPS. "I just want to see her really quick, if that's okay."

"Yeah. It's fine. Don't stress it." He puts on a gentle smile for me, following the route.

Before I know it, we've made it to Teagan's apartment complex. He parks in front of her building, letting out a loud sigh as he kills the engine.

"Gonna feel good to stretch these legs," he groans, pushing the car door open. He steps out and stretches his arms above his head, then twists his torso to crack his back.

I hop out with Callie in my arms, but she insists on being put down. I grab her leash, clip it to her collar, and place her down.

"This way."

I head for the stairs, going up to apartment 6A. After knocking twice, Teagan answers and at first, she smiles, but when she sees my face in full, she gasps.

"Oh my God, Gabby! What in the hell happened to you!" she screeches, grabbing my arm and hauling me inside. She turns toward Marcel with a vicious scowl. "Did you do this to her?" Her voice is full of rage as she shoves him backward with all her might. He hardly budges.

"Teagan! He didn't do this! He's helping me!" I yell before she can shove him again.

Marcel's hands are in the air now, his eyes wide and confused.

Teagan settles down a bit, glaring over her shoulder at me. "He's helping you do what?" she snaps.

"Get away from *Kyle!*"

When it registers to her, her mouth clamps shut, and her eyes get bigger. "Oh my God." She rushes my way again, holding my upper arms. "Oh my God, Gabby!" She reels me in for a hug, and this hug is powerful, which threatens me with tears, but I refuse to let them fall. I'm tired of feeling weak about what Kyle did to me. I'm stronger than this and I know it, so I keep my tears at bay for now, focusing on my best friend's face again as she looks me all over. "Kyle did this to you? Are you *serious*?"

I nod. "He found out about Marcel."

The rims of her eyes thicken with tears. "Shit! I'm so sorry this happened, G! I can't believe this!"

"It's okay," I whisper. "Don't worry. I'm okay now."

"I'm gonna take Callie for a walk, let you two talk," Marcel mumbles behind Teagan.

Teagan turns, looking him over in his white T-shirt and dark jeans. "I'm so sorry for hitting you. It was just a reaction—I didn't think it all the way through."

Marcel gives her a swift nod. "You're just lookin' out for your friend. I get it." He scoops Callie up. "But for the record, I would never hurt a woman, especially a woman like Gabby."

Teagan nods and Marcel turns away, walking out the door. One of his cheeks tips up in a smile as he focuses on me, before shutting the door behind him.

"Fuck," Teagan deadpans.

"What?"

"Why is he so damn *hot*? When my hands were on his chest, I almost forgot what I'd pushed him for!"

"Oh my God, Teagan!" I can't help the laugh that bubbles out of me as I wipe the dampness from under my eyes.

This is why I needed to see her. She always lifts my spirit, even when she isn't trying.

"What? It's true!" She drags me to the sofa. "But enough about that! I'm glad he brought you all the way up here. Most guys wouldn't even bother."

"Yeah, he's been a lifesaver."

"Good. That's exactly what you need right now."

"I hope I didn't interrupt your plans or anything."

"Nah. I was going to go to the movies with Josh, but you called and that was much more important. I told him I needed a raincheck. I think he's a little upset, considering we hardly ever get to go out as it is, and I canceled."

"What? Well, don't let me stop you! I can always come back!" I start to stand but she grabs my hand, forcing me back down.

"No—don't even try it! Sit down." She's looking me deep in the eyes now. "How did this happen, G?"

I throw my hands in the air, at a loss for words. I know this won't be my last time hearing this question, so I might as well get used to answering it. "Kyle found out about Marcel."

"I figured as much, but *how*, G?"

"I don't know, but from what he's said to me, he's had his suspicions about it for a while. He found Marcel's business card on our kitchen floor, the day after the table broke."

Teagan gasps.

"Then when I was on the way home after spending those three days with Marcel, Kyle was already there. It's like he was *waiting* for me. He saw me when I got home and told me to get in the house, and as soon as we were inside, he, um…he grabbed me by the throat and pushed me against the wall."

"Oh my God." Teagan's eyes close softly.

"He finally let me go, told me I was pathetic, then he kicked me in the face." I point at myself as nonchalantly as possible. "That's how I got this lovely bruise." I force a smile, but everything about it pains me.

"Fuck that! This isn't a joke! Nothing about that bruise is lovely, Gabby!" She sits up higher, grabbing my hands and squeezing them. "I thought you said things had gotten better with him! Has he been hitting you all this time?"

I half-shrug. "It wasn't constant. Just holding me too aggressively sometimes, which always left marks or small bruises. Little stuff that I shrugged off. He hasn't exactly *hit* or choked me since the night I came running here the last time."

Teagan releases an annoyed breath. "I hate that you waited until now to walk away."

I drop my head. "I know. Me too. I wasn't going to walk away at first, though."

Teagan frowns. "What do you mean?"

"I mean…the day after Kyle found out, Marcel stopped by to give me my wedding band. I'd forgotten it at the villa. Marcel saw my face, and he flipped out. He wanted to rip Kyle in half, but instead he told me to pack a bag and to come with him. I packed one, but Kyle showed up as soon as we were leaving and reminded me why I couldn't."

"What do you mean? Why the hell couldn't you?"

"Because of my family, T. You know about the situation with my mom, and what Kyle did for Ricky. And to make matters worse, my dad sold his docking business to Kyle's investment company. My dad will rely on whatever money he can get from that, but after walking away, Kyle will terminate that, I'm sure of it. He'll do everything he can to get to me—he's threatened to kill me before."

"That's so fucked up, Gabby! You have to stay the hell away from him! And he's an idiot if he drags business into something personal."

My throat feels raw and tight again. I'm on the verge of another breakdown, but I do my best to hold it together.

With a shaky voice, I say, "I haven't told Marcel this but...Kyle *raped* me before I got the courage to walk out. It happened in the kitchen. It was worse than the first time he did it."

Teagan sits forward. "*What?* Are you fucking serious?"

I nod. "He kept asking me how I had sex with Marcel—kept acting like he really wanted to know how we did things. He forced me on top of him and told me to—"

I can't even finish. I hate thinking about it. Every single second of that day was misery.

"Hey, hey. It's okay." Teagan wraps her arms around me, and it's now I realize I'm doing exactly what I said I wouldn't do. *Crying*. She holds me tight, and I rest my cheek on her chest. "You got away from that shithead. That's all that matters. Fuck him. If things go a little off-course with the family, it will suck, yes, but there are always ways to build back up. They've survived for this long, I'm sure they'll keep doing what they need to do to survive. But if something happens to you, they won't survive, Gabby. It would kill them if they got to the bottom of why something happened. If they found out you were severely hurt or even killed because you didn't want your family to suffer, that would make matters even worse for them. They'd blame themselves for the rest of their lives. You did the right thing by running away from Kyle, trust me."

She's so right, but it's not so much that I'm worried about my parents. I know they'll make a way—they've done it all their lives. It's more so the fact that I know Kyle well enough to know that he will not let this go. He will hunt me down. He'll make my life a living hell and possibly even hurt me or someone else that I care about. It's a horrible thing, to live in fear.

"I'm just worried. What if I did the wrong thing by walking away? I know cheating was wrong—I understand that—but I can't help thinking that maybe if I hadn't hired Marcel in the first place, none of this would have happened. We would have tried to be happier and gotten Kyle some help." I sniffle and swipe at my face. "Shit…I don't know. I don't even know what I'm saying."

Teagan forces me to sit back up then wipes one of my stray tears away. "Listen to me, Gabby. You are the greatest woman I know, okay? You can't let something like this tear you down or think this is all your fault. It's not your fault Kyle is the way he is. When I first met you, I was so envious of you—I still am—but only because you are everything I aspire to be. You're beautiful, funny, and maybe even slightly more sarcastic than I am."

I bubble out a laugh.

"You are an amazing person who deserves so much

more than the shit Kyle gave you. I can tell Marcel is a good guy—the kind of guy you *need*. It doesn't matter how you met him. At the end of the day, you were clearly supposed to meet him. You're hurting, and this all seems so fucking surreal—and not in the best way—but there are people who are here for you. Don't be afraid to ask for help when you need it. Okay?"

I nod as her misty eyes lock on mine. "'Kay."

She lets out another sigh then pulls me in for a tighter hug. I hug her back this time, and as we do, there's a knock at the door. Teagan gets up to open it, and Marcel is on the other side.

"Okay to come in?" His deep voice carries through the apartment.

"Yeah, come in."

He steps inside, placing Callie down after shutting the door. He smiles at me as I wipe my tears away. "Should I look for a hotel?" he asks.

"What?" Teagan shakes her head. "Hell no, save your money. You guys can sleep here. That couch is a pull out. Gabby can sleep there with you, or she can share the bed with me."

I smile. "I'll take the pull out with him, T. It's okay. I don't want to intrude too much."

"Oh, please. You know I don't mind. The only time I care is when your armpit ends up in my face."

Marcel breaks out in smile. "Is it like that?"

"No!" I laugh, shaking my head. "It is nothing like that!"

"It really is!" Teagan shouts. "You might want to watch out, Marcel! You don't want to end up with a mouth full of armpit!"

The laughter continues, and damn, does it feel good. This is exactly what I needed. Being out of Hilton Head has already been a relief, but to be here laughing with my best friend is gold.

"Let me grab some blankets." Teagan walks off, still laughing, and Marcel's brows shift up as he focuses on me.

"Everything okay?" he murmurs, stepping closer.

"Yeah. Everything's good."

"Good. So, interesting thing just happened. Got a phone call, and the person left a voicemail."

"Who was it from?"

He takes his cell out of his back pocket. "Your husband."

My heart gallops, quick and unhinged. Marcel hands me his phone, which is already on the voicemail app. I press the phone to my ear after tapping play, and Kyle's British accent sends my heart plummeting to my stomach.

*"Gabby, I know you're probably fucking Ward right now. Just know if you aren't back home within the next two days, I will proceed with cutting off all of your ties. Don't forget everything I've done for you. The loans I have paid off for your sake. The house I bought for you to be fucking happy in. I don't understand how a woman in your position can be so ungrateful. There are so many others who would kill to be where you are—to be with me. Get your ass home immediately, or I will find you."*

I lower the phone, handing it to him like it's caught fire. "Delete it."

Marcel looks me over. "No. You can use this as proof that he's a threat to you."

He's right. I didn't think of it that way.

"Okay. Well, we have to see my parents by tomorrow. He said two days. That's plenty of time for us to fill them in so they can prepare themselves."

"He's going to leave you with nothing, Gabby. It'll be tough for a while. Are you prepared for that?"

"I don't care. I went into it with nothing. I'll be fine in the end."

He nods, as if he likes that answer.

Teagan returns with a sheet and a blanket, and we help her set up the pullout couch.

After she opens up a bottle of wine to share while I discuss the plan with my parents tomorrow, we're all exhausted and curling into bed.

I rest on Marcel's chest, letting out a long sigh. It's nearing midnight—I see it on Teagan's microwave in neon blue numbers. Callie is sleeping on her dog bed next to the pullout.

"What's wrong?" Marcel asks.

"I don't know. I guess I'm surprised you've stuck around after everything. Most people would bail."

"You shouldn't be surprised. I like helpin' people."

"What about your company? You're missing work for a big job, right?"

"It's handled. Told the guys I'll be back in a few days. Rob is in charge for now. If anything goes bad, he knows to call me."

I nod, glad to hear that.

We're quiet again.

"Marcel?"

"Hmm?" He's rubbing circles on my upper arm.

"Are there other things about you I should know before this gets any deeper?"

The circles on my arm stops, and he's quiet for so long I assume he isn't going to answer the question. But then he says, "There are a lot of things about me you don't know, Gabby, but right now, I'm focusing on *you*. We'll get to my shit eventually."

I'm not upset by those words, nor am I comforted by them. I'd like to know what more there is to him, and if it will make or break us, but at the same time, who am I to question his past when my skeletons have all tumbled out of the closet? I didn't tell him anything, and now we're both reaping what I've sowed.

I don't think what he's given me is false. I really do think he likes me, and that he has fallen for me.

I've fallen for him too…but I'm hoping that falling for him isn't going to end up being another giant mistake.

## CHAPTER ELEVEN

### MARCEL

Teagan wakes up early to make coffee and pancakes. She said she had to work in a few hours and that we were free to make ourselves comfortable, but after chowing down on the breakfast, Gabby decides it's time to leave.

"It's better to get this over with now." Gabby throws her arms around the back of Teagan's neck. They hug for a long time, standing in the parking lot of the apartment complex. I put Callie in the truck and wait by the passenger door. "Thank you for letting us barge in. I know you had better things to do," Gabby says.

"Oh, please. I'll always make time for you. You know that." Teagan smiles, holding Gabby by the upper arms. "Stay strong, okay? No matter what happens, promise me you'll keep your head up."

Gabby nods. "I will. I promise."

"Good. Love you," Teagan says after a kiss to Gabby's cheek.

"Love you, too."

Teagan waves goodbye to me, and I wave back. She then climbs into her Hyundai as Gabby climbs into the passenger seat of my truck. I start the ignition, waiting for Gabby to give me instruction.

When she's quiet for a moment too long, I ask, "What's wrong?"

"My parents," she mutters. "I already know they're going to freak out."

"Better to get it over with now, right? Get to them before he can."

"Yeah. True. I'm just..." She crosses her fingers in her lap with a huff. "I'm worried."

"About what?"

"Disappointing them."

"I think they'll be much more disappointed in him than you, Gabby. If they aren't, that's on them, not you. And we all make mistakes. I met your parents, and they seem like the kind of people who know all about learning from their mistakes. You should trust them the most with stuff like this, right?"

"I do…I just…I remember how badly they wanted me to marry Kyle. They were so *in* for it, you know? He had money, and the looks, and the charm. They love him."

"Yeah, but it clearly wasn't the *real* him, and once they find that out, they'll be grateful you left his sorry ass." I grip the steering wheel. "Where to?"

She doesn't need the GPS this time. She points ahead and says, "Make a right out of here."

I leave Teagan's apartment complex, taking the first right, then I reach over and grab her hand.

"Be strong, Gabby."

She locks her glistening eyes on mine. "I will."

∼

We arrive at her parents' house in about forty minutes.

The house is simple. Quaint. A two-story home painted a very pale yellow. Brown shutters and a deep, wooden porch that's set up with cushioned rocking chairs.

I shut the car door behind me. Gabby is already out of the truck, with Callie in her arms. She stares ahead at the house then shifts her eyes over to the car in the driveway. There's a white Camry parked there.

"My dad's not here." She walks up the cement driveway, heading straight for the door. She gives the doorbell a ring, and I wait behind her.

"Do you want me to wait in the truck?" I ask.

"No, it's okay." She looks at me over her shoulder.

I let out a steady breath. I don't know if it's a good idea having me around with all that's going on. Who's to say her parents won't blame me for what happened? They don't seem like the kind of people who would jump at my throat, but it would make matters much more complicated if they do.

It takes a while for the door to open, but when it does, I spot the familiar petite Colombian woman on the other side of the screened door, only this time she isn't all dolled up in a dress, heels, and makeup.

She's wearing a black V-neck shirt tucked into high-waisted jeans. Her face is curious as she spots me first, but when her eyes drop and focus on Gabby, her half-smile completely collapses.

She swings the door open rapidly, screaming, "OH MY GOD! WHAT THE HELL HAPPENED TO YOU?" Cupping Gabby's face in her hands, her eyes immediately fill with tears. "Gabby? *Que pasó*, huh? What the hell is going on?" Her eyes shoot up to mine, and just like Teagan, she's already on the fence, probably assuming I have something to do with this. What do they think, I've kidnapped her and am bringing her around to say her goodbyes?

"Can I come in, Mamá?" I can hear the emotion in Gabby's voice as she asks.

"Yes, get in here!" Her mother opens the door wider, grabbing Gabby's hand and escorting her into the house.

I hesitate going inside when her mother gives me a death stare over the shoulder.

"It wasn't him, Mamá." Gabby glances at me. "Kyle did this."

Mrs. Lewis turns and frowns deep as she looks Gabby over. "Kyle? What do you mean *he did this*?"

"He choked me and kicked me in the face several days ago."

"He *kicked* you! Are you fucking kidding me?" Mrs. Lewis's voice is shrill.

"Mamá, calm down. It's okay." Gabby is holding her mother by the shoulders now, almost like she's soothing a child throwing a tantrum.

"No! This is not okay! How could he do that to you? How!"

Gabby closes her eyes very briefly and inhales, before opening them again and exhaling. "I'll explain everything to you, okay? Can you make some coffee or tea or something? Take a minute to calm down?"

Mrs. Lewis doesn't look like she wants to pull away from Gabby for one second, but she finally does, nodding as she twists around hastily for the kitchen.

She says something in Spanish as she storms away, and from the sound of it, I can tell she's pissed. Angry muttering continues from the kitchen as utensils rattle and drawers slam.

Gabby sighs, looking back at me. "There's a TV there, if you want to watch it. I know you're tired of hearing my sob story." She forces a laugh.

"Stop that." I rub her shoulder. "I'm fine, but if you want to talk to her privately, I understand. I'll just take Callie out for a walk."

"Sure. That'll be good."

"You got it."

I go for the door, pushing it open and letting the dog out. When it shuts, I look back, watching Gabby walk to the kitchen.

I can't help wondering if she's hiding something from me. There's something in her eyes—the way she looks at me, with so much guilt and apprehension. It's like she wants to tell me something but hasn't found the right words to say it.

I walk Callie around the neighborhood for about twenty minutes, but when we circle back to the Lewis home, I notice another car pulling into the driveway. This car is a blue Subaru.

Mr. Lewis steps out of the car as I walk across the street. He frowns when he spots me walking in his direction, then drops his eyes to Callie.

"Marcel?" He's confused, eyes narrowed. "What in the world are you doing all the way in Virginia?"

"I'm here with Gabby, sir," I answer.

"Gabby?" Mr. Lewis is still confused. His eyes shift from mine to the door. "Is she in the house?"

"Yes."

"But that doesn't explain why *you're* here. She didn't tell me she was visiting."

"It was an unplanned trip. I offered to drive her here after what happened."

"Well, what the hell happened?"

"I suggest you go find out for yourself, sir. She's inside waitin'."

Instead of asking another question, he marches toward the house and goes right inside.

I walk Callie to the door and go inside too, and from where I stand, I can see Gabby hugging her father in the kitchen.

"What is going on? What in the hell happened to you?" he asks, voice laced with worry. He has her face in his hands and is rubbing it with the pads of his thumbs.

I unclip Callie's leash from her collar, standing upright.

"Kyle happened," Gabby sighs.

"Kyle? What do you mean? I'm not understanding what's going on. And, I'm sorry, but why is your *yard guy* with you?"

*Landscape architect, jackass.*

Gabby focuses on me as I walk toward the kitchen. "He saved me from him. Offered to bring me here to see you guys."

"I'm so confused—"

"Dad—just sit. Okay?" Gabby's hands are in the air, her eyes now shut. I can tell she's tired of his interrogation.

When I'm in the kitchen, Gabby looks at me and points to the four-top table in the corner. There is a carafe of coffee on top of it, set up with creamer and sugar. I sit as Gabby and her mom do, but when I look up, Mr. Lewis is staring right at me, still standing in front of his chair.

"Do you two have something going on?" he demands.

Gabby frowns at him. "Dad—is that really your biggest concern right now?"

"I mean, if so, it's pretty damn obvious, Gabby."

She shakes her head, pouring some coffee into my mug. I thank her, reaching for the creamer and sugar. "I've already told Má what happened, so now I'm going to tell you."

"Tell me what?"

"How about you sit, and maybe I'll fill you in."

Mr. Lewis blows out a breath, placing his tall frame on the chair.

Gabby dumps sugar and creamer into her coffee, stirs, and then sips it. She then looks up at her father and says, "Kyle found out about me and Marcel a few days ago. When he did, he choked me and then kicked me in the face."

"HE DID WHAT?!" Mr. Lewis shoves out of his chair, as if Kyle is in the room and he's going to pummel him into the ground.

I know exactly how he feels. I wanted to beat that fucker into a pulp when I first saw her face, so I can't imagine what her own father wants to do to him.

"Sit, Will. Please," Mrs. Lewis pleads, but her husband is still seething. He sits back down but leans toward Gabby.

"How in the hell did this happen, Gabby? I mean, why would he choke and kick you? That doesn't sound like him at all!"

"It's been happening for a while, Dad. He's never kicked me before, but he has hit me before." Gabby's throat bobs. "A few days after we got back from our honeymoon, he choked me. That was the first time."

"But that was *months* ago," Mr. Lewis croaks.

"I know."

"And you didn't tell me?" He glances over at his wife. "Did you tell your mother?"

"No, the only person who knew about it was Teagan, and Kyle, of course. I didn't know how to tell you guys, especially since we'd just gotten married. I considered it a mistake, and he promised he'd never do it again. He was drunk when it happened—"

"Drunk or not, he doesn't have the right to fucking hurt you like that!"

Gabby lowers her head, focusing on her lap. "I thought it would stop there, but with every month, he seemed to get more controlling. When we moved, he grabbed me more. Held me tighter. I started to pull away, I guess, but I ended up focusing too much on Marcel, and I'm assuming Kyle noticed too. I didn't mean for the affair to happen, it just did, and things got a little carried away…" Her voice thickens, and she huffs, like she's frustrated with herself.

I clench a fist beneath the table. I hate hearing the pain in her voice.

"I slipped up, and Kyle grew suspicious about it. He said he had to work out of town for a couple days last week, but now that I think about it, I don't think he had to. I think he waited around somewhere and watched me leave, then checked my emails or something. That, or he followed me. I'll never know."

"How long has this been going on with you two?" Mr. Lewis asks, sliding his eyes over to me before focusing on his daughter again.

"Since April…" Gabby answers.

"Jesus." Mr. Lewis plants an elbow on the table and drags a hand over his face. He then looks up at Gabby, bringing that same hand forward to clasp her chin between his fingers. "Look, I know you feel bad about what you did, but you can't live your life with regrets like that. He never should have put his hands on you. *Ever*. Doesn't matter what you did."

Gabby's eyes are instantly damp, the tears falling when she closes them. "You sold the docking company to him, Dad. Why would you do that?"

Mr. Lewis withdraws, eyes widening. "He told you?"

"I saw papers on his desk last week. He's going to ruin everything I care about, which means he'll cancel whatever arrangement he made with you. It will take a while to get your assets back. You could lose a lot of money."

Mr. Lewis huffs out a breath, sitting back against the chair. He stares absently past Gabby then lowers his gaze.

"When did you sell it? You never told me about this." Mrs. Lewis is staring a hole through the side of her husband's head with a deep scowl.

"I sold it completely a couple months ago, but before

that, he'd only been investing in it to keep business going, so I could settle some of my debts, renovate, and so on."

Mrs. Lewis groans and pinches the bridge of her nose. "I can't believe you didn't tell me, Will!"

Gabby asks, "Why, though? Why sell it to Kyle?"

"Because I was losing money," he answers, slightly frustrated. "People aren't coming to rent boats anymore and most are building their own docks. Fredericksburg is just a small blip on the radar. There aren't as many tourists as there used to be. I had heard about Kyle's investment company years before selling it and was told if I ever needed to sell it or have someone invest in it in a reasonable time, to go to him." He sits forward, shoving his fingers through his peppery hair. I can tell something's bothering him—something deeper than all of this. "Mariana, Marcel, I need a word with Gabby alone, please."

Mrs. Lewis lets out an aggravated sigh. I push to a stand, taking my coffee mug with me.

"I'd love to check out your backyard, Mrs. Lewis," I offer. "I noticed the front yard is well kept."

"Sure." Mrs. Lewis waves a hand, going for the backdoor. "Come on."

Callie is right at my heels, following me out the door. I look back at Gabby, but she doesn't look my way.

She's staring at her father, and even I can tell that what he's about to say to her will end up breaking her even more.

## CHAPTER TWELVE

### GABBY

Dad gets up and walks straight to the fridge.

I push out of my chair, going to the counter opposite of him and resting my lower back against the edge of it.

"Why would you make a deal with him anyway?" I ask.

Dad is quiet, pulling out lunchmeat, bread, mayo, and a few other ingredients.

"Dad?"

"I had no choice, Gabby."

"There is always a choice."

"I was losing money, and a good friend of mine told me about Kyle and his company in New York, so I went there to check it out and to see if he could help."

"And?"

"And…I ended up hearing more than I should have the day I met with him." He side-eyes me.

"What do you mean?"

He takes two slices of bread out. He's going to make his

infamous turkey club sandwich. He makes them when he's stressed, otherwise my mom is the one making them for him.

"Okay, look." He sighs, stepping away from the counter and holding his hands in the air. "The first time I went for a meeting, I overheard Kyle talking to his mother."

My frown deepens, but I don't speak. I wait for him to go on.

"I overheard his mother asking about his dating life and telling him he needed to hurry and get out there so he could get a wife. Just a bunch of stuff that was clearly annoying for him to hear, and like she'd told him about it plenty of times before. She left out, and Kyle called me into his office moments later. I had my papers and was hoping for a small investment at least, but he turned it down. I was a little annoyed that he'd turned me down so quickly without even giving me a chance, so I told him I'd overheard his conversation with his mother." Dad looks at me warily, eyes glistening. "I told him I could help with his…*situation.*"

"Help? How?" I snap, and he groans, dragging both palms of his hands over his face.

"Gabby, look…" He hesitates, avoiding my eyes. "What I'm about to tell you might upset you, but I want you know I did it for all of us."

"Oh my God, Dad, just spit it out already!"

"Okay—fine. It's just…well, the relationship you have with Kyle was, in lack of better words, *arranged*. I told Kyle I had a daughter who was finishing up college. I showed him a picture of you, and he told me he would go to the place you worked and see you for himself. I guess he liked you, because he called me a few days later and told me he was willing to invest."

*Wow.*

I was *not* expecting that.

If I thought the kick from Kyle was a big blow, this one feels even worse. This blow is stronger, and I'm surprised it doesn't knock the wind out of me just as much as Kyle's kick did.

I don't even know what to say to him right now. I can only stare into my father's eyes—the eyes I inherited.

All this time, I thought Kyle was coming to Nuni's out of sheer coincidence, but it turns out it was all *planned*? By my own *father*?

"Dad..." I feel like all my words have been lodged in my throat. "How could you do something like that? All for your *company*?"

"I didn't want to, Gabby, trust me, but I was desperate! You were already struggling with getting through college, and we were close to losing this house!" He throws his hands in the air. "I didn't know what else to do, so I took what I heard and threw it right back at him!"

"Is that why you were so adamant about me marrying him? He asked me to marry him almost a year later, and you were all for it! You even met him before I'd even introduced you to him, but pretended you didn't know him at all! Who does something like that?" I'm shouting now, something I've never done to my father out of respect, but I don't care right now. I feel victimized.

That rich man in Nuni's only wanted me because of a recommendation from another man—and not just any other man. My own goddamn *father*. Kyle would have never met me otherwise. Hell, if it weren't for my dad, I never would have fallen for Kyle, which would have spared me from the trouble I'm in now.

I can't believe this shit!

Rage takes hold of me, boiling in my bloodstream. My rage is horrible, but it can't be controlled until it's unleashed.

I can't even remember the last time I was this pissed. This hurts so much more than what Kyle did to me. So. Much. More.

I step toward my dad, pointing a firm finger in his face, "You know what, Dad? You've always been selfish. Ever since I can remember, all you've ever cared about is yourself! When you cheated on Mom, Ricky and I didn't bat an eye! Mom pretended it was nothing, but it was bullshit! She should have made you *pay* for what you did instead of forgiving you so quickly!" I shout in his face. "I always wondered how you could do that to her, but now I see. You cheated because you're a self-centered, inconsiderate, *stupid* man! Any man who can sell out his own *daughter* instead of keeping his dignity is no man at all!"

"Gabby, please listen to me, sweetheart! I didn't know he was that kind of person! I thought he was good for you and that you really liked him, so I didn't want to ruin—"

"No!" I growl. "No! You *do not* get to decide what is good for me and what isn't! You don't get to make those decisions for me!"

Tears have blinded me. My heart aches when I notice a tear sliding down his cheek, but I refuse to cave.

I turn around and rush for the back door before any drop of sympathy can course through my bloodstream.

Marcel is outside talking to my mom, but when they

hear the door slam, they look back with confused expressions.

"Marcel, let's go!" I yell.

He frowns in my direction. "What's wrong?"

"Let's just get the hell out of here. Please." I pick Callie up as she runs to me then I walk around the house.

I can hear my dad calling my name before I can get too far.

"Gabrielle!" My mom screams. "Honey, where are you going? What happened?"

I come to a sudden halt, swinging around to face her. "I don't know, Mamá! How about you go ask Dad, huh? He's the one with all the big secrets these days!" She's confused, but she stops chasing after me, allowing it to digest.

I hurry to Marcel's truck, climbing into the passenger seat. I wait for Marcel to get inside and as soon as he does, he looks at me.

"What the hell happened?" he pants.

"I don't want to talk about it here! Let's just go! Please!"

He's quiet as he looks me over, but he starts the truck anyway.

My dad is walking down the driveway, waving a hand, trying to get my attention. Marcel drives off, and I'm glad, because I don't want to see my dad's face anymore.

"Gonna tell me what the hell happened?" Marcel asks as I swipe an angry tear off my face.

"I just thought of all people, my dad would be the last to hurt me, but he fucking did. He's no better than Kyle." My voice breaks, and I turn away, squeezing my eyes shut and holding back a sob.

Marcel doesn't ask any more questions after that. Frankly, I don't expect him to.

He drives for hours, glancing at me every so often. I only know it's been hours because we passed the "You are now leaving Virginia" sign a while ago. The sun begins to sink, and, eventually, Marcel gets off the freeway, pulling up to a hotel.

"Why are we stopping?" I probe.

"Because we need to rest. We'll stay the night and head back to Hilton in the morning." He glances down at Callie, who is on my lap. "It's pet-friendly. Be right back."

Marcel climbs out of the truck, shutting the door behind him. He goes inside, most likely to book a room, and returns several minutes later, opening the passenger door.

I step out, Callie tucked beneath my arm, then he grabs the suitcases from the back row.

I place Callie down, and she immediately runs off to pee.

When I'm inside the hotel room, I dump some food and water into Callie's bowls then sit on the edge of the bed.

Marcel lets out a long, weary sigh, and walks to the bathroom.

"Why don't you hit the shower? Maybe that'll help a little."

I peer up at him as he stands by the bathroom door. Then I stand, too, walking his direction.

"This is all too much for you," I whisper.

He clasps my chin between his fingers. "How so?"

"I can just tell. I feel like I'm dragging you through my shit. You don't deserve this."

His head shakes. "I told you I'm not goin' anywhere, Gabby."

"Yeah, but I just…" I trail off with a huff. I don't even have the words right now. I feel betrayed and so, so stupid.

I go for my suitcase to take out my toiletries and then walk past him to the bathroom.

Once the shower has been started up, I strip out of my clothes. He's watching me from the door, but not in a hawkish way. More so like he's concerned.

"Shower with me," I insist.

"You sure?"

I nod. I don't know why, but I'm afraid that if I shower alone, Marcel would be gone when I get out. Would he do something like that? After everything he's had to deal with because of me, it wouldn't surprise me, but I'm not sure I could handle it if he did.

I stand beneath the warm stream of water, closing my eyes and soaking in it. When I turn my back to the shower-head, Marcel is stepping in, too.

We stare at each other for several seconds before I finally tear my gaze away and turn toward the water again. The heat of his body meets my backside, and I feel the ridge of his soft cock on my ass.

I sigh, because I love the comfort of his body so much.

"I don't know what else to do," I mumble.

Marcel wraps his arms around my midsection, pulling me closer to him. "You stay with me," he murmurs. "You fight."

"Are you sure that's what you really want? I'm technically still married, and you've seen firsthand who I'm married to. It would be complicated."

"Complicated may as well be my middle name," he says with a light chuckle. "It's all my life has ever been."

I can't help smiling a little at that, even though my heart still hurts.

When he pulls away, we both wash up, rinse well, and get out of the shower. As he searches for clothes, I sit on the bed again in just a towel, my hair damp and on my shoulders.

"I want to know more about you," I murmur.

Marcel looks back at me as he slides into a pair of briefs. "What do you wanna know?"

"If there is anything about you that you haven't told anyone. Other than the information about how you lost your sister."

He looks away, toward the window. He's quiet for a really long time, going to the side of the bed to sit with his back to me.

"Marcel, I can't stay with you if I don't know you," I say after a while.

"I know."

"So, tell me something. Who is the guy you fought at the bar? You got charged for assault for it? Why?"

"Jesus." He pinches the bridge of his nose.

"Tell me."

He lets out an agitated breath. "He was Shayla's ex-boyfriend. She used to hang out with him a lot. The fight happened right before I moved to Hilton. He was at the bar the same night I was, and he was really drunk. He started blaming me for her death, calling me a bunch of different names. For a while, I sat there and took it, but then he called me a name I didn't like."

I turn to fully look at him, but he's not looking my way at all. "What name?"

*"Murderer."*

I study his hunched shoulders. He stands, fists clenched, as if the memory itself is enough to infuriate him.

"I slammed his face on the counter. He was with a few friends, and one of them tried to join in on the fight. It was bloody, so I got arrested. Tommy, Shayla's ex, decided not to press charges, probably because he was no longer drunk and realized he'd said some pretty fucked up things to me. Also, if it hadn't been for him almost getting busted, she wouldn't have needed a ride from me anyway. The police let me go after a few days."

"Wow… Oh my God, Marcel. I'm so sorry that happened—that he called you that."

He shrugs. "It is what it is."

We're both quiet a beat.

"Mind if I ask you somethin'?"

"Depends on what it is…"

"I don't know why I'm curious about it, but were you plannin' on havin' kids with him?"

My brows dip when I meet his eyes. "Um…he wanted them sooner than I did. We couldn't agree, so we left the topic alone for a while."

"Oh."

I drop my arms and walk around the bed, pulling the comforter down and lying on the bed.

Marcel stands with a grunt and makes his way to the bed. When we're under the sheets, Callie jumps up and starts to snuggle in the blanket at the foot of the bed.

I lie on my back, staring up at the ceiling for a while.

Marcel has told me his truths. I can't keep holding mine back from him.

"When Kyle and I first got married, right after our honeymoon, we got into an argument about having kids. That was the first night he choked me."

He's quiet after I air my statement, but I can tell he's listening.

"His mom was so obsessed with the idea of us having a baby. I told her I wasn't ready yet, at a dinner that happened shortly after our honeymoon. I mean, we'd just gotten married. I wanted to enjoy the married life a little while longer before bringing a baby into it."

"I understand that."

I roll over, curling up to his side. My pulse quickens with what I'm about to tell him. "The day when you were about to take me with you, Kyle did something to me that I can't, for the life of me, forget about. I mean, it happened before, but not to this extreme. I've been having nightmares about it, that's how bad it is."

Marcel finally moves, turning his head to meet my eyes. "What did he do?"

I close my eyes, fighting the burn that's taken hold of them. "He kept asking me about you—about how we...*did* things. How we had...*sex*..." I draw in a sharp breath and a deep growl forms in the pit of Marcel's throat. "He was in a rage, almost like another person. He threw me over the table and *raped* me."

"*WHAT?* Are you fuckin' serious?" Marcel sits up straight, his back against the headboard. "I swear to God, Gabby that is the last fuckin' straw! I'm gonna break his goddamn neck!" He shoves the sheets away and jumps out of bed, pacing the room, flinging his arms in the air. "I don't give a fuck if he charges me with assault, Gabby! I don't! He's a worthless piece of shit who needs to be taught a goddamn lesson!"

I climb out of bed, stepping in front of him. I grab his hands and shake my head. "Marcel, it doesn't matter what you do! He's not going to let you get away with it!"

"I don't give a shit! He's hurt you multiple times, Gabby! If you don't report it, then I'm going to beat his ass, plain and simple!"

"I don't want you getting in trouble because of me, okay? I'm not kidding! If you want me to report it, I will! Just promise me you won't put yourself in that position because I *need* you! I can't afford to lose you right now!" My voice breaks, and his seething eases. That frown of his slowly melts away. My hands are shaking now, my throat raw. "I don't know how it's happened, okay? I don't know when this feeling took over me, but I realize now it's not just that I have fallen for you! I *love you*, Marcel! I love you a lot, and I was trying to deny it, but the more I'm around you, the more I realize that's exactly what I feel! I fucking love you, okay?"

He's looking me all over, eyes wide, breaths leveling out. "How can you love me?" he rasps. "After everything I've told you—everything you know about me—"

"I don't care about any of that! I don't care that you had to do what you had to do to survive. And what happened with Shayla was an accident. I don't care that you were almost charged with assault—but if you get charged again, you won't just be in there for one night or even one week. Kyle will make sure you're in there for *months*. He will ruin your life like he did mine, so just promise me, right now." I try keeping my voice steady, but it's breaking terribly. "Promise me you won't put your life at risk for me." I squeeze his hands. "I need you right now, so promise me that you won't hurt him unless he hurts you or me first."

He studies my face, and it doesn't take long for him to cup it in his hands. "I can do you one better."

Bringing his face forward, he kisses me so passionately that every emotional fiber inside me ignites.

I throw my arms up and curl my fingers in his hair as he picks me up by the waist. My legs lock around his hips instantly, and he carries me to the bed, laying me down gently and continuing the kisses.

We maneuver to the middle of the bed, my heart racing and my mind gone. I'm greedy for more of him, kissing feverishly, like one kiss at a time will never be enough.

He sucks on my bottom lip and trails his lips down to the crook of my neck, sucking there before lowering his mouth to the cut of my shirt. He snatches the shirt down, sucking one of my erect nipples into his mouth.

"Make me forget," I breathe. "Please. I want to forget it."

He peers up at me with hooded blue eyes, and with no hesitation at all, he lowers my shorts. He's between my legs in seconds, kissing my lips, drinking me in. I snatch my mouth away to force his boxers down, and his cock lands on my thigh, hot and heavy.

"Are you sure? I don't want to hurt—"

"No. Stop." I press a finger to his lips. I am still sore, uncertain, but I need him right now. I want to erase that pain—replace it, even. I know Marcel can do that. "This won't hurt me. I need it."

As if my words are everything he needs in this moment, he wastes no time pushing between my thighs. He's inside me with ease, kissing me fiercely as he stills for just a second.

"Oh, fuck," he groans, mouth dropping to the crook of my neck.

I moan.

"You're too precious to hurt, Gabby." He lifts one of my legs, thrusting even deeper. I cry out in bliss and pleasure, arching my back. "You are fuckin' gold. You're perfect."

"I don't want you to leave me," I breathe out, and I know I sound desperate, but it's the truth. I don't want him to leave. I never thought I'd want another man as much as I'd wanted Kyle, yet here I am, wanting Marcel Ward more than anything on this earth.

"I'm not goin' anywhere. You already know that," he rumbles in my ear, and his voice is so deep it's almost orgasmic. Everything about it makes me want to come.

He cups the back of my neck, and his mouth lands on mine again. As we kiss and he strokes, the fire builds up, roaring like a flame. Every single thing outside of this moment is meaningless.

The bruise on my face means nothing.

The pain I felt mere days ago? That's gone.

Why? Because he's erasing that pain. He's taking it all away.

I meant every word of what I said to him. I love Marcel, and I know Kyle. He will not rest until Marcel is taken down, and if Marcel lays a finger on him first, he will make sure that his life is ruined.

He's already ruined mine. I refuse to let him do the same to this insanely beautiful, wonderful man, who has already been through so much.

With several more thrusts, I feel my climax building. He's closer and closer, and my back begins to arch again.

Marcel unleashes a deep groan, and before I know it, we're both letting out noises like animals. He's groaning and I'm moaning, and I realize what this is: we're both letting go at the same time. It's a release that shoots us over the moon and past the stars.

I've never done this with Kyle—never had the pleasure of coming when he's coming, but this sensation is fucking amazing. I feel even more connected to him than I did moments ago, and when he kisses me, I sigh, loving every bit of this.

After our bodies have died down, we slide up to the pillows and I lay my head on his chest, hiding my smile.

We catch our breaths for just a moment, my arm curled around him and his hand on my waist.

"I'm going to file for a divorce," I whisper after a few minutes have ticked by.

"I've been waiting to hear you say that," he says, and I can hear the smile in his voice.

I run my hand down his chest, over his toned stomach. "When we get back, I'll go to the police station and file a domestic report, too. He's not getting away with what he did that easily."

Marcel tips my chin, planting a kiss on my lips. "Good," he rumbles. "That's my girl."

## CHAPTER THIRTEEN

**GABBY**

MARCEL PURCHASES a phone for me as soon as we are back in Hilton Head.

He told me point blank that he needs to be able to call and check in with me, so he added me to his phone plan. With Kyle's threats hanging over my head, I'm glad he's taking this seriously.

Marcel has been doing so much for me lately that I almost can't allow myself to accept some of it. I feel like he's taken on my burdens, and since we're just now getting to know each other, the feeling always makes me icky. He deserves better than to deal with my mess, let alone help clean it up.

As soon as I received the phone, I gave my mother a call —using the number on the folded sheet of paper I wrote it on, during the little trip to Virginia, where I asked her for it —but of course, she gave my number to Dad, who has been calling me and leaving voicemails for the past five days.

I haven't answered any of his calls. I haven't even answered my mom's after he started calling, because I know she'll give him the phone, and I refuse to hear his excuses.

What he did is unacceptable. Though I understand he thought he was doing what he needed to do to save the family and his business, I do blame him for thinking I was some kind of object he could auction.

Surprisingly enough, Ricky has been calling too. I didn't answer at first, because he's just like Dad, thinking everything is no big deal, but today I do.

"What the hell is going on?" is the first thing Ricky asks when I finally answer the phone.

"I'm sure you've talked to Dad," I say as I pull out a pair of shorts and a top.

"Yeah, and Má. She told me he used you to get to Kyle somehow. I don't know all the details about what went down with you two, but it sounds messed up."

"He more than *used* me. He sent Kyle to me, as some kind of incentive to buy the dock. He knew all about us, even before I introduced Kyle to the family."

"Shit. Seriously?" I can tell Ricky is shaking his head. "Where are you now? Do I need to come and get you? You know you can always stay with me."

"No, it's okay. I'm in Hilton right now, staying with a friend." I walk out of the bedroom, looking at the door Marcel just walked out of to go to work less than twenty minutes ago.

"Is it that landscape guy?" he asks.

"Yeah." I tuck my hair behind my ears. "Is that dumb?"

"Is he keeping you safe?"

"Yeah. He bought me this phone and checks in every hour."

"Then no, it's not dumb, staying with someone who has your back."

I smile at his statement.

"Anyway, I'll be busy this weekend, but I wanted to hear your voice. I'll try and come out to see you soon if I can."

"Okay, Ricky."

"And do me a favor, Gabby?"

"What?"

"Answer Dad's call the next time. I know you don't want to hear it, but he told me you ran out before he had time to completely explain himself."

I scoff. "What more is there to explain, Ricky? He set this whole thing up, and all that time I thought what Kyle and I had was real. It wasn't, and now I have a bruise on my face because Dad cared more about his business than anything else!"

"It's not like he knew Kyle was abusive, Gabby! Look, from what Dad told me over the phone, he went to Kyle and told him to cancel the investments he'd made to the docking company when you two were about to get married. He wasn't happy with what he'd done and was willing to let his company take the fall, but of course Kyle declined. The contract had already gone into effect and couldn't be voided for another year. You guys were getting married sooner than that. I assume he only sold it to Kyle in full because he thought things were working out between you and Kyle."

I blink quickly. "Wait…what? Are you serious?"

"Yeah. Apparently, Dad didn't want to tell you about the investments to the dock in the beginning because he knew you would have gotten upset and probably would have stayed with Kyle anyway, and if he'd told you about the whole setup, you would have lashed out then, too. All it would have done was back you into a corner. He felt guilty, Gabby. He saw it was going too far, but he was desperate, and I know he did it for us. He wanted to tell you, but Kyle told him there was no going back and not to mention the arrangement at all to you. Kyle threatened that if he said anything about the arrangement to you, he'd find a way to cancel the contract. Dad didn't want to lose everything, including you, so I guess he swallowed his pride and kept quiet about it. Just sucks you had to find out this way."

I sit on the edge of the sofa, staring down at the floor. "Wow."

"Yeah. So, not saying you have to answer him right away, but you should consider it. Dad has done a lot of fucked-up shit, yes, but I don't think he completely sold you out. He just jumped the gun a little too quickly and did what he thought was right to help the fam. He most likely assumed this would get his foot in the door with Kyle, but didn't expect it to get *that* serious between the two of you." He clears his throat. "Besides, you're his favorite," he chuckles. "He wouldn't do you dirty like that."

I huff a laugh. "Thanks for telling me, Ricky."

"No problem."

"Talk to you soon."

I hang up, placing my phone on the coffee table and running my palms over my face. I have no idea what to do or what to believe anymore.

I get up to clean a bit, but it's not distraction enough. As I feed Callie and make myself a mug of coffee, I can't help thinking about one woman who plays a major role in Kyle's life.

His mother.

She knows all about him. She wanted this marriage to happen just as badly as my father.

I'm sure once she hears that I'm filing for divorce, she'll come running, and when she does, I *will* seek answers.

Her son wasn't made a monster overnight. They allowed this to happen…and I want to know how it all started.

## CHAPTER FOURTEEN

**MARCEL**

"I can't take that." Gabby's voice is firm as she glares down at the white envelope in my hand.

"You can and you will." I toss it on the bed beside her.

She unfolds her arms to pick it up and then stands, grabbing my hand and placing it in my palm again. "I won't take *your* money to help me get through *my* divorce, Marcel. Seriously. This is my fight. I'll figure out a way to pay for everything."

"Didn't I tell you I'm here to help? I have money to spare, Gabby. This is just enough for you to do what you need to do in New York, like book a hotel or rent a car."

"Yeah, but I can't take this money from you. You've already done so much for me and—"

"*And* I will do much more, so just take it." I hand it back to her, and she sighs, looking down at it. "I want you out of that fucked-up marriage. I don't care how much I have to hand over for it to happen."

Her eyes swoop up to mine. "You are either the craziest person I've ever met, or the sweetest." Her lips smash together. "Thank you. Seriously."

"Don't mention it." I give her a smile, heading for the fridge. "Just find yourself a good pro bono lawyer so you can get the process started."

"I've been doing some research already for pro bono lawyers in New York who deal specifically with domestic cases. I haven't been here long enough to make a case in South Carolina, but I can in New York, since that's where Kyle and I filed our marriage certificate. There are a few good lawyers there that may be able to help me." She sits on the sofa. "The one I found deals with domestic circumstances a lot, and all of her domestic cases have been won."

"That's good. Keep me updated on all of it." I take a beer out of the fridge.

"I will. Do you mind if I use your laptop?"

I look at my bag on the sofa, and my heart beats a little faster. "I was actually about to do some work on it. You need it right now?"

She shrugs and laughs a little. "Doesn't have to be *right now*. I was just going to show you the lawyer's firm, get your opinion of it."

I avoid her eyes. "Yeah. After I finish some work, it's all yours." I put on a lopsided smile, opening my beer and then picking up the laptop bag, going to the table.

I'm glad she doesn't notice my hesitation. Instead she gets off the couch and picks up Callie's leash. "Okay. I'm going to give Callie a quick walk." On her way out the door, as I'm setting up at the table and taking out paperwork, she kisses me on the cheek.

When she's gone, I log into the computer and close the browser I was on before getting home, then I blow out a breath, raking my fingers through my hair.

Now that she's staying with me, I have to get used to her asking to use my stuff. I'm almost certain the last thing I searched for would require a lot of explanation, and I'm really not in the mood to talk about it right now. Not only that, but she's already going through a lot right now.

I told myself I'd let this go a long time ago, but I still haven't.

I need to get myself under control before Gabby catches on and I ruin this too.

## CHAPTER FIFTEEN

### GABBY

Four days later, I fly to New York, thanks to Ricky buying a ticket for me, and am now seated behind Jasinda Humphrey's desk.

I went to file a report at the police station about my domestic abuse shortly after we got back from Virginia, then Marcel took me to Venice Heights the following day—a Saturday—to see if Kyle would be arrested.

We camped out for about two hours before the cops showed up and took him in, but he wasn't in handcuffs, so we followed them to the police station and waited four more hours. Luckily, Marcel had time to kill.

Kyle walked right back out of the station, but he wasn't alone. There was a man in a suit at his side.

By the vein bulging on Kyle's forehead, it was clear he was pissed. I was pissed because he walked out with a simple slap on the wrist.

"Doesn't matter," Marcel muttered. "You made the report; it'll be in the system when you file for a separation and take this to a hearing."

I guess he was right, but it didn't make me any happier to know he was still walking around like nothing had ever happened.

The walls of Mrs. Humphrey's office are a robin's egg blue, the tile floors shiny and spotless. She has her college degree tacked to the wall behind her, and on her desk are several photos of her with other people. She's shaking their hands in front of her office door, so I assume they are her clients. Each person is smiling, which I hope means their case was won.

There is one photo that stands out the most to me—an image of Jasinda with a man who is slightly taller. They're wearing sombreros and holding margaritas, smiling at the camera together. I assume the man in the photo is her husband. It's nice to see her in a relaxed state, because right now she's dressed to impress, and at first sight, she is sort of intimidating.

"Can I get you some coffee? Water?" Mrs. Humphrey asks as she steps around her desk.

"Oh, no thank you. I'm okay."

"Okay." She smiles, sitting down with bright red lips and long brown hair. Her eyes are hazel, and there are fine lines around her mouth and eyes. She has beautiful brown skin. If I had to guess, I'd say she's in her mid-forties. "So, I read your email and I have to say, I find this case very fascinating—not fascinating about what you've gone through, of course, but the case itself." She pauses. "Apologies. I just love my job and fighting for cases like these." She gives me a cautious smile.

"No apologies necessary." I smile a bit wider to let her know her comment didn't offend me.

Pressing her lips, she picks up a sheet of paper in front of her to read over it. "So, you mentioned in the paperwork that your father knew Mr. Moore before you did, and that the relationship was arranged without your knowledge?"

"Yes."

"If you could give me a number of times Kyle visited the restaurant, how many would you say?"

"Um…" I think on it, chewing on my bottom lip. "Maybe fifteen to twenty times. He came over the span of three months, maybe a little more. Around the third month we got a little more serious, but prior to that it was just a lot of flirting and exchanging questions."

She writes something down, nodding. "Okay, and when you met him, did you see any signs that he might be abusive?"

My head shakes. "No. None. I thought he was a genuine, sweet guy."

She points at me with her pen. "Before I go on, did you take pictures of what he did to your face?"

"I had my friend do it, yes."

"Good. I will need you to email those to me, as they will come in handy. Is there anyone you think would be able to write up a testimony as a witness, other than your friend, Mr. Ward?"

"My best friend Teagan could. I went to her the first night he hit me. She saw the bruise around my eye and the bruises from the first time, when he choked me. Also my neighbor, Meredith. She took me in and even saw Kyle get aggressive with me and threaten me."

"That's good."

I sit forward a little. "Would Marcel be able to write one?"

She gives her head a simple shake. "For your case, it won't look too good if the man you had an affair with is sharing his thoughts. The judge will consider his statement biased, and if Kyle has good lawyers, they will definitely catch onto that and make it a point. That, or they'll direct the attention to the affair, make both of you seem like the bad people instead of Kyle. It's better if Marcel takes no part in this at all, so that it is only about you, Kyle, the abuse, and getting a divorce."

I nod, sighing. "I get it. I don't want that for him."

"Neither do I. You mentioned your parents saw you days after the last assault?"

"Yes. My best friend saw the bruise, as well as my mom and my dad."

"And do you think all three are willing to write a testimony against Kyle?"

"I believe they would, yes."

"You'll have to talk to them, let them know they may need to write statements. The one who will get questioned the most is you, to see if your story wavers, but if you're telling me the whole truth, I have no doubt it will be fine. My mission is to make Kyle seem as guilty as possible. Whoever the judge is, they will see the images of your face and have no choice but to be shocked, but I have to warn you, the system can get a bit tricky when it comes to domestic divorces that involve an affair and *a lot* of money.

Considering the fact that Kyle is a very wealthy man, he will fight hard to make sure he goes out of the divorce without owing you much and without tainting his reputation. If he's willing to go to trial over this, then we will have to call him out on his abuse and possibly get the judge to recognize the *other things* Kyle has done to you." She allows a brief pause. "Do you understand where I'm coming from when I say that, Gabby?"

I nod, twisting my fingers in my lap. "Yes, I think so."

"He raped you. You mentioned that in the email."

I swallow hard, my eyes burning now. I look away and bob my head.

"We can try hard to let it be known that he did that to you, but there are complications when it comes to situations like this. If anything, we may not even be able to use it in court. You are married to him. Not saying sex with your spouse is always consensual, but you were the only one there, therefore there are no witnesses, which means it's your word against Kyle's. He can easily lie and say it was consensual. Without evidence, it's difficult to prove."

"That's bullshit," I huff, wiping the tears out of my eyes.

"You're frustrated. I know. Trust me." She picks up a box of tissue from her desk, offering one to me. I snatch one out, dabbing the corners of my eyes with it. "May I ask you what you want out of this? Is it money?" she inquires.

"No." I focus on her eyes. "I mean, money would be great, but I honestly just want my freedom back. I don't really care about his money."

"You should get something out of this disaster. It will be hard to pick up and rebuild a new life without money."

"So what do you suggest?"

"I was thinking I could reach out to Kyle's attorney and make him a settlement offer."

"What would the offer be?"

"I could ask his attorney to request Kyle to willingly release all your assets and to give you enough money to get back on your feet. If he agrees to that, then we can let him know you will not take it to trial."

"You can try, but I'm telling you, he won't do it. He'll want to see me in court, try and intimidate me. He's a jackass that way."

"We will try. If he turns the offer down, we will proceed with getting a hearing for your case. Even so, when it comes to divorce, you must be separated from your spouse for at least six months."

"Really? That long?" I blow out an agitated breath.

"Yes, but with your restraining order in effect that should make things a little easier for you.

"Okay." I nod. "That would be good."

"Great. In the meantime, I want you to think about your story with Mr. Ward, and think hard. Figure out why you had the affair with him. If this goes to court, Kyle's attorney will grill you about that affair, so you have to make every word count. Make it so believable that the judge will have no choice but to sympathize with you."

I nod, pushing to a stand as she does. "I will."

"Good." She extends her arm, offering a hand. I shake her hand then walk around the chair. "If there is anything else you'd like me to know, please feel free to call or email me," she says when we're outside the office.

I tell her I will do that, and then I head out to the rental car Marcel booked for me. I watch Mrs. Humphrey go back into the building, and when she's gone, I rest my forehead on the steering wheel, taking a moment to breathe.

As badly as I want to cry, I don't. This is in motion now. I know for a fact Kyle won't take a settlement. He has too much pride for that. He'd much rather take the opportunity to make me look like an idiot or a whore.

But if he's willing to fight, so am I.

∼

I'm not the least bit surprised when I get an email stating that Kyle has turned down the settlement.

I read over Mrs. Humphrey's email several times, sitting on the sofa next to Marcel. I got home about two hours ago.

She got a response much faster than I expected, but this is Kyle. He probably shot the idea down before his attorney even had the chance to finish his sentence.

"What's up?" Marcel asks, looking from the TV to me.

"Kyle turned down the settlement." I sigh.

He sighs too, pulling his arm off the top of the couch and wrapping it around my shoulders. "You knew this would happen. I guess it's time for you to gear up, huh?"

"I guess so." I get off the couch. "I'm gonna make a call."

He nods, and I walk out the back door. I study the phone for a while, at the number on the screen, then I cave and push the call button.

It rings a couple times, and then there is an answer.

"Gabby?" Dad's voice is full of surprise.

"Hey, Dad."

He wastes no time launching in. "I'm glad to be hearing

from you! Listen, sweetheart, I am *so sorry* about what I did. I didn't mean for all of this to happen. I just wanted what was best for you and the family, and I was at a low point. I didn't want to lose the house and I wanted to help your mom stay here, and also wanted to help you get through school without worrying about your loans and—"

"Dad, stop. It's fine. I'm putting it behind us."

"You are?" He sounds surprised.

"Yes, but only if you promise to help me in every way possible from now on."

"Of course, Gabby. I'll do whatever you need me to do."

"Good, because I'm filing for a divorce from Kyle. My attorney made him an offer to settle, but he turned it down, so we'll be taking it to court for a hearing."

"Well, shit."

"I'm not surprised. But I will need you to write a statement telling everything you heard about Kyle, about his mom and how she wanted him to have a wife, about how it was all arranged. I need you to let my attorney know that I had no idea about any of it, and that Kyle did, and used it against me and you."

"I have no problem doing that."

"Are you sure? I know you have the company…"

"Yes, but he can't break the contract anytime soon. I read through the clauses carefully. He can't break it for another four months. That gives me plenty of time to save my money and come up with a plan."

"I'm glad to hear that."

We're quiet a second.

"How much will all of this be?" he asks.

"She's a pro-bono lawyer, so it won't cost me anything."

"Oh, well that's good. I'm glad you're doing this. He shouldn't get away with what he did."

"No, he shouldn't."

"Whatever else you need, just know I'm here. I've got your back, sweetheart. Never forget that."

I close my eyes, cooling the burn in them. "I know you do, Dad."

And I really do. Yes, my father has done some really stupid things. He's not perfect, but then again, no one is. Not even me.

I was livid about what he did, don't get me wrong, but only because my father is supposed to be the man who protects me at all costs. In a way, meeting Kyle did save me, but only financially. I have no debt, thanks to Kyle, and I'm sure my father was only thinking about the financial status of my future.

My father had no idea that Kyle was abusive, and I'm sure if he had, he *never* would have done what he did.

He thought Kyle was a good man who met me and fell in love with me, and I *was* genuinely happy with Kyle…for a while. I remember repeatedly telling my parents that I loved Kyle so much, and that I was ready to marry him and be with him for the rest of my life.

I guess I wouldn't have expected my father to ruin all of that by telling me my relationship was at his orchestration.

"I know it's late, but tell mom everything when you can. Okay?"

"I will. Keep me updated on everything and have a good night."

"Goodnight, Dad."

When I'm back inside, Marcel asks, "Who did you call?"

"My dad."

Marcel looks surprised. "How did that go?"

"Pretty good, I think. I told him I'll need his help and support and he agreed to be there through it all."

"That's amazing."

"Mrs. Humphrey told me we need to avoid having you testify." I sit beside him again.

"Why not?" He straightens his back, looking me over.

"Because we had an affair. It automatically makes me look bad. If you write a testimony, Kyle's lawyer will get to ask both of us questions about our relationship. They'll make us look like we're the reason Kyle lashed out."

"If they have questions, I can handle it, I'm sure."

"But I can't, Marcel."

His Adam's apple shifts up and then back down. He looks away, focusing on the TV.

"That's bullshit," he mutters. "I should get the chance to tell them what I saw too. What I went through with you after what he did to you."

"It's better this way," I murmur. "Trust me. You've already done so much for me. You have nothing to do with what Kyle did. He would have hit me again either way."

He looks sideways at me then wraps an arm around me, puling me close to his body. "Is what you said the other day true?"

"About what?"

"That you love me?"

I smile at him. "Yes. I do love you."

"Well, guess what?"

"What?"

"I think I love you too."

"You think?" I laugh, climbing on his lap and holding his face in my hands.

"All right, all right. I *know* I love you."

I can't fight my grin. I kiss him deeply, and he cups my ass in his hands with a deep groan.

I swear, I love being around this man.

## CHAPTER SIXTEEN

**GABBY**

My hearing is happening in twelve days.

That is way too much time to think about everything that could possibly go wrong, but I've been gearing up for it.

Jasinda told me she has done some research on Kyle's attorney, and, apparently, he's a very good lawyer who has worked for a lot of famous people.

She believes they will dig up anything to make me look like the immoral one instead of the victim, so she's been warning me to not get carried away when I'm on the stand and to remain calm when I am questioned.

Things have been going great with Marcel, though. He comes home early now, around seven or eight most nights, and kisses me each time. He holds me tight in his bed at night, and kisses me before he goes off to work in the mornings. He's a sweet man…but I've noticed some strange behavior.

For instance, the way he is with his phone and laptop is

odd. He doesn't mind that I use his laptop, but when I do, he always hovers over me to watch what I'm doing.

He's way too cautious with the laptop. Then again, he does a lot of work on his computer, so maybe he doesn't want me to mess up a certain document or something.

Even so, I try not to dig too deep. He's still warming up to the idea of having me in his house every day. The last thing I want to do is upset him or make him feel uncomfortable in his own home.

On Sunday morning, I leave out early to grab some groceries. I want to make a nice breakfast and dinner for him today. He's been working hard.

When I'm back, I walk through the door with a handful of grocery bags. Marcel is sitting at the table, and when he sees me, he immediately closes his laptop and pushes out of his chair. He tries to do it casually, but there's something about the way he does it, and the look in his eyes, that seems a little off.

"Everything okay?" I ask when he meets up to me to take the groceries.

"Yeah, everything's good."

I study his back before meeting him in the kitchen. As I take some of the groceries out and start placing them in their designated areas, I ask, "Is there something wrong, Marcel?"

He looks sideways at me, grabbing the container of chocolate ice cream and putting it in the freezer. "No. Everything's all good. Why do you ask?"

I shrug, playing it cool. "Just asking."

I don't believe him for a second, but this is supposed to

be a pleasant Sunday. It's his only day off this week, and I'll let it go…for now.

~

Later on, after taking a much-needed shower after all my cooking, I walk out of the bathroom, but Marcel isn't in the bedroom.

I hear murmuring and walk to the bedroom door to see where he is.

His back is to me as he stands by the dining table. He's talking too quietly to hear at first, but then I hear him say a little louder, "I can't meet you right now, but you can come to my office tomorrow. We'll talk then."

*Who is he talking to?*

I go to the bedroom and get changed before he returns.

"You okay?" I tread as carefully as possible, not wanting him to know that I was eavesdropping.

"Yeah. All good."

"Oh. Okay." I force a smile. *Maybe it was a work call*, I think.

I try not to let it get to me.

Like I said, all of this with Marcel is new. He has a lot going on in his life, and I'm honestly just a complication. He won't admit it, but I know I am. I try to do everything I can around here to make it less stressful for him, like cooking dinner for him and cleaning, but I'm not used to this, and neither is he.

It was all so sudden, and a part of me is afraid that this lovely bond between us will end up crashing and burning.

But it can't die.

I don't want it to.

"Have you ever been to Mitchelville Beach?" I ask him when we're in bed. He's spooning me, his chin on my shoulder.

"One time. Wasn't much to see, though. Coligny is better."

"I want to go there, see what it's like."

"What makes you want to go there?"

"I don't know. I saw pictures of it before moving to Hilton Head. I told myself I'd visit one day, see what it was like, but haven't had the chance. I'd love to go watch the sun set there one day."

"Hmm. We should go then." He sounds tired. "We should go to a lot of places, do a lot of different things. Get your mind away from all of the mess that's happened here."

I smile, squeezing his hand that's on my belly. "That would be nice."

"I'll take you places," he murmurs, then kisses the top of my shoulder. "You deserve to see the world and more, little thing."

I laugh. "Promise?"

"Guaranteed."

When Marcel falls asleep, I fight the urges trying to take over me, but I can't hold off for long. Eventually, as he rolls onto his back, throwing an arm over his eyes, I reach over to grab his phone. There's a passcode that needs to be entered.

I hesitate for a bit, fighting an internal war, then I sigh, putting the phone back in place and lying back down. I can't invade his privacy like this. Who am I to check his stuff or question him?

I mean, technically, we aren't together. We just live

together for now, because I have no place else to go. I don't know what we are, but we have to be something serious after everything we've been through, right? He's never claimed me as his girlfriend. Right now, we're sort of stuck in the middle, with a situation that's tricky to define.

I finally calm my mind by reminding myself that I have no reason to be worried. I didn't ask Marcel to do anything, except pick me up that night. Maybe all of the shit with Kyle is really getting to my head.

But when it all boils down, I really hope Marcel isn't hiding anything from me. The last thing I need is for another man I care about to disappoint me.

## CHAPTER SEVENTEEN

**MARCEL**

I TAP the end of the pen on my desk, waiting for the clock to strike twelve.

When I hear the brakes of a car squeal lightly, I look out of the window, spotting a green Volkswagen parking in front of my office building.

I push out of my chair and walk to the door, watching Lucy come my way. Her face is paler than I've ever seen it, her blonde hair strewn all over the place. She's wearing a leather jacket and is hugging it tightly to her body. She has on a gray dress beneath it with black sandals.

She called me last night and asked if she could see me. I told her I couldn't right then because I had Gabby, but that she could meet me here in my office today.

"Hi, Marcel," she breathes when she's inside the building. "Wow, look at you! You look so great!"

"Thank you. I would say the same, but you look like somethin' is botherin' you. What's goin' on?"

Her throat moves up and down, then she points at the coffee station in the corner, blinking her tears away. "Can I make a cup?"

"Sure. Go right ahead."

I watch her go through the motions. After she's dumped several packets of sugar and cream into it, she sips and then walks to my office, sitting in one of the chairs behind the desk.

I walk around the desk warily, glancing at her before sitting too. She sips slowly, quietly, then she places her cup down on the end of my desk, drops her face into her hands, and breaks down in a sob.

I'm shocked and not quite sure what to do. I'm not that great with women crying on me. Gabby I can handle, but Lucy and I are in a different position.

Leaning forward I ask, "Lucy? What the hell is goin' on? What happened?"

"I'm sorry," she says, voice thick. "I—I didn't mean to lay all this on you."

"It's fine, but tell me what's goin' on."

She picks her head up, her eyes and nose red. "Wilson died."

I narrow my eyes, confused. "Who the hell is Wilson?"

"The fiancé I told you about. The one I said I was quitting escorting for. He passed away yesterday. Heart attack. I was driving, because he'd been drinking too much at an event we went to. I looked over and…he was clutching his chest, and his eyes were really big. I took him straight to the hospital but he…he didn't make it!"

"Oh. *Shit*." I don't even know what to say. I slouch back in my chair, lowering my gaze. "Damn, Luce. I'm so sorry."

"I didn't know who else to go to," she says through a sob. "The women at my job won't care. The boss was mad that I quit for Wilson, so he sure doesn't want to hear my sad story." She rolls her eyes and swipes under her eyes with a sniffle. "None of my family lives here in Hilton, and even if they did, they wouldn't have cared either. They didn't approve of me marrying him."

I walk around the desk, grabbing her elbow and bringing her to a stand. "Don't apologize. We're friends, Luce. I told you I'm always here if you need to talk." I reel her in for a hug, and she sobs on my chest even harder.

I let her cry for a moment, then pull back, holding her by the shoulders. "You're more than welcome to see me for anything."

She nods, taking a hand away and swiping her face with the back of it. "Thank you. I really needed to hear that from someone." She draws in a shuddering breath, then puts on a smile that I can tell pains her to do. "You've always been such a good guy, Marcel."

"You don't have to do that. Don't make it about me. You're here for you."

"I know, I just…well, thinking about it is so exhausting." Her voice breaks. "We were supposed to be getting married in August. It was going to be a beautiful fall wedding, and I had even chosen my gown—it's hanging right up in his closet, but now I'll never wear it!" Her voice is thick again, the tears lining the rims of her eyes. She blinks it away then reaches up to stroke the side of my face. "Is everything okay with you, though? You look much happier. How is everything with the girl you like? She lives with you now?"

She smiles and pulls her hand down, but before I can respond, I hear a door shut and look past her.

My heart plummets when I spot Gabby standing by the door with a plastic bag in hand. Her olive eyes are wide, lips parted.

Gabby looks from me to Lucy, who glances over her shoulder and pulls away from me.

"Gabby, hey—uh, this is Lucy," I tell her, stepping around Luce.

She frowns. "Lucy? Your *escort*?"

"No, it's not like that anymore. She's—"

"No, you know what?" Gabby holds a firm hand in the air. "Please don't even explain. I thought I'd come by and surprise you with lunch, seeing as I felt guilty for thinking you could possibly be hiding anything from me, but now I know my suspicions were right." She tosses the bag on the floor and turns around, marching out of the office.

"Shit!" I rush around Lucy, dashing out of the office. Gabby is already inside the rental car when I make it outside. I rush to the driver's side of it, pulling on the handle, but it's locked.

"Gabby! Come on! Would you just let me explain?" She starts the car up, but I bang on the window. "Gabby! She's not here for that! You have it all wrong! She only stopped by to talk!"

She glares up at me, her eyes glistening, the hurt in them very, very clear.

"Gabby, come on. Please?" I plead. "You can't run away from all your problems like this!"

She frowns at my statement then narrows her brows.

"Watch me," she snaps back then she presses on the gas and takes off.

I leap back, watching her speed out of the parking lot to get on the main road.

"Goddamn it!" I plant my hands on my waist, dropping my head.

When I look up again, Lucy is walking out of my office with a stunned expression as she looks toward the road then back at me. "Oh my God, Marcel! I am so sorry! I—I knew I shouldn't have come here! This is all my fault! Do you want me to help you find her and tell her this wasn't what she thought it was?"

"No." I shake my head, releasing a ragged breath. "It's not your fault, Luce. It's mine. Don't worry yourself. You have enough to deal with."

"Okay." Lucy shifts on her feet and swipes her nose. "I'm gonna leave you alone. I don't wanna cause you any more trouble."

"Sure, yeah. I'm gonna go after her." I catch her arm before she can walk past me to her car. "Will you be okay?"

She bobs her head slowly. "I hope so. I think I'm going to drive to North Carolina and stay with a good friend of mine until the funeral. Wilson's family doesn't want me helping with the arrangements." She shrugs, on the verge of tears again. Poor Luce. "I'll call you if I need anything."

She forces a smile at me before walking away. I'm tempted to get her to stick around, maybe help her somehow, but if I do that, I'll be blowing off one of the biggest moments of my life.

I watch Lucy go, too, then walk to the curb to sit and think.

I rake my fingers through my hair, trying to figure out where Gabby would go.

She wouldn't go back to my house, that I know for sure. I also know she won't go to Meredith's, because she lives in the same neighborhood as Kyle.

But where the hell else would she go?

I think for a minute, and then it hits me.

Rushing into the office to grab my keys, I lock up and then hustle to my truck, going after my girl.

As bad as I feel for Lucy, Gabby is so much more important to me.

## CHAPTER EIGHTEEN

### GABBY

I SHOULD BE USED to disappointment by now. My life has been full of disappointments, after all. Perhaps this is Karma kicking me in the ass for cheating on my husband.

Even as a child, life seemed to have a way of letting me down. Mainly because my parents didn't have the money or the time. They worked a lot to keep a roof over our heads.

By the time Mamá decided to stay home and be with us more often, it was a little too late. I'd pretty much grown into my own person. I was used to not getting my way, so I dealt with it.

Maybe that's why I dealt with Kyle for so long. He had his way with me many times, and I allowed it. I didn't really expect any better after the first time he let me down.

I'm starting to think maybe it isn't other people who are the problem. It's me.

With my legs pulled up to my chest, I stare ahead at the rippling ocean. The sun sits on the horizon, the sky layered with creamy orange, lavender, and cotton candy blues. Seagulls caw, making their way home before it gets dark.

I'm sitting on Mitchelville Beach, surrounded by seashells and sand, dunes, grass, and even trees stacked behind me. It isn't your average beach, and I think that's what attracted me to it. It's quiet here. Peaceful. A place where nature can actually *be*.

Standing up, I walk to the water, letting it surround my ankles. I close my eyes and lift my arms, taking in the salty breeze that whips at my hair. The waves are cool around my ankles before sliding back to the large body of water.

There's a tightness in my chest, and I don't know how, but tears have slid down my cheeks. I don't wipe them away, though.

I can't.

I simply drop my arms, keeping my eyes closed, trying to figure out exactly what my purpose is in this world.

At one point in time, I thought I was supposed to be married and happy. I thought that perhaps I was only supposed to be a wife who was devoted to her husband—the kind of wife who loved cooking and cleaning and giving her husband everything he ever wanted.

I realize now that I am not that kind of woman. I have *never* been that kind of woman, and I knew it when Kyle asked me to marry him, yet I went through with it anyway.

I had dreams—goals. I went to college and got a degree in art history, hoping one day I could become an artist myself, maybe make a little money doing what I loved.

I let that all go for Kyle.

Like a fool, I set myself back, just to make *someone else*

happy. I've done that my entire life—never giving myself the chance to live, chase my dreams, and be happy.

*God. What is wrong with me?*

The tears are thicker now, droplets landing on my chest. I feel something warm touch my cheek, then it runs over the length of my cheekbone. It touches the other side, and my eyes flutter open.

I'm met with apologetic eyes as blue as the Mediterranean Sea, parted pink lips, and a strong chin sprinkled with stubble.

"Marcel," I whisper, almost like I'm imagining him here, but I know he's here. I smell him, his familiar scent taking over every single one of my senses.

"I'm so sorry, Gabby" he pleads, his eyes sincere.

I blink some of my tears away, stumbling back a little. "How did you find me?"

"You mentioned this beach last night. I hoped maybe you'd come here. Glad I was right."

He actually remembers? It's surprising, considering the fact that most men would have forgotten a conversation like that as soon as it was over.

Even so, I can't bring myself to be fully relieved that he found me. I don't know if this is right for us at all. Maybe we aren't meant for each other, but were placed in each other's lives as a means to save one another.

I turn away, grabbing my sandals and rushing though the sand, toward the wooden bridge that's in between a line of trees.

"Gabby, wait!" Marcel calls after me. "Stop runnin' away from your problems!"

"No!" I shout back, trudging through the sand.

"Just listen to me! I'm here with you right now! Doesn't that mean somethin' to you? If I was really hidin' somethin' like that, do you think I would have come here to find you?"

"I don't know!" I scream back.

I hear him huff, and before I know it, he's jogging around me. He stops in front of me, holding his hands up, a silent plea for me to stop and listen. I try going around him, but he extends his long arms out, catching me.

"Please, Marcel! Just leave me alone, okay? You don't deserve to be stuck with someone like me! You need better!"

"I'm not stuck with you!" He grabs my hands, holding them tight. I try and yank them away, but he continues holding on. "Quit thinkin' that shit! Quit tryin' to push me away! I'm not goin' anywhere, and I've told you that a million fuckin' times!"

"I don't care!" I lower my gaze, and when I am finally able to yank my hands away successfully, I swipe hard at my tears. "I'm *so tired* of being disappointed, Marcel! I'm tired of everyone in my life treating me like I'm not worth a damn thing!"

"I know you are, Gabby? Okay? Trust me, I get it, and the last thing I want to do is disappoint you or make you feel that way. I swear." His voice is so gentle that it makes my heart ache even more.

"So why did you?" My voice cracks as I meet his eyes again.

"I—" He sighs, looking me over before pinching the bridge of his nose. "I never intended to. Lucy called me last night, told me she wanted to see me because something bad had happened, and I told her I couldn't because I was with you. I told her she could meet me at my office today."

"Well what the hell happened to her?"

"Her fiancé died."

"Oh." I blink rapidly.

"He died from a heart attack last night. I told her many times before if she *ever* needed a friend or a shoulder to cry on, that I was here. She doesn't have any family in Hilton and neither do I, so she wanted to talk to me. I know it sounds weird, especially knowin' she was my escort before, but I promise you, her meetin' me today wasn't like that, Gabby. Despite what we did, she was my friend, and I help my friends no matter what. If that offends you then I'm sorry. I know I should have told you, but I just…I fucked up, all right?"

"Wow," I let out a small breath, tucking my hair behind my ears. Now I feel like a total bitch. "I just wish you would have told me she was meeting you there."

"I know, I know, but I didn't know how you would take it, Gabby. I figured you'd worry the whole time, and I really didn't know what happened, either."

I shake my head, pulling my gaze away. I sometimes loathe the fact that he knows me so well.

He moves closer, taking my hands in his and squeezing them lightly. "I would *never* do somethin' like that to you. After everything you've been through, the last thing I want to do is hurt you. I fuckin' love you, and you mean *everything* to me. Yes, I should have told you about the call, but I'm just…I guess I'm not used to tellin' people every little thing that goes on in my life. I'm used to bein' on my own, doin' my own thing, but I see now that all of that has to change. It has to, if I want to keep you."

His words. Ugh. I love them so much. It takes me a

while to block the emotion enough to speak. "I'm sorry," I whisper brokenly. "Lately I feel like I'm in your way—like I'm invading your space. I don't know."

"You're not, Gabby." He cups my face in his hands, forcing me to put my eyes on his. "I promise you. Havin' you around has been the best thing to happen to me in a very long time, believe it or not. It feels good havin' someone at home waitin' for me."

"Well if that's the case, why do you close your laptop so quickly when I come around? And every time I ask to use it, you're always so weird about it. It seems like you're hiding something from me."

He looks me over, leaning back a bit. "You've noticed that?" He releases my hands, running his fingers through his hair.

"Tell me what's goin' on with you, Marcel. I understand the thing with Lucy. You're a good person with a good heart, but I feel like there is more I should know."

He's quiet a beat too long. Then he says, "There are things I never thought I'd have to share. Secrets I've carried for years. It's not usually like me to tell people about it." He scoffs. "I'm fuckin' ashamed about it, if we're bein' honest."

"Ashamed about what?"

He drops his head.

I take a step closer. "I want to know what it is, Marcel. Please, tell me."

He sighs. Sand collects on his feet as he turns sideways, looking at the ocean.

"Is it *that* bad?" I ask.

"It may have you lookin' at me differently, and I don't want your views of me to change."

*Shit.* What does that mean? Now I'm starting to freak out.

I twist my fingers around each other as I wait for him to say something.

He grabs my hand, leading the way past the wooden bridge. He walks until he finds an open spot on the sand, right under a tall tree. We sit at the same time, surrounded by tall grass. I can still hear the ocean roaring.

His tongue runs over his dry lips before he begins.

"After Shayla died, I stopped lookin' for work. I couldn't afford a funeral, so I had her cremated and then dumped her ashes in Charleston beach." He drops his head, bringing his legs up and wrapping his arms around his knees. "Since I wasn't workin', I got evicted from the apartment I was stayin' in. I had to sleep in my truck for a few weeks, but I did start lookin' for jobs. There was one day when I had finally gotten a job interview for a maintenance technician position at some fancy condos. A woman interviewed me, but she didn't give me the job because I didn't meet her education requirements, she said. Not only that, but later I found out the woman who'd interviewed me for the job saw me sleepin' in my truck before I came in. Anyway, before I left, she told me she could pay me if I fixed some things around her house, ran errands, and all that stuff. I didn't have any other options, so I agreed."

My heart is racing. Now we're talking about a woman? I don't like where this is going one bit, but I pretend to be calm and nod my head, urging him to go on.

"At the time, I had absolutely nothin' to lose. I had no money to my name or anything, so I met that woman at her house at the time she told me to. She had me cut her grass, trim the hedges, and clean out the gutters. She was married, I later found out, and the couple offered to let me live with them for as long as I needed to, as long as I did all the errands and maintenance…but there was more of a catch to all of it."

"What else was there?"

His throat bobs up and down, and his head shakes. "She *wanted* me."

"Wanted you? Like to *sleep* with you?"

Marcel sighs, and his leg is bouncing, like he doesn't want to talk about this anymore. He's making me nervous as hell. "Yes, but I didn't want her. I mean, don't get me wrong, I was grateful that she and her husband had let me stay in their home, but I wasn't really into her that way."

I twist my fingers in my lap, confused now.

"The couple had let me stay in their house, gave me a room to sleep in until I could save money, and they paid me well. I was savin' up so I could move into my own place, but I needed a little bit more money before I was comfortable movin' out, and they knew that. One day, after they had dinner and she went to bed, her husband made me an offer. He wanted me to have sex with his wife once a week until she got pregnant."

My eyes stretch wide. "Wait…*what?*"

"Yeah," he mumbles, looking into the distance. "He told me they'd been havin' a hard time havin' a kid. Apparently, he was havin' functional issues, so he said he'd give me two grand each time I had sex with her, and that I had to finish inside her. I did it around the time she was fertile—sometimes more than once a night—and he gave me two grand for each time I had sex with her. That money, on top of the money they were giving me for maintenance, added up."

"What the hell, Marcel? They sound twisted."

"Yeah, well, I wouldn't have found it so strange if he weren't sittin' there watchin' us. It was another catch of theirs, and it was always hard to finish with him right there starin' at us, but he loved her, and somethin' told me it wasn't their first time doin' somethin' like this. Maybe before, they weren't tryin' to get pregnant while he watched, but this time they were. They were havin' trouble havin' kids, had this random, healthy man helpin' out around the house and livin' there, so they turned to me."

"I—I don't get it. What does this have to do with the laptop?"

"Because I saw that same couple two weeks ago. It looked like they were on vacation or somethin'. They were walkin' with a kid—a little boy with dark hair. He had to be about seven years old. He didn't look anything like the dad."

My eyes nearly bulge out of my head. "With *your* kid?" I whisper. "So, she actually ended up *pregnant* by you?"

Marcel can't do anything but blink. It's confirmation enough.

"That's…" I don't even know what to say to that. "What did they say when they saw you?"

"They didn't see me. I saw them leavin' the grocery store when I got in my truck. I started to get out and say somethin' to them, but they looked so happy, and I couldn't bring myself to do it. I knew it was what they wanted—to have a kid at any cost—but seein' them surprised the hell out of me. I had no idea she'd even gotten pregnant." His throat bobs as he swallows. "I was just the sperm donor, and her husband had made that very clear when we made the agreement. After the second month, I couldn't do it anymore. It was gettin' weird around the house, and she hadn't gotten pregnant the first month, so I figured it wasn't workin'. I had already been looking for cheap apartments, found one, and was lucky enough to moved out within a few weeks, but before I left, her husband told me not to reach out to them ever again. I thought he'd told me that because he was jealous and didn't want his wife comin' to me behind his back, but now that I've had time to think about it, and after seein' them at that store, he must've known then that she was pregnant. I had no clue until two weeks ago."

"Wow." I hold my hands up, trying to process all of this. "This is a little too much to take in right now. Why didn't you tell me this before?"

"I didn't know how, Gabby. I saw them around the time you were going through the shit with Kyle and your parents. You were trying to cope with what'd happened to you. I didn't want to add more worry to your life with somethin' like that. At the time, I wasn't even sure if it was my kid, but considerin' his age and his looks, I'm certain he's mine."

"Wow," I huff, looking toward the water. "You biologically have a kid walking around out there."

"I know."

"That's just—" My head sways side to side.

"You aren't tempted to find out what he might doing?"

"That's why I was on the laptop. I look the couple up every night now, ever since I saw them. I found them on Facebook—the couple. Richard and Sherry Briar. Sherry posts more than Richard does. The kid is a good kid. He plays soccer, gets good grades, and loves the color red. He has my eyes and my hair. I mean, he looks just like me, Gabby. It's kind of crazy."

I face him full on, flabbergasted.

"He's happy in his photos. They look happy. I know I can't interfere and throw a wrench into their lives, so it's better to watch him grow from a distance, I guess." He shrugs, picking at a loose string on his jeans. "When I was on Facebook, I searched for Sherry a lot. I didn't want you to see it and think I was out here with another woman." He shrugs. "I know it's stupid, but like I told you, my life has been complicated."

I look away, unsure what to say to that. I can't exactly be angry about it. This was before he ever even met me, and he was going through a rough time after the loss of his sister, so of course his head wasn't on straight.

Not only that, but the couple *wanted* it, and now they don't want him having anything to do with the kid. I know that bothers him. He seems like the kind of guy who would want to at least get to know someone he helped create, but at the same time, he knows it would cause too much tension and unnecessary drama for the kid.

Marcel isn't a selfish man. He'd never taint an innocent child's happiness all for his sake.

"Does that bother you?" he asks when I'm quiet for a little too long.

I side-eye him. "That another woman beat me to the punch? Oh, for sure."

Marcel laughs. "Beat you to the punch? So, you *want* my babies, too? I knew it," he grins.

I shake my head, fighting a laugh. "It is a little weird, but it's more so the couple whom I find strange. Women are surrogating all the time, though most aren't getting banged by the husband in order for it to happen. You were just the sperm donor, though they could have been a little classier and had you come in a jar or something, not straight out bang the wife while he watched."

"I'm certain they did that for their own personal desires more than anything else. She was attracted to me—I could tell from the day I met her—and he was the kind of man who would do anything to please his wife. I got the feeling they were swingers of some sort."

I nod. I do get it. "Is that all?" I ask. "No more secrets?"

"Well, let me think. I lost my virginity when I was sixteen. When I was twenty-one, I got so drunk I ended up getting alcohol poisoning. You know about Lucy and how I hired her, but that was over way before you and I ever even did anything. You also know what happened to my parents and my sister, so, yeah, I think that's about it." He smirks, reaching for my hand and kissing the back of it. "No more secrets, little thing."

"You're sure?"

"I'm positive."

I inhale deeply before exhaling. "Alcohol poisoning. That must have been horrible."

"Oh, it was. Trust me. Wouldn't wish it on anyone… well, except Kyle. He deserves several rounds of alcohol poisoning."

I break out in a laugh, as does he.

"I think we need to get away," he murmurs after our laughter has faded. "Take a trip again. Just you and me."

"Where would we go?"

"Anywhere you wanna go. I feel like the stress here is

really gettin' to us. We can go somewhere, clear our minds, then come back and handle everything properly."

"Aw, we don't have to. I know you have a lot of work to do."

He reaches for my hand and gives it a squeeze. "I want to, Gabby. Besides, I don't vacation much because I work so much. It's about time I start livin' a little."

I smile a little. "Well, where would we even go?"

"I don't know. Maybe Florida? Las Vegas? New Orleans?"

I gasp. "Wait—I've never been to New Orleans. That would actually be really fun."

"You've never been?" He looks at me with a boyish grin. "I've been once, but it was for a work trip. Didn't get to have fun like I wanted. We can go there. Get drunk, let loose."

I lock on his eyes. "You're serious?"

"As a heart attack."

I wince. "Whoa. That was *way* too soon!"

He busts out laughing then throws his hands in the air with a shrug.

"Okay. New Orleans it is then," I declare.

He looks me over. There's heat in his eyes, and I don't know how I could ever think he doesn't want me. That look says it all, smoldering and unquestionable.

"Come here." He drops his legs, and I move to his lap, wrapping my arms around the back of his neck. "Know what would make me a happy man right now?"

"What?"

"To fuck you under this tree."

My heartbeat picks up speed as he reaches under my dress to tug on the strap of my panties. "But there are people walking the beach," I say, though I can't pretend I'm not excited.

"They won't see us," he assures me. "The grass is too tall. Now get up."

I perch up on my knees while he remains seated and pulls my panties the rest of the way down. When they're low enough, I work my way out of them, then lower back down on his lap.

"Right here? Really?" I whisper on his mouth as he reaches down to undo his jeans.

"It'll be quick," he rasps, pulling his cock out. "If we can't see them, they can't see us."

My mouth parts on his as he positions himself at my entrance then brings a hand to my hip to lower me.

"Oh, God," I breathe, squeezing my eyes shut. I still have to get used to his size. "We're really doing this. So crazy," I breathe.

I ride him slowly, planting my mouth on his. A groan catches in his throat as he cups my ass, guiding me up and down the length of his thick cock.

"Damn, baby," he groans. "This is a dream. You're a dream."

His words are so beautiful, completing me in so many ways. I may not be everything to one man, but I am everything to this man, so I ride him faster, our skin softly clapping together while rays of sunlight kiss my back.

Panting raggedly, I curl my fingers in his hair, shifting up and then back down.

"Perfect pussy," he rumbles on my neck. "Perfect body. Perfect woman."

Every word brings me closer. I drop down, and he takes

initiative, flipping me onto my back, bringing one of my legs over his waist and thrusting powerfully into me.

He doesn't slow down either. I meet him with my hips, watching his eyes and the way they swim with lust and so much love.

I love everything about this. Where we are. How we're doing it. He's right; no one can see us from here. The grass and even the trees around us block most of the view from where we are.

Bringing a thumb down, he places the pad of it on my clit and rubs in slow, gentle circles.

"Yes," I moan, and he thrusts forward, filling me with his hard cock again. Sand is in my hair, but I don't care. As he continues rubbing small circles on my clit, my body bucks, and I breathe his name.

"Shit, baby. You're comin' all over my dick," he groans.

With one more push inside me, his cock fills me up as his hips remain still, and then he lowers his body, his mouth connecting to mine as he comes.

I cup his face in my hands and kiss him back, and his moan becomes mine. When our lips separate, we lock on each other's eyes again.

"No more secrets," he reassures me. "From now on, I'm an open book. I'm all yours." He runs a finger over my bottom lip, and his cock pulses inside me one last time. "And you're all mine."

"Yeah," I smile. "I'm all yours."

## CHAPTER NINETEEN

**MARCEL**

A LOT of people won't be able to accept the fact that I've fallen in love with a married woman.

To many, it may seem like I came in the way of Gabby's marriage, but the truth is, I saved her from that terrible matrimony.

This woman…there is just something about her. She makes my heart race in ways I've never felt before. When she's next to me, I feel whole. I haven't felt whole since my sister died eight years ago.

I have Gabby now, which is exactly what I've wanted for a while now. Being with her is surreal. The circumstances aren't great, but I'm going to help her get through this shit any way I can.

Her battles have become my own. The scars she wears from months of abuse have been marked on me too. I won't let her go through this alone.

After we leave the beach, we go back home, and I make

love to her in bed—*our* bed. She fits in my hands like the perfect puzzle piece.

Her husband was a fool to let her go—to abuse someone so wonderful. I know for a fact that I'll never let it happen again.

She's with me now, and I'll do everything I can to make sure she's here to stay.

~

After planning the mini getaway to New Orleans the following morning, I check in at work for a few hours, and then take Gabby to the mall, like I agreed.

Gabby is running low on clothes, and I don't have much to wear for leisure, so we're going shopping for new outfits, seeing as our trip is happening in three days.

Gabby and I talked a little more this morning over breakfast about the kid that I'll most likely never get to meet. I've come to terms with the fact that I'll never meet him. For that kid's sake, I'll stay away and let him live a happy, oblivious life. They seem like great parents, too. I can't ruin what they have, no matter how much it bothers me.

I personally would love to have a kid of my own one day, but I never saw it in the plans for me. Maybe that's why I became a bit obsessive with staying updated on that family after seeing them at the store.

His name is Wylie Briar. Maybe when Wylie's older and out of school, his parents will feel the need to lay the truth on the table for their own peace of mind and tell him who his real father is.

They know I'm a good man. Then again, when I think

about it, they weren't the kind of people who *couldn't* keep a secret. After all, they had many.

Deep down I know I may never get the chance to formally meet the kid, and that bothers me. But as of today, I'm putting a stop to the Facebook stalking and research. I'm only torturing myself by doing it. I'll still check in, but I know I need to end the obsession. I'm only hurting myself.

After hitting our fourth store in the mall, I already have what I need tucked inside my shopping bags, but of course Gabby is still shopping.

While Gabby roams to the next store, I sit in the corner inside, letting her shop in peace. I scroll through my emails as someone else walks into the store, a bell chiming to alert their presence.

I don't pay much attention to the person at first, but in a matter of seconds, Gabby is rushing in my direction, her face panicked.

"We have to get out of here," she says hurriedly.

"Why? What happened?"

She looks over her shoulder and I stand, looking in the direction she's looking.

There is an older, Asian woman standing in the women's section, shuffling through a rack. She side-eyes us, then continues to shuffle through the rack.

"That's Kyle's mom."

*Shit.*

"Let's go," she insists, grabbing my hand and heading for the exit of the store, but before she can make it out, her name is called, and she freezes.

"Gabrielle?" The voice calls again, and Gabby releases my hand turning toward the voice.

I look with her and now that the woman is closer, I can see hints of Kyle in her. The eyes and nose. The dark hair. The woman puts on a faint smile as she looks from Gabby to me.

"I didn't expect to see you here," the woman says. Her accent is different. I can hear the British, but there's another accent mixed with it that I can't place.

Gabby shrugs. "Just shopping."

The woman takes a step forward while Gabby takes one back. As if the woman notices Gabby's cautiousness, she stops and straightens her back. "Is this the young man you had the affair with?"

Gabby frowns. "This is Marcel, the man who *saved* me from Kyle, yes."

The woman tips her chin, that faint smile still on her red lips. "You know, I was actually hoping I would run into you. Do you mind having coffee or tea with me? We can go any place you'd like."

Gabby looks at me warily before focusing on her. "Not if Kyle will be around."

"He won't be around, love. I assure you." She smiles wider then looks me in the eyes. "I would prefer that it is only us, if that is okay."

I drop my eyes to Gabby's. Gabby shifts on her feet, then she finally nods. "Fine. Coffee it is."

"Are you sure?" I ask.

"Yeah. Just wait for me around here. I'll call you when I'm done." She takes a step toward Kyle's mom. "There's a coffeeshop upstairs. Let's go there."

"Very well." The woman sashays past Gabby, but she pauses in front of me, looking me up and down.

Shaking her head, she walks away, and I frown, watching her go.

"Bitch," I grumble. "If shit goes south, Gabby—"

Gabby places a hand on my chest. "I'll call you, I promise. There are a few things I want to talk about with her and then we'll go. This shouldn't take long."

I watch her walk off too, but I don't feel good about any of it. What are the odds that Kyle's mother runs into Gabby at an outlet? She doesn't even look like the kind of person who would shop in a place like this.

Something is fishy.

For all I know, this whole thing is just a set up.

## CHAPTER TWENTY

**GABBY**

The aromas of roasted coffee beans and sugar are thick in the air of the coffee shop.

The walls are painted a light brown, the floors made of dark wood. The accent colors of the shop are ivory and blue.

I'm seated across from Mrs. Moore, latte in my hand, while she sips tea from a white teacup.

I fold my arms, leaning against the back of my chair. She hasn't said much since we've gotten here. She's been fixing her tea to her liking, pouring honey into it, acting like she has all the time in the world.

"Why are you here?" I finally ask when I'm tired of waiting.

"To see my son, of course," she answers.

"No, I mean *here*. At the mall. You told me once that you have a designer who gets your clothes and arranges your wardrobe. You knew I'd be here."

Her face remains stoic as she looks me over. "I hired a private investigator who knows where Mr. Ward lives. He told me you two were here, so I came to see you."

"Wow. Are you serious? So, you're stalking me now?"

"No. I'm just keeping my family ahead of the situation. Keeping tabs. How was the meeting with the attorney?"

I narrow my eyes at her. "Wow. Your whole family is clearly insane."

"No, Gabrielle. We are just cautious." She sighs. "Don't worry, Kyle has no idea I am meeting with you right now. I wanted to get the chance to talk to you alone."

I narrow my eyes. "To talk about what?"

"Kyle, of course."

"If that's the case, there's nothing for us to talk about. Kyle hit me many times and *raped* me. That means he is dead to me. I'm sure he's told you his sob story, though, and you'll believe him over me."

"How can your husband rape you?" she asks, and her voice is so cynical. I want to throw my coffee in her face. She is the kind of woman who makes others feel like they're in the wrong. Now I see where Kyle gets it from, and I see why so many rape victims don't come out to let people know they've been raped.

I scoff and push out of my chair. "You know what? I'm not about to let you try and undermine me. If there's nothing to talk about, I'm leaving."

"Gabrielle, sit," she demands as I turn. "*Please*," she adds, and I know that took a lot of pride for her to request.

I stop, not because of her demand, but because I really do have questions, and I know she's the only one who can give them to me.

Despite how much I am not a fan of Kyle's, I face her again, taking my seat and leaning toward her. "For the record, your son is a heartless coward, Mrs. Moore. He choked me twice. Kicked me in my face. Raped me over the dining table *you* gave to him as a gift. Your son is a fucking *monster*. I thought I'd let you know that before you try and convince me to change my mind about any of this."

"I'm not here to change your mind. I simply want to talk." She folds her fingers on top of the table, studying my eyes. Realizing how dead serious I am, she drops her gaze to her cup of tea, picking up the spoon beside it and stirring it. "I suppose I shouldn't be surprised about what's happening. I had a feeling it would happen again."

I frown. "What do you mean again?"

"Kyle hasn't always been like this."

"Frankly, I can't tell. He's been abusing me since shortly after the wedding."

She's quiet a moment. "Dan isn't Kyle's real father," she says, matter-of-factly, and I close my mouth.

"What? How?"

"His real father was British as well. He visited Malaysia here and there for work, and that's how I met him, but I didn't realize he was such a horrible person. Kyle was severely abused by his biological father." Her throat bobs. "After our divorce, I made the terrible mistake of letting my son live with his father for a few years so he could go to a popular boarding school that was hard to get into at the time. His father had connections with one of the men who accepted applications at the school and only agreed to talk to the man at the school *if* I let Kyle live with him during the school season. I could only have him on summers and winter breaks. While he stayed with his biological father, however, he was being abused the entire time. I didn't find out about the abuse until I picked him up one day for an optometrist appointment and saw him with a faded black eye. I took him away immediately, filed a report, and went to court over it, where he was found guilty, and we have not seen his father ever since. I met Dan a year later, and he took on the role of being Kyle's father without a problem, moved us to America, and we rebuilt from there. He even offered to give Kyle his last name, as a way for him to start fresh."

I can't help staring at her. I didn't know any of this about Kyle. Why didn't he tell me? Not that it would have made a difference, but all this time I thought I was doing something wrong.

"Kyle was placed in therapy for a few years and seemed to be improving," she goes on. "I thought he was fine…until he got a little older and had his first real girlfriend. He hit her once after school in his car, gave her a busted lip, and her parents pressed charges. They dropped the charges, but only because we wrote them a very large check and asked them to dismiss it. I didn't want it on his record, you see."

"Wow."

She sips her tea delicately. "All I've ever wanted was for Kyle to find his happy place. To find a woman who would help him change. I thought it would be you, but he has hit you as well, which proves to me that perhaps my son will never change."

"You knew this about him all along and didn't warn me?"

"I didn't feel the need to. He seemed genuinely happy

with you. He had changed while he was with you. I thought it was for the better."

I scoff and look away.

"I told Kyle not to take the divorce to the hearing. I told him to go through with a settlement so that it doesn't have to go to court, but he refuses. He claims that because you had the affair with Mr. Ward, that you deserve to get called out for it. He is being spiteful. He's hurt and angry—"

"*He's* hurt?" I spit out. "Wait—are you serious right now?"

She presses her red lips.

I sit forward, digging my phone out of my back pocket. I unlock it quickly, then go to my pictures app. When I find the photo of my face, I turn the phone toward her, practically shoving it into her face.

"This is what Kyle did to me. This happened because of him and I've had to deal with that and so much more, so I don't want to hear *shit* about him being hurt."

She puts a hand on the phone to lower it, shaking her head. "I understand your anger, Gabrielle. I really do, but you have to realize that Kyle has a lot of money. Even if you win the judge over at the hearing, it won't hurt him. He won't lose much of anything, and we will make sure he doesn't do any jail time. The most he'll get is community service of some sort, or going to required therapy."

"I don't care. It's still happening." I shove out of my chair. "Tell Kyle to take the settlement or get ready to be put to shame in court."

I give her my back, but before I can go, she says, "He knows where Marcel Ward lives."

I freeze again, turning her way, this time much slower

than before. "How?"

"He knew about my private investigator and asked him to find out where you were staying."

I plant my hands on the table, getting in her face. "I dare him to show up. It will give Marcel even more permission to beat his sorry ass again."

She narrows her eyes, focused on mine. "You've fallen for that man."

I pull back, looking her over. "Does it matter?"

"May I ask you something?"

I frown, but I don't move, which she takes as permission to ask.

"Were you ever in love with Kyle at any point?"

I shrug, stepping away. "I thought I was…but it turns out I was only in love with the idea of him."

"I see." She picks up her cup of tea. "Until next time, Gabrielle."

I turn away. I no longer want to see her face because all I see is Kyle. They look just alike.

I leave the coffee shop, taking my phone out and giving Marcel a call.

It's a relief spotting him in the food court, waiting for me by the exit with one of his hands in his pockets, our shopping bags in the other. He looks so anxious, and his worry warms my heart. He truly cares.

When I'm closer, he opens his arms and reels me in to plant a kiss on my forehead.

"How did it go?" he asks.

"Not so well. She hired a private investigator. That's how she found me." I pause before saying, "The investigator also told Kyle where you live."

He frowns. "You think he'll show up at my house?"

"I don't know, but if he does, you'll have every right to hurt him if he feels like a threat. He'd be trespassing."

"That's true. Don't even worry. I'll keep an eye out. You ready to get out of here?"

"Yes," I sigh. "Please."

We leave the mall and head to his truck. As I look over my shoulder, toward the entrance of the mall, I spot a black SUV pulling up to the front.

Mrs. Moore is going toward it, and a man climbs out of the driver seat to open the back door as she walks around with her chin high and lips pursed. I watch as she climbs inside in her pantsuit and heels, but I'm almost certain that on the other side of the backseat is a man.

And not just any man.

By the dark hair and beige skin, it's clear to me that Kyle is in the backseat too. Fortunately, they don't see us, and we've met at Marcel's truck, out of plain sight, but that doesn't stop my heart from banging in my chest.

Marcel starts his truck, but I watch the SUV drive away as I clip my seatbelt. When I can no longer see the SUV, a flood of questions hit me.

Did he send his mother in there, thinking I would cave? Is she even the one who hired the private investigator, or was it a cover-up for Kyle? Because now that I think about it, he's exactly the kind of person who would hire a PI, and she's the kind of person who would cover for him.

Wow.

I'm realizing this is no longer a game to Kyle. This is a war.

And he won't stop until he takes me down.

# CHAPTER TWENTY-ONE

**GABBY**

I'm having a hard time forgetting about that sitting with Mrs. Moore. Seeing Kyle in that SUV has boggled me.

Kyle knew I was in the mall. Did he see me leaving, too? The thought of it has me on edge for the rest of the night and checking the windows every few minutes to see if some random car will be camped out, watching us.

Marcel tells me that I need to calm down—that no one is going to harm me while I'm with him—but with Kyle and his fucked-up ways, we can't be too sure.

Later that night, I take Callie out while Marcel takes a shower. I would have waited for him to be done, but she was scratching at the door, so it seemed like an urgent situation. He doesn't like her going in the backyard, so I suck it up and head out.

"Come on, girl," I coo when she stops by the mailbox to sniff at something. I continue walking down the street, where the streetlights pave the way. The sun set over half an hour ago, the sky a deep, dark blue.

There is a home for sale two houses over from Marcel's that Callie likes to go to. The grass is tall, and she always pees there. I move to the sidewalk and she trots over to the grass.

As I wait for her to finish, I hear footsteps approaching and look back, thinking it's Marcel. When I first moved in, he'd come outside to check on me to make sure nothing bad happened.

But when I see the person, I realize I am completely wrong. It's not Marcel at all.

The person walks my way casually, in a pair of black dress pants and a white button-down shirt. His hair is disheveled, like he's constantly been shoving his fingers through it, anxiously waiting for this moment.

My heart drops to my stomach, and it isn't usually like me to freeze, but I do when I see him coming.

I had my guard up, lowered it for just a moment, and he showed up, just like I knew he would.

"Gabs, look at you," Kyle sighs, and beneath the lamp posts his smile is eerie. His dark eyes are glassy, and even from several steps away, I can tell he's drunk.

"W-what the hell are you doing here, Kyle? I swear to God if you don't leave now, I'll call the cops! You're not supposed to be near me!"

Kyle scoffs, still walking. "How exactly can you call the cops if I do this?"

I grimace. "What the hell are you talking about?"

Kyle reaches around me, and I flinch, expecting him to

strike me, but he doesn't. Instead, he retracts, but with my cellphone in his hand.

"I guess old habits never die."

"Give it back! Now!" I yell, sticking my hand out for it. I know it's a hopeless act.

"You'll have to ask nicely." He smirks.

I back away. I don't have time for this. He can keep the damn phone for all I care.

I tug on Callie's leash as she starts to bark at Kyle, then rush toward the street, abandoning him on the sidewalk.

I glance over my shoulder, hustling in the direction of Marcel's house, but he follows me.

"Did you think I wouldn't find you, Gabby? You are forgetting that I am your husband! You are mine! This is just a little falling out, but I'm sure we can sort this out, just like last time!"

My heart beats louder. I pick up speed and run toward the house. The footsteps behind me are heavier, quicker.

I rush across the street when I'm closer to Marcel's house, but as soon as I reach the lawn, I'm tackled to the ground, face-planting the grass.

I scream loud as Kyle flips me over, but a hand that isn't mine comes up to firmly cup my mouth.

"Shh, shh, shh," Kyle hisses. "Don't want to disturb your temporary neighbors, do you?"

My screams are muffled, and Callie barks at Kyle. He's on top of me, his weight keeping me pinned to the ground.

Staring into my eyes, he sighs, then uses his other hand to stroke my cheek. I buck beneath him, trying to shove him off, but he keeps me pinned down.

"I drove my car here after getting the address to this

place from my investigator. He's told me all about you and Marcel. How you left town together, went to see your parents. He told me about how you lay on the couch with him, and even when you two have sex in his bedroom." My eyes widen at his statement. "You've had your fun now, but that's over. Here's what's going to happen: I'm going to take you to the car I rented and drive you back *home* where you belong, then you're going to apologize to my mother for dragging her all this way for nothing." His throat bobs as he looks me over. "This is just…it's a falling out," he croaks, and his breath is heavy with the scent of bourbon. "Husbands and wives fight all the time, right? But they patch things up. The only difference between myself and other men is that if you try and leave for good, I will really have to hurt you, and I can't be so sure that I'll hold back. We don't want that, do we?" he asks.

I shake my head, eyes still wide.

"Good." He slowly pulls his hand away, and when he does, I spit in his face. His eyes squeeze shut, and even with them closed, I can tell he's pissed. His eyes shoot open again as he swipes the spit away with his arm.

"Fuck you!" I snarl. "I am *never* going back with you!"

Kyle's eyes flare with rage, and his hand comes down to lock around my throat when I try to scream again.

Callie barks even louder, and then I hear a loud thud, followed by the heavy pounding of footsteps.

My oxygen is nearly depleted as Kyle stares down at me, nostrils flared and teeth bared, but in an instant, I'm sucking in a breath, and all I see is a dark shadow running by me, tackling Kyle to the ground.

Coughing, I roll over and press a hand to my chest,

struggling for air. From where I am, I can see a shirtless Marcel on top of Kyle. He's punching him repeatedly.

"I told you to *stay the fuck* away from her!" Marcel hollers.

Another punch.

"Marcel!" I yell, but my voice cracks from the damage to my throat.

Sluggishly, I push off the ground and go to him, grabbing his arm and pulling him off of Kyle. It takes all the strength I have, because he's trying to punch him again, but I manage.

"Marcel, don't! Let it go!" I plead.

But he doesn't listen, or either he doesn't hear me through his rage. Marcel lunges forward, trying to get at Kyle, who is sliding backward on his palms. There are people standing outside their homes now, confused and in shock.

"Marcel!" I scream.

"He hurt you Gabby! I'm tired of him gettin' away with this shit! He came to my property and hurt you! He fuckin' deserves it!"

"I know, I know," I plead, stepping around him and grabbing his hands. "But this is not you," I cry. My vision is blurring, but I don't pull my eyes away from him. "Look at me," I command lightly.

He's breathing like a raging bull, glaring at Kyle like he wants to kill him. I didn't think Marcel possessed that kind of power, but I'm certain that if I don't calm him down, he just might do what he has in mind.

"Please, Marcel, just look at me."

Marcel finally lowers his head, putting his gaze on mine.

His heavy breathing steadies just a bit, but his jaw is clenched, as well as his fists.

"He hurt you, Gabby," he says again.

"I know, but in order for you to stay here with me, you can't do what you really want to do to him. Okay? You were protecting me, and that's fine, but you have to let it go. You can't go to jail right now. There are people watching—you can't hurt him more than you have already—and I can't be alone here without you."

He frowns, but his eyes swirl with understanding. He gets where I'm coming from, I can tell by the way he staggers backward and looks around at the couple across the street.

I turn away, looking at Kyle who is just now standing up. He stumbles toward the street.

"You are both idiots," Kyle barks, swiping the blood off his mouth. There's a red mark near his eye too. "I can't believe how pathetic you are! All this time, I thought I married a smart woman! You are no different than the rest of them! If anyone should be calling the cops, it's me!"

"No, it isn't!" Marcel barks back. "You came onto *my* property and put your hands on a woman! I had every right to beat your sorry ass!"

Kyle spits in our direction then digs in his pocket, chucking my phone toward me. Luckily, it lands on the grass.

"I suggest you reconsider what you're doing, Gabs," Kyle growls at me. "I'd hate for something tragic to happen."

"Like what?" I snap. "You can't do anything to my parents! They are preparing themselves for whatever you do!

And the worst you could do to me would still be better than being your wife!"

Kyle's eyes are rounder as he stops in front of the blue Honda that I didn't even realize was parked beneath the tree of the house across the street from Marcel's. I thought it was one of the neighbors' cars. Kyle would normally never be seen driving a Honda. This proves how low he'll go just to get to me.

Opening the door of his car, he yells, "You'll regret it! Trust me, I know you!" and then climbs inside, slamming the door behind him. He drives away, his tires screeching as he leaves the neighborhood.

When I can no longer see his taillights, my thundering heartbeat settles, and I walk toward my phone to pick it up. When I look up, the neighbors are retreating, but not without looking back at us a dozen times. They probably think we're crazy.

"Are you okay?" Marcel asks, grabbing my face and tilting it up. He brushes his knuckles across my neck and shakes his head.

"I'm okay." I grab his hand, checking his knuckles. They're a little red, but not split, thank goodness. "This won't be the last time we see him, Marcel," I whisper.

Letting out a sigh, Marcel drops his hand to grab mine and leads the way into the house. After Callie is inside, he shuts the door behind him and meets me at the couch.

"This is getting ridiculous, Gabby," he mutters.

"I know."

Marcel picks up my phone and hands it to me. I take it. "Call the cops. You need to report this too."

I nod and call the cops, who arrive within an hour to take my report, as well as the neighbors across the street.

After the police leave, Marcel and I go back inside. He cracks open a beer, sits on the couch, and growls, "I wanted to murder him." "I swear if you hadn't pulled me off, I would have killed that son of a bitch."

I walk to him, grabbing his face and leaving him no choice but to focus on my eyes. "I appreciate what you did, Marcel, but you can't do anything that will risk your freedom or your safety, okay? Once we have the hearing and get through the rest of this, we'll be better. Jasinda is going to fight really hard for me."

Marcel nods. Nothing more.

"Let's go to bed," I offer, and I'm glad he accepts. He walks to the bedroom before me, but not without grabbing my hand and leading the way. I follow him, climbing into bed.

Even though we're laying down, neither of us can sleep. My heart is still beating rapidly as I steal glances at the windows. Thankfully the curtains are closed, but it doesn't settle my paranoia. That investigator could be trying to watch now, or even Kyle.

"And we're supposed to be goin' on a trip tomorrow," Marcel mutters sarcastically. "That just ruined my whole fuckin' mood. Don't even wanna go anymore."

"No. We have to." I rub his chest, sighing. "We can't let him ruin our fun. That's what he wants. Plus, he's not as likely to be able to follow us there."

Marcel makes a throaty noise but doesn't say anything. Exhaling deeply, he tugs me closer and holds me tight.

"Well, like I said before, I've got you. I'm here."

"I know." My eyes sting, but I close them before any tears can fall.

I know without a doubt that Marcel is here for me…but with so much going on, it wouldn't surprise me if this was more than he signed up for.

There is only so much a man can take. Dealing with a stalker-ish, possessive husband is a lot to handle, and is baggage that he definitely doesn't need.

## CHAPTER TWENTY-TWO

**GABBY**

The following day, after eating breakfast, Marcel takes me to the store to grab a few last minute travel toiletries before we leave.

I'm sure Kyle has been arrested. And if he hasn't, he should be well on his way to jail. There's no other place he'd go but home. He most likely won't be sitting in jail for long, but this makes two counts of domestic abuse on his record. They have to count for something when we face the judge at the hearing, I hope.

When we get back to Marcel's house, we try and let go of our awful night and pack up for our three-day trip to New Orleans. After the shit that happened last night, I know this trip will do us some good, although my paranoia is at an all-time high.

I can't even bring myself to go to Meredith's house after the brawl. She had to meet us someplace outside of Venice

Heights to get Callie. I felt bad for having to make her do it, but after I told her what happened with Kyle last night, she was more than happy to meet me.

I need to have a good time somehow. Getting out of Hilton Head Island will be a good start...but who's to say Kyle won't follow us there, too? If he does, he's fucking sick.

Even if he doesn't, he could always send that damn investigator he hired and that thought alone bugs me.

Despite knowing it, I can't let him stop me from living my life and having fun. The bruise he created has mostly faded away. There is a small purple hue, but it's easy to cover with concealer. I need this trip. The hearing will be happening very soon, and once I'm back, my game face will be on.

And besides, I need to spend more time with the one man who wants to really get to know me.

I feel like I've been so wrapped up with my hatred for Kyle, and worried about the divorce, that I haven't actually gotten the chance to give Marcel my fullest attention.

Last night really made me question whether or not I should just walk away and stay with my parents until this is all over. I'd be further away from Kyle, and Marcel wouldn't have to deal with my shit. He wouldn't have to worry about getting into fights or possibly getting tossed in jail.

Though I'm sure he understands, I know he deserves better. But...he wants me to stay. And I can't bring myself to leave.

This weekend, I'm making a promise to give more of myself to him.

As soon as we land in New Orleans, we are in a rental car and on our way to the hotel. Even in July, the city of New Orleans is lively.

It's extremely humid out, and I can tell a fresh shower of rain has just passed because the roads are slick and the air is sticky. Even so, we have the windows rolled down, taking in the many people crossing the streets.

Some are dressed like they are in a parade, and others very casually. There's a mix of regulars and others looking for their next party, and I love it. New Orleans clearly isn't just for one person. It's for everybody—whether they have an eccentric soul or a meek spirit.

Once we've checked in to the hotel, we grab something to eat in the restaurant next door. Marcel chooses a burger, while I go for the tuna melt and a sparkling water.

"I'm glad the hearing is next week. You ready for it?" Marcel asks after taking a bite of his burger.

I shrug. "I don't know."

"You don't know?"

I glance up at him before focusing on my plate again. "Marcel, I really don't want to talk about that while we're here."

"Why not?" he asks, and though I'm glad he's in a much better mood than last night, I'm not up for this conversation.

"Because this is our time, you know? I feel like we should enjoy the freedom we have. When we go back, I'm sure we'll be stressed all over again."

He looks me over twice then leans back in his chair. "You're sayin' all this, but you seem bothered right now. I get you're upset about what happened last night, but we're here now. He can't get to us here."

I frown at him, pick up my drink, and take a sip.

"Tell me what's on your mind, Gabby."

I sigh, placing the drink down and then propping my elbows on top of the table. "I don't know. I just...I keep wondering if he sent that investigator after us. Like is he here right now? Watching us? Or maybe Kyle will show up again and ruin this whole trip for us." I do a hard sweep of the restaurant, like I'll see some man in a trench coat and sunglasses hiding behind a newspaper. I know—overboard—but it's all I can imagine.

"I'd say that's a little extreme." Marcel finishes off his burger. "He showed up at my house, which is less than twenty minutes from his, yeah, but to come *all the way* to New Orleans would be fuckin' ridiculous."

"Yeah, but it's not beneath Kyle. He has the money to do it."

"And I have the fists to beat his ass again, as well as that investigator's ass if he crosses my path," he shoots back with a mouth half-full. Marcel gives me a smug smile, but I don't cave. Noticing that I'm still on edge, he swallows the bite in his mouth then reaches across the table, taking one of my hands in both of his. "Look, we're here to have a good time, Gabby. Say Kyle did send the investigator here. He can't bother us publicly, otherwise he's not good at his damn job. And if he's around takin' pictures or somethin', it won't affect anything. What we're doin' now has nothin' to do with the divorce. Focus on that. Understand?"

"I'm trying, but everything is really getting to me after last night. The more I think about it, the more I'm convinced that his mom didn't hire the investigator. Kyle did. It's something he would do, but she always takes the fall for the shit he does."

"Well, that's on her, not you. We're here to have a little fun, right?"

"Right," I reply sullenly.

"Then let's do that. Fuck Kyle. Fuck the divorce right now. Fuck what happened last night. You filed a report, I'm sure they've arrested his as, so that means he can't be here. It's just you and me, Miss Gabby."

I smile at the nickname, and he puts on a smirk while tipping my chin.

"Fine. You and me. But if that's the case, what's the plan? The only way I'll be able to forget about all of that shit back at home is if I get super wasted!"

"You wanna get wasted? I can get you wasted. Don't even worry about that," he boasts, finishing up his meal.

"Well, let's do it then!" I finish my tuna sandwich, and after Marcel pays, we go upstairs to shower and change clothes. Then he takes me to Bourbon Street.

The sun has dipped in the sky, the streets packed with so many moving bodies. There are bands playing on drums made of old paint containers and pots, and there is even a jazz band standing in front of a restaurant, tooting trumpets and other horns that I can't help but shake my hips to.

We stop by one of the many bars around, and I order a hurricane. Shit, why not? My life has felt like one big hurricane lately. It's the perfect drink to have right now. Marcel orders one too, and we walk the streets, sipping on our fruity drinks arm-in-arm and laughing.

It's not Mardi Gras, but there are many women walking

around with only bras on. Some are so drunk that they actually flash their boobs for club owners so they can get in for free. Half the time, it doesn't even work.

I laugh, and I can tell this drink is hitting me hard, because I'm slowly starting to forget what's happened back in Hilton.

"Let's go in there!" I shout to Marcel, grabbing his hand and rushing to one of the clubs that has a neon purple sign above the door. It's dark inside the club, but the wall behind the bar is lit by even more neon signs and glowing lights on the shelves.

At the bar, I order myself another drink, and Marcel does the same.

A song by Drake comes on, and if my mouth weren't full of slushy, fruity alcohol, I would scream. My eyes get bigger and Marcel asks, "What?"

I grab his hand and push my way to the middle of the dance floor, holding my drink in the air with my other hand so it doesn't spill. "Let's dance!" I yell over the music.

"Oh, no, no!" Marcel shakes his head and waves his hands. "I'm not good at dancin'!"

"Oh, come on! You're here to have a good time, remember? Lower your guard!"

His head shakes again, but he can't stop smiling as he watches my body sway. I turn around, pressing my ass to his groin, leaving him no choice but to take me full on. He holds his drink in the air as I circle my hips while Drake raps about single women. Everyone in this club is dancing, smiling and sweaty, and I love it.

I'm not usually the one to enjoy nights at a club, but

with Marcel, I do. I feel him growing hard, his erection digging into my backside as his hips rock in sync with mine.

He's lowered his guard, his mouth on the crook of my neck, where it feels oh-so-good. Knowing how badly he wants me right now makes me so much happier than I thought it would.

## CHAPTER TWENTY-THREE

**MARCEL**

I'VE NEVER SEEN Gabby so relaxed—so outgoing.

I didn't know she was such a good dancer, either. Her full ass feels way too good on my dick as she grinds and dips. If there weren't so many people around, I'd fuck her right in this club.

She brings the straw of her drink up to her lips and shakes her hips as she sips, throwing one arm around the back of my neck.

I bury my nose into the crook of her neck again, letting her sweet, honey-cream scent fill every one of my senses.

She isn't the only one who has had too much to drink. I've had one too many, and I'm glad the hotel is a quick walk away. She's turning me the hell on, and I swear, one more dip of those hips and I'll erupt.

"Fuck this. Come with me," I growl in her ear.

She turns around and I grab her hand, leading her

around the corner. There is no line for the bathroom, so I walk right in and lock the door behind me.

The bathroom has a bold, red neon sign on the wall, and a red lightbulb above the sink. It's fucking hypnotic, and Gabby looks breathless and sexy beneath it. Her hair is down, dark tight curls surrounding her face. Her lips are full and parted, eyes glazed with a familiar lust.

I don't even give myself the chance to think this through, because the shit I want to do to her, I can't even put in words.

I place my drink on the counter, and she does the same, clashing into me. She moans as I pick her up to sit her on the counter. One of the drinks topples over. I feel it splash on my leg as it hits the floor. It'll leave a mess, but right now, I don't give a damn.

I shove Gabby's dress up to her waist, tug her panties down, pick her up in my arms, and slowly guide her pussy down until it's wrapped tight around my dick.

"Oh, fuck," I groan, and she gasps as I shift her up and then back down. She looks me in the eyes, hers glossy and heated.

"Oh my God," she breathes. "I can't believe we're doing this."

"I can." I grip her ass even tighter. She moans loudly, but with the bass thumping and the people yelling, I'm sure it will blend in with the rest of the noise.

I don't hold back as I place her upper back on the nearest wall and stroke swiftly. Beads of sweat appear on her forehead, and I feel my own sweat dripping down the side of my face. She's gripping the hell out of my dick right now, and I'm so fucking drunk, losing control.

"Fuck, I'm close," I growl, and she sighs, kissing my neck, my chin, and then my lips again.

I pick her up off the wall and drop her down on my swollen cock one more time, and she cries out just as I explode, coming quick in her tight, wet pussy.

"Oh shit," I groan, putting her back on the wall again, trying to remain steady. "Fuck, you're so damn good, baby."

"You're amazing," she breathes and then there's a banging on the door.

"Hurry the hell up, whoever you are! I have to pee!" some girl screams on the other side of the door.

We look at each other and bust out laughing while still trying to catch our breath.

I help her clean up and then grab the drink from the counter. I pick up the cup I dropped, but the shit we spilled is a lost cause.

When Gabby unlocks the door, the girl screams, "Finally!" and shoves right past us. She starts to lower her shorts, but I close the door before she can show too much. She's trashed, that much is clear.

We visit two more clubs, where we share even more drinks, laugh, and dance a little more. Eventually, as we walk the lit streets of New Orleans, that buzz dies down, and we stop by one last bar, taking a spot at the counter. This bar is much quieter—a sports bar with pool tables and TVs in every corner.

Gabby orders a water to rinse some of the alcohol away. When she receives it, she swirls the straw in her cup, fiddling with the ice.

"I know I tell you this all the time, but you're so different, Marcel," she says to me after a while.

"Am I?" I'm turned toward her on the barstool, my knees touching the side of her thigh.

"Yeah. I mean, you're rugged, yet you have a soft heart. You're careless but carefree all the same. You're the first person I've met who actually speaks his mind about how he really feels about someone." She shrugs and releases the straw. "I love it, honestly. It's nice being around someone *real*."

"I'm glad you think so highly of me."

She looks me over, placing a fist beneath her chin. "What do you like about me?"

"Everything."

"No, come on!" She laughs. "Go into detail. Every day I wonder what attracted you to me. Is it my looks?"

"Yeah right. You're beautiful, yes, but if you think I've only stuck around because of *that*, you're sadly mistaken." I point a finger at her chest. "You have a good heart."

She blushes and grins, lowering her gaze.

"Believe it or not, when I first met you, you reminded me a lot of Shayla."

"Really?" Her eyes stretch a little. "How?"

"Well, for starters, my sister had this odd fascination with art, and you are an artist. The day I met you, you had all that shit on your hands and paint on your clothes." I huff a laugh. "Shay was also super sarcastic, just like you can be sometimes. She underestimated herself a lot too…just like you. Never believed she was worth more than she had." Gabby sucks in a breath, locking eyes with me. "Every day I wish I could tell Shayla that she was amazing, and that she could do whatever the hell she put her mind to." I pause a moment. "This might sound crazy, but sometimes I think maybe that's why I met you, so I can tell you every day that you are amazing, and that you can do whatever the hell you want, so long as it makes you happy."

The rims of her eyes shimmer with tears. She blinks it all away quickly and shakes her head. "Sometimes I feel like I don't deserve whatever I want. I can't believe I was so stupid with Kyle. I let him do that stuff to me, like I had no value whatsoever."

"You were afraid. You can't blame yourself for feeling that way after what he did to you."

"Yeah, but I always ask myself *why*? Why didn't I fight back? Why did I just sit there and *take* it? He did a lot for me and my family, yeah, but I just…I don't get why I never spoke up until now. Before now, I always felt like I owed him my life, which sounds insane!"

"I guess you just needed that push. Luckily, I more like shoved your crybaby ass to get a move on."

She breaks out in giggles. "You're such a jackass."

"I'm *your* jackass." I lean forward. "Now kiss me."

She cradles one side of my face, kissing me tenderly.

"Your lips are so soft," I murmur. I swear they are. They mold perfectly to mine. "You wanna know what else is soft?" I ask.

"What?" she mumbles on my mouth.

"That ass of yours."

"Oh my gosh!" She tosses her head back and laughs again. "Stop! You are so corny!"

I laugh too, then prop my hands on the counter. "Ready to get out of here?"

"Yeah." She hops off the stool and grabs my hand when I stand. "Let's go back to our room."

We walk hand-in-hand on Bourbon Street, making our way over to Canal, where our hotel is.

During the walk, all I can do is listen to her. She talks about wanting to open an art studio where she can physically teach students how to paint, sculpt, and other creative things.

She also talks about how she twisted her ankle running away from a raccoon when she was twelve. She can hardly tell the story because she's laughing so hard, and I laugh because she can't stop laughing, swearing that the raccoon was going to give her rabies if she hadn't run.

I may sound like a sappy bitch, but I love seeing a smile on this woman's face. I love seeing her *happy*. She deserves that and so much more, and how any man can deny her these beautiful smiles astounds the hell out of me.

## CHAPTER TWENTY-FOUR

**GABBY**

Everything goes by in a blur the next day.

We drink and laugh and have a good time, putting aside everything bad that has happened the last few weeks.

We party hard, living life with no worries. For once in my life, I am *living*, and it's with a man I admire so much.

Having sex with him in the bathroom of that club was so damn erotic. I never thought I'd have sex in a public place, but we did, and it was better than I ever could have imagined. I'm almost certain I would never have done something like that with Kyle.

On Sunday morning, I roll over in the hotel bed and notice Marcel is already looking at me.

"Are you watching me?" I murmur, my voice still tired.

"I am."

"Why?"

"'Cause you're fuckin' gorgeous."

Even this early, I blush.

Marcel climbs on top of me as I rest on my back. I caress his cheek and say, "I don't want it to be our last day."

"Doesn't have to be. We could stay here forever."

"No, we can't," I giggle. "I have a hearing, and you have to work."

"Damn. Forgot all about that. Responsibilities kinda suck." He smirks, planting a kiss on my cheek. "Did you have fun this weekend, though?"

"I did."

"We need to do this more often—little getaways like this."

"Yeah," I breathe when he parts my thighs with his knee, spreading them wider apart.

I help him lower his boxers, and before I know it, he's inside me and a heavy moan has run through my lips.

"I want you to know somethin'," he hums on my mouth.

"What's that?" I ask, breathless.

"I want you to know that when we go back home, I'm here for you, no matter what." He cups the back of my neck, lowering his lips to the crook of it. "You're an amazin' woman, and I'm never lettin' you go."

His words are so romantic.

I hate thinking about it while we are in such an intimate position, but Kyle has never spoken to me this way. Ever. How did I get so lucky after all of that?

Kyle has never made me feel important, but Marcel is a whole other breed. He is all male, and he knows what he wants, and nothing makes a man sexier.

Though he'd never admit it, I know Marcel is a hopeless romantic, just like me.

For the rest of the day, we walk the streets of New Orleans then ride around, grabbing some of the best beignets in the city and exploring other interesting places.

New Orleans is a magical place, and now I see why everyone raves about it. It's fun here, the perfect getaway for someone who has a lot on their mind. This place will leave you no choice but to forget about the bullshit and to enjoy the moment.

It's a desolate feeling to be packing up when we head back to the hotel, but I know we must get back.

I got an email from Jasinda letting me know that my hearing has been pushed a day ahead. I don't know how it will turn out, but I need to get my head in the game.

We check out, head to the airport, and fly home. From the airport in Hilton, we catch an Uber to Marcel's house to get his truck then drive to Venice Heights to pick Callie up from Meredith.

When we leave, I can't help looking across the street at the place I once called home.

The porch lights are on, and there is a black SUV parked at the curb, which proves that Kyle's mother is still around. I have a feeling she won't leave until she knows how this all plays out. Also probably so she can keep an eye on her demented son, so he doesn't do something else crazy.

On the way home, Marcel grabs my hand and gives it a comforting squeeze. "You sure you don't want me at the hearing?"

"No. It's okay. Jasinda said it will be best if I show up alone."

"All right." He sighs, and I stroke Callie's back with my free hand. I missed my sweet girl. "Don't even worry about the hearing. You have enough evidence."

"I hope so." Truth be told, I am nervous as hell. What if we're appointed a judge who couldn't give a shit about our case? What if Kyle pulls something out of his sorry ass that sets me back?

I don't know how the hearing will go, but I do know that I have to remain confident.

This is my life, and I refuse to let Kyle take any more of it away from me.

# CHAPTER TWENTY-FIVE

## GABBY

My hair is brushed and tied in a sleek bun that took me an hour to straighten before styling.

I'm wearing a conservative sky-blue dress I found at Banana Republic, with pumps to match. I stare at myself in the mirror of Jasinda's restroom, focusing mostly on my eyes.

"I can do this," I tell myself. "I can do this."

My heart beats faster with every word. *I can do this.* With the words repeating in my head, I pick up my clutch and leave the restroom, going to Jasinda's office before I talk myself out of it.

"You ready?" she asks when she spots me.

"Yeah. Let's do this."

From her office, we ride to the hearing together, and along the way, she gives me the rundown.

She tells me to remain calm when I see Kyle, and to not speak unless I am spoken to in the courtroom. I can do that.

For a split second, I feel pretty confident about doing this, but as soon as we pull up to the courthouse, my heart drops to my stomach.

Kyle is standing in front of the courthouse beside his attorney. My heart drums in my chest, but I get out of the car anyway when Jasinda does. She locks her car, and I follow her up the steps.

"Don't panic," Jasinda says quietly as we walk toward the entrance of the courthouse. She notices Kyle too. She knows exactly what he looks like after I showed her the images of him. "Don't even look at him. Just keep walking."

I do as she instructs, sticking by her side. I can feel Kyle's eyes on me as I pass him a short distance away. Even as I walk up the stairs, I can still feel his hot glare on me, one of disapproval and loathing. Before coming up, I noticed the cut on his cheek and his lip, courtesy of Marcel. He's lucky he didn't end up with a black eye.

When I'm inside, the cool air in the building swallows me whole, and I draw in a deep breath before exhaling.

"You're much better than some of my other clients. Most end up getting into it before the hearing even begins." Jasinda smiles, then digs into her briefcase, taking out a pack of mints. "Here, suck on one of these. I know it sounds weird, but I swear the mint always works as a good distraction."

I take the case and dump one into my hand, popping it into my mouth.

"Courtroom's this way."

She leads the way. Once we're inside, surrounded by brown benches, tables, and American flags, Jasinda places her briefcase down on one of the tables. I take the seat next to hers, sucking on the mint while studying my surroundings.

I have never been inside a courthouse before, let alone a courtroom. Luckily, no one will be here but us, and not some grand jury like all the movies have.

Several minutes later, the doors behind us swing open and Kyle saunters in behind his attorney. They take the desk just across the aisle from us, and Kyle's attorney takes several papers out of his briefcase then takes a seat, straightening his tie.

The judge enters the room moments later, swathed in black with a head full of peppery hair, and the bailiff introduces him as Judge Walker as we all stand.

After the judge tells us to be seated, the hearing begins by Jasinda pleading my case, and telling the judge about the history of domestic abuse between me and Kyle, then proceeds to request a restraining order.

I can hear Kyle scoffing as his attorney writes down notes. I steal a glance at Kyle and he's shaking his head, as if all of this is preposterous. After Jasinda presents all the proof of Kyle's abuse, including the domestic reports I filed at the police station, and even the voicemail he left on Marcel's phone—which Kyle did not see coming—Judge Walker is pleased to hear that I already have a restraining order.

He informs us that that I can proceed with the divorce trial after six months, since the law requires us to be separated for six months or more. Since Kyle still refuses to go with a settlement, we have no choice but to take this to trial.

Six months seems like an eternity, but as long as I don't have to be around him, I will get through it.

It all happens so quickly—much quicker than I had anticipated. I'm more than relieved when I'm out of that courtroom.

"I'm going to run to the restroom really quick," I tell Jasinda.

"Okay. I'll meet you outside." She trots away, and I go down the hall to find the ladies room.

After I wash my hands and dry them, I leave the restroom, but as I turn the corner, I catch a familiar pair of dark-brown eyes.

I gasp as Kyle pushes off the wall, standing in a dark blue Armani suit. My heart slams against my ribcage, and I make an effort to get around him, but he catches me by the elbow and swings me back in front of him.

"Leave me the hell alone, Kyle," I hiss at him, shoving his hand away.

"Gabby, aren't you tired of this charade?" he asks, his voice calm.

"This is not a fucking charade, and the fact that you think it is proves how fucking *insane* you are."

His eyes narrow, and I swear they turn a shade darker as he steps closer to me. "You do realize that I am the one with all of the money? I have your car. Your art. I have everything you love—hell, I may as well *own* you. You will walk out of this with absolutely nothing to your name, and when that happens, everyone will look at you like *you* are the fool. Not me. I'm advising you, as your husband, to not go through with this, and to save your future while you can."

I get closer to his face, but even so, my heart booms even louder. "You are *not* my fucking husband anymore," I snarl.

His upper lip twitches, and he brings a hand up, grabbing my upper arm tight and slamming me as gently as possible into the wall.

I fight a gasp as he cages me in with both arms. He does it so casually that to any passerby, we seem like a couple in deep discussion.

"You are a stupid fucking girl," he snarls back. "I gave you *everything*. I made you my *wife*! Do you think you are the only woman who has wanted me? The only woman who has had a taste of me? My assistant was very good at sucking my cock during the times you wouldn't, but I still came home to you. I didn't run off with her, so it makes no sense whatsoever for you to run off with another man."

My eyes stretch wider as I digest the pill of truth he just delivered. My instincts were right. I knew it. He was sleeping around with his assistant Joanna. It shouldn't bother me, but I wonder how long it's been going on or when it even started. Was it before we got married or after?

"You're a fucking pig," I spit at him.

"If you say so, but before you think about bringing that up in court, don't bother. My lovely assistant has already been told not to say a thing, and there is absolutely no proof that we have done anything together. And even if there was, it's all been erased." His jaw flexes. "I am giving you another chance here, Gabs, and you're willing to throw it all down the drain? Are you forgetting you spread your legs and let another man have what was mine? You started this." He drops his hand, attempting to grab the sensitive area between my legs, but I duck under his arm and back away as quickly as I can in my heels.

"Fuck you, you piece of shit!" I shout then I twist around and rush down the hallway.

As if she heard my voice, Jasinda rounds the corner with knitted brows and wide eyes. She looks at me and then over my shoulder, eyes widening as she sees Kyle standing there.

"Come on," she murmurs, wrapping an arm around me and ushering me toward the exit. "Let's get you out here."

I want to nod, but I can't, because I'm desperately trying to hold back on the tears that are threatening to fall. He was never happy with me. Knowing he's been sleeping with his assistant proves that, and all this time I thought he'd been faithful to me, which resulted in enormous waves of guilt.

"Don't forget all I've done for you, Gabs!" Kyle yells.

Jasinda stops when she sees Kyle coming after us. "And you, Mr. Moore, should not forget that you are under a restraining order. If you come within one hundred yards of my client again, you will be arrested again, and that will not look good for you at trial."

I glance over my shoulder, and Kyle stops walking, lifting his chin. He grimaces at me, jaw clenching, fists tight.

I snatch my eyes away and leave the courthouse with Jasinda, thankful that he'll never be able to lay his hands on me again.

# CHAPTER TWENTY-SIX

**MARCEL**

I'M glad to know Gabby's hearing went well, but kind of pissed that she has to be tied to that dipshit for six more months.

Knowing that he touched her again, and I wasn't there to protect her, definitely pissed me the fuck off. When she told me, I wanted so badly to go to his house, kick the door in, and hand it to him, but Gabby calmed me down, as usual. She's good at that, I notice.

I'm not surprised he had an affair, either. I could see a prick like him messing around behind Gabby's back, but now that she knows, she's even more upset and questioning the whole marriage.

None of it was real. Yes, she knew that, once her father told her about the arrangement, but to know that she'd invested the time in him as a true wife and he never took it seriously is painful to her.

I can't blame her for feeling that hurt. No one wants to

be used like that—made to feel insignificant. Trust me, I know all about it.

Several weeks pass, and I do notice her mood changing. At first, I think nothing of it, assuming the stress of the separation is weighing her down.

But it's more than that. The spark she had before is gone. As the days go on, she lays around in hoodies and sweatpants, watching TV, and it's unlike her. She's usually very outgoing, wanting to take walks or go out for runs, shop or try a new recipe.

I almost start to wonder if *I'm* doing something wrong. What can I do to make her happier? Should I buy her chocolates and flowers? Perhaps I'm not doing enough. I'm still getting used to all of this—being in a relationship, that is.

I remember that I'm not supposed to keep anything from her, so I finally cave after she makes us pasta and ask her what's going on.

"Why does something have to be going on with me?" she snaps, and her attitude catches me way off guard.

"I'm just curious. You've been mopin' around for the last few weeks. Seems like somethin' is wrong."

"It's just this stupid separation," she mutters. "Jasinda called today and told me Tom, Kyle's attorney, has the emails between you and me."

"Really?"

"Yes. He'll send them to the judge. He's trying to make me look bad."

"Nothing looks as bad as a man hitting a woman."

"Yeah, that's in our world, Marcel, but in court it's different. What if he requests more time on the separation?

I read somewhere that judges can do that if they think the couple can do mediation and work it out."

"That won't happen, though. You have the restraining order, so the judge wouldn't do that because he's a threat to you."

"Yes, but the order is only until the trial happens. He could easily change his mind." She uses her fork to fiddle with her food, resting a fist beneath her chin with the other.

"You just need to take a moment to relax, Gabby."

"Oh my God! Please stop telling me to relax, okay?" She drops her fork and pushes out of her chair. "I can't exactly *relax* when I don't know what my future will look like, so stop saying it, Marcel!"

I frown as I watch her storm to the bedroom, then I push out of my chair too, chasing after her.

"Gabby, what the fuck is wrong with you? All I'm tryin' to do is talk you through this shit! What are you gettin' mad at me for?"

"Because you keep asking questions, and you keep saying things, and I'm just so fucking sick of all of it! None of this would even be happening if I hadn't had a damn affair!"

"Yes the hell it would!" I snap. "Kyle would still be beatin' your ass, and you'd be pretendin' nothin' is goin' the fuck on! Pardon me for wantin' to know how you're feelin'! Next time, I won't even fuckin' ask." I turn away as her mouth drops open, going to the door and grabbing Callie's leash.

Callie hears the leash jingle and rushes to me right away, tail wagging. After I've clipped it to her collar and grabbed my keys, I open the door, slamming it behind me.

As I walk Callie, I can't help wondering if maybe this is all fucking wrong. I love Gabby—trust me, I do—but I don't know if this is what she really wants. The stress is eating her alive, and I get that. I'd be stressed, too, but people always tell the truth when they're fed up or angry, and she's just confessed her truth.

Maybe she's not used to being asked about so much going on in her life after being with Kyle, but I'm a different man and she knows that—she knew it since the very first day she met me. I care about her feelings. I want to know what is going on inside her head, unlike him.

I let out a slow breath, sitting on the curb in front of my house as Callie sniffs around. "Your momma's fuckin' crazy," I mumble when Callie stands on her paws, sniffing my face. "But I love her."

Callie sits in front of me. I can tell she's ready to go inside. We've been out here for about thirty minutes, anyway.

With a sigh, I stand up, but I don't go in the house. I go to my truck, place Callie in the passenger seat, start the engine, and leave.

## CHAPTER TWENTY-SEVEN

**MARCEL**

When I get back to my house, I walk with Callie to the front door and lock it behind me when I'm inside.

I check the bedroom for Gabby. She's not there. When I walk back to the living room, I notice the light for the back porch is on.

Stepping out, I look to the left, at the patio furniture I have set up out back. Gabby is sitting on one of the chairs, her legs drawn to her chest. Her hair is up in a messy, curly bun, her chin on her knees.

"Hey," I murmur. "I got you something."

She frowns in my direction. If looks could kill, boy, I'd be dead.

I hold up three white canvases in one hand, and a pack of paintbrushes in the other.

Her eyes light up, and then they instantly fill with guilt.

"I wasn't sure what kind of paint you used, but I stopped

by the bank and took some money out so you can go and get whatever you want."

She nods, blinking the tears away. "Thank you." She pauses. "I thought you left to do something crazy."

I give my head a shake, placing the art stuff against the wall of the house. With a long, tired sigh, I take the chair beside hers, and we sit quietly for a moment. She's staring ahead at the line of trees.

"I'm sorry," she finally says, looking my way.

"Don't apologize for how you feel."

"But I am sorry. I don't regret being with you, Marcel, I swear." She reaches for my hand, entwining our fingers.

"I know you don't, Gabby." I give her hand a squeeze. "Trust me. I know all about sayin' shit I don't mean. You're stressed and tired, but this will all be over soon."

She bobs her head in agreement, resting her head on my shoulder.

"Even so, I need you to understand that I'm *nothin'* like Kyle, Gabby. I'm not sure how you grew up at home, or if you had to grow up keepin' all of your thoughts and secrets to yourself, but I didn't grow up that way. I didn't become that way until after all of my family died. But as a family, we all knew that if someone had somethin' to say, they said it. You are my family now, so if you have somethin' on your chest, you let it out. Period. Don't hold that shit back."

She peers up at me with glistening eyes.

"I told you I'm here for you every step of the way, and I mean that. Yeah, some days are hard as fuck, but that will never change the way I feel about you."

"Good," she whispers, "because I can be a bitch sometimes." She drops her legs with a coy smile and walks my way, sitting on my lap. She curls up to me, the side of her head on my collarbone. "You deserve better than me, Marcel."

"No." My head shakes as I tip her chin. I press a gentle kiss to her lips, and she sighs. "There is no one better than you, little thing."

Her eyes sparkle. "Do you think we're meant to be?"

"I don't know. But I know I'm committed. The question is, are you? You were committed to him for so long; it would be understandable if you want to be on your own again for a while."

She laughs dryly, shaking her head. "With Kyle, I may as well have been alone. He put effort into winning me, but after the engagement, everything sort of went downhill. I tried to appreciate him, but I think I ended up putting him too high on a pedestal. I made him seem like some god and myself, a measly peasant."

"Well it's not like that anymore. And you're not a peasant, you are a fuckin' goddess. You run your own world. Remember that."

She wraps her arms around me, drawing in a deep breath and exhaling. I do the same, and we sit here for a while, just like this, the two of us in my backyard, letting the cool breeze dance in our hair.

"Thank you for the canvases and brushes. I can't wait to paint. It'll ease some of the stress for sure."

"I figured it would."

She hugs me around the neck and kisses my cheek. "I don't regret this," she says again. "I really do love you."

I smile, sweeping my knuckles over her chin. "I love you, too."

I guess I was right about what I'd said before. She's stressed, and stress will wear any person out, but one thing I've learned is to never say something I don't mean, no matter how hard life gets. The last thing I said to my sister still haunts me to this day.

We sit like this for a long time, and before I know it, she's fallen asleep on my chest. With a grunt, I stand, her body lax in my arms, carrying her into the house.

I place her on the bed, but I can't help watching her sleep for a while.

I think every kind of relationship has its doubts and its tests. I'm trying to remember that it's okay to fall out, just so long as we forgive and forget. My mother always told me that, and now I see why she abided by that one rule. Now I see why she stuck with my dad until his dying breath.

Loyalty runs in my blood. I can't escape it. My love is fierce, always burning like a gas-fueled flame, extremely hard to put out.

Something tells me Gabby's love is just as fierce…she just needs to break through the old mold to see it for herself.

## CHAPTER TWENTY-EIGHT

### GABBY

THE SIX MONTHS fly by much faster than I anticipated. It hasn't been easy, either.

Kyle still refuses to go with a settlement and is still playing the role of victim, because I had an affair.

Thankfully, I haven't seen Kyle since the restraining order was placed, and Marcel has been consistent and devoted to me through all of the ups and downs.

Dad has called every single day to check on me, although it has been a struggle for him with work and his docks, he has gathered a plan to relaunch the docking business on his own since Kyle terminated the contract. It will require a lot of money and renovations, but he's ready to work, and Ricky plans on investing to keep things going.

Apparently, Kyle terminated the contract as soon as he possibly could. We weren't too disappointed, because we saw it coming and I'm glad Dad was preparing for it, but I couldn't help feeling like Kyle was right about my Dad. He had no backup plan, and now the dock is at risk again, and he's the only one who can save it. I hope, with Ricky's help, he can.

I can't help feeling like this is all my fault, but my dad insists that it's no one's fault but his. If he hadn't been so eager to get a deal, none of this ever would have happened.

Life is tough, and there are many lessons to be learned for sure, but the only thing we can do is learn from our mistakes and keep going. I will admit that I have never felt closer to my family than right now, and that says a lot, because we were pretty tight before.

The trial is today, totaling to a grueling seven months, and I'm a nervous wreck. Fortunately, we didn't have to wait too long. Seeing as we have been legally separated for six months, and there are domestic reports in the system for Kyle, Judge Walker decided to rush our trial.

Kyle has a good attorney. Mine is great, but I have a list of demands, some of which involve money. While I didn't bring anything financial to the relationship, he encouraged me to not get a full-time job, and the pain and suffering he put me through ought to be worth something. But, it's his money, and the judge will probably go with that. I just want something from him, an acknowledgment that he didn't win and that what he's done to me was wrong, otherwise he'll just keep doing it.

I'm walking away now, but who's to say another woman won't be harmed later on?

Jasinda has informed me many times that since I committed adultery, this case may not be as simple as she'd hoped, and that alone terrifies me.

I stand in the women's bathroom in the courthouse,

staring at my reflection in the mirror. The bruise I had months ago has healed completely, but even so, I've put on foundation and brushed my hair into a slick ponytail to look presentable today.

I take in my pink blouse and black pencil skirt. I look good enough. I'm praying things go my way.

There's a knock at the door, and I hear Jasinda's voice. "Gabrielle? Everything okay?"

"Yeah!" I call back. "I'm fine." I wash my hands, dry them off, and then walk out in black heels. Jasinda is standing off to the right, waiting for me.

"Nervous?" she asks, handing me her pack of mints.

I take the pack, dumping one into my palm. "A little."

"It's okay to be nervous, but don't forget what I told you. Remain confident and only tell the truth. Tom has agreed to only call you to the stand for testimony, if we don't call Kyle for his testimony. This is good, because if the judge only hears your side of it, you may sway him. We have the witness statements with the judge as well, so I have a good feeling about this one."

"Yeah. Got it." We walk to our appointed courtroom, and Jasinda leads the way to the desk on the right.

On the left side of the room is Kyle and his attorney, and in the row behind them are his parents. I catch his mother's eyes, but look away before she can hook me in.

Dan, Kyle's step-dad, starts to smile at me, but then he withdraws and looks away when Mrs. Moore bumps his shoulder. I actually really like Dan. He's always seemed like a nice man, and he supported my art. Not only that, but after what Mrs. Moore told me about him taking Kyle under his wing, it proves he has a good heart. Too bad he's stuck with Kyle and Sophon. Not sure what he did to deserve that kind of torture.

My parents, Ricky, and Teagan are behind me. And in the very back of the room is Marcel, with his arms folded over his broad chest. He promised Jasinda he'd keep his distance and keep his remarks to himself. I know that's going to be hard for him to do, though. He hates Kyle.

I look back at him, smiling. He returns a small smile, mouthing the words, "You've got this."

I focus on my parents next. My mom sticks up a thumb, and Dad winks. Ricky gives me a head nod, while Teagan gives me a big, reassuring smile.

The bailiff tells us to rise, and we stand as the judge walks in.

"You may sit," Judge Walker orders.

Judge Walker tells Jasinda and Tom to come up after a few readings. As they walk up, I feel eyes on me and look to my left. Kyle is looking right at me, his fingers folded on top of the desk, eyes narrowed.

I look away, clearing my throat and watching Jasinda return to the table.

They go over several procedural statements and then Jasinda begins to plead my case. She goes on about how I was set up to be married to Kyle by my father, and that Kyle took that and ran with it. She mentions that I married him a year later and that several days after our honeymoon Kyle hit me for the first time.

"She described it as Mr. Moore choking her until she couldn't breathe. He was upset that she said she wasn't ready to have kids yet, and frankly, Your Honor, that is the woman's decision and right as to whether she is ready or not."

Kyle's attorney objects.

The judge waves a hand, overruling it.

Jasinda nods, thanks the judge, and comes back to the desk.

"Your Honor, may I call Mrs. Gabrielle Moore to the stand?" Kyle's attorney asks. I've come to know his name is Tom Cavalier. Tom is an ambitious little shit. He reminds me of a weasel, which is never good.

"Granted," the judge says.

I stand, walking around the desk. I knew this time would come, but it doesn't stop my heart from nearly beating out of my damn chest.

I take the stand, place my hand on the Bible to swear to tell the truth, then take a seat.

Tom walks toward my stand with his hands behind his back. I can tell from the hungry look in his eyes that this is his time to shine, and he's going to make it hurt.

"Mrs. Moore," Tom starts, "was there a time you were in love with Kyle?"

"I thought so. But I was young, and just in love with the idea of him."

"Explain that a bit more, if you would."

I sigh. "I worked at a restaurant, and we went out on dates. I had never had a real boyfriend until Kyle, and I thought we were meant to be."

"When did you realize that it wasn't meant to be?"

"The first time he hit me."

"Which happened to be over a year ago, correct?"

"Yes."

"So why didn't you just leave for good at that time? Why go back to him if you were no longer in love?"

"Because he promised he wouldn't do it again. We'd just gotten married, and I didn't want to believe that I'd been so wrong about him, that the investment of my time and energy was going down the drain."

"Mrs. Moore, did your affair with your landscape architect have any say so in your desire for a divorce?"

"Objection, Your Honor! Speculation!" Jasinda calls out.

"Judge Walker starts to speak, but I speak up.

"No," I answer.

Tom looks surprised that I answered. "So, you mean to tell me that if you'd never met the architect, you would have wanted a divorce anyway?"

I swallow hard, looking back at Marcel.

He shakes his head.

My eyes then shift to Jasinda, who does a subtle nod.

"I'm certain I would have divorced him eventually, if for no other reason than to protect myself. My landscape architect had nothing to do with me wanting a divorce. The decision was fully mine."

"Okay. So, it is clear to me that you were well taken care of while with my client. He provided financially for you, and bought a home where you had a full art studio and could work from home. Now, you are requesting his money. Apologies if this sounds harsh, but I have reason to believe you stuck around with Mr. Moore, despite what he'd done, just to have access to his money. Would that be true?"

"What?" I frown at Tom, and then at Kyle, who is smirking. My eyes shift over to Jasinda, who shakes her head. I remember not to get riled up like she told me not to, so with a leveled voice I say, "No. Kyle's money didn't, and still doesn't, matter to me."

"So why ask for money in your settlement? Why not just ask him to sign the papers and just go about your way?"

I glance at Judge Walker, who is also waiting for my answer.

"Because...he hurt me," I say, my voice almost breaking. "He took advantage of me and ruined my life. I strongly feel that he doesn't deserve to walk out of this with just a signature on a paper."

Tom looks me over, before focusing on the judge.

"No further questions, Your Honor." Tom walks away and Jasinda stands, studying me carefully, most likely giving me a moment to breathe. I take the opportunity, drawing in a deep breath before exhaling.

"Gabby, can you tell me your full name?"

"Gabrielle Angel Lewis-Moore."

"Are you proud of that very last name? Moore?"

"Not anymore," I confess with a huff.

"Why is that?"

"At one point in time, I was proud of it. But when I got to know who Kyle really is, I became ashamed of the name."

"And why is that?" Jasinda questions.

"Because...I still used the name like a badge of honor, despite what he'd done to me."

"Can you describe what you felt the first time Mr. Kyle Moore physically abused you?"

"Fear," I say right away. "I never knew when he'd attack me again, so that fear continued."

"If you had a friend who was being physically abused by

her husband, would you suggest she stay in the marriage and make it work, or would you tell her to get out as soon as possible?"

My throat goes dry, but I swallow before answering. "I would tell her to run as fast and as far away as she possibly can, because she deserves better."

Jasinda nods. "No further questions, your Honor."

"You may go back to your seat," Judge Walker murmurs to me. I leave the stand, but my legs are shaking. Fortunately, I make it back without collapsing.

"Good job, baby," Mamá whispers in my ear.

"Mrs. Humphrey, what exactly does the defendant want as far as settlement?" Judge Walker asks.

Jasinda stands. "My client would simply like a settlement of two hundred thousand dollars, and for Mr. Moore to never speak to her or reach out to her again."

"And you're telling me that is too much to ask for, Mr. Moore?" Judge Walker asks, one brow dipped as he focuses on Kyle.

Tom whispers something to Kyle, and Kyle stands, straightens his tie, and says, "Your Honor. My wife is a very greedy woman. As my attorney clearly pointed out, she stuck around because she knew my money would come in handy. All of a sudden, after *she cheats*, she wants to leave with a hand full of cash? I'm sorry, but I just don't buy it, Your Honor, and I don't think it's fair when I've worked so hard for my money."

"Wow," I mutter, shaking my head.

"Right now, she says that she wants two hundred thousand, Your Honor, but she and her family have been getting money from me for *years* now. I paid off her school loans and have spent more than three hundred thousand dollars on her family alone. Because of that, I don't feel like I owe her anything."

"You caused this woman physical harm," Judge Walker states with a frown. "I'm looking right at the photos, and reading what you've done to her, and you mean to tell me you feel like you don't owe her anything? You are a very wealthy man, Mr. Moore. I'm certain you can afford what she's asking and still be well off."

Tom whispers something else.

Kyle sits and Tom stands.

"Your Honor, my client has a history of being abused himself. He has needed therapy for what he went through. It was even stated in this paper from his therapist, when he was twelve, that there could be lashing out in his future. Gabrielle was warned of this by Kyle's mother, yet she stuck around anyway."

*"What?"* I hiss, sitting forward with my hands on the desk. "Are you fucking kidding me? She told me about that *after* I filed for divorce!" I hiss at Jasinda.

"It's okay," Jasinda whispers, patting my hand.

I sit back with a scowl and a huff. I cannot believe this. They're lying now!

Tom shuffles through a few papers, then hands it one the bailiff, who hands it to Judge Walker.

"As you can see, my client is not very stable, and has even agreed to go to therapy again, but that does require a lot of time and money."

"Your Honor, Mr. Moore has *more* than enough money to cover his own therapy and pay my client for the mental and physical damage he has caused her. Who is to say she won't need therapy after trying to recover from an abusive spouse?" Jasinda asks, standing now with her palms planted on the table.

Judge Walker sighs, and Tom and Jasinda remain focused on him, waiting for his response. I swear, if a pen dropped, everyone would hear it. That's how quiet it is in here.

"Mr. Moore, Mrs. Moore, please rise."

Kyle stands, fixing his tie and the lapel of his suit. I stand too, folding my fingers in front of me.

"I am a very simple man," Judge Walker declares. "Although adultery is lawfully a crime that tends to often go unpunished, a domestic crime is a much, much bigger one that doesn't. I grew up with the idea grounded in me that a man should *never* put his hands on a woman, no matter the circumstances, and that a man should *never* have sex with a woman unless it is consensual."

I straighten my back, my heart beating madly.

"This case, honestly and truly, is a simple one for me, after studying all of the facts. I have morals grounded into me, and after seeing the bruise that covered that young woman's face—your *wife's* face—and after reading the police reports, as well as these terrifying testimonies from people who thought highly of you at one point, I have been given every reason to not let you walk out of my courtroom with all of that pride you are so happily carrying, Mr. Moore."

Kyle's smug smile slips to a frown.

Judge Walker stacks his papers and slides them aside. "Adultery is wrong, yes, but that is your *wife*, and you caused her harm in multiple ways. I won't allow it. What I will allow is both parties an opportunity to come up with an agreement during recess. If no agreement is made, then Mr. Moore will be required to give over half of his yearly salary to Gabrielle Moore every year and will have to attend mandatory anger management for a full year. Mrs. Moore will go to therapy for eight months to recover from her abuse, and in the meantime, the divorce will be finalized, and the restraining order will remain in effect for the next five years. Is that clear?"

"Yes, Your Honor," Tom says quickly.

Jasinda smiles. "Understood, Your Honor."

"Good. See you all in forty-five minutes." Judge Walker stands up in his black gown, leaving the courtroom.

I look over at Tom and Kyle. Kyle is seething, fists clenched, while Tom tries to calm him down.

Deep inside, I'm happy as hell. I look back at Marcel, who is standing and smiling wide. I bite a grin when he winks at me, then I look down at my parents.

My mom has her face cupped in her hands, like she can't believe what just happened, and Teagan is about to burst with excitement.

We all know that I may just win this thing.

## CHAPTER TWENTY-NINE

### GABBY

Since the mediation rooms were full, we're seated in an Italian restaurant nearby. Only the four of us—Jasinda, Tom, Kyle, and me.

I don't like being this close to Kyle. He's right across from me, looking at me with flared nostrils and dark, furious eyes.

"Let's get started, shall we?" Tom says, clearing his throat.

"Yes. Let's. So, my client has agreed that if her demands are not met, she will be happy to take half of Kyle's yearly salary and do the therapy requested by the judge. Now, in order for that not to happen, she has to get what she wants out of this," Jasinda states. "The judge is a fair man. We have much more proof, and it is clear he is not happy with what Kyle has done. Judge Walker considers the act of domestic violence a much bigger crime than adultery. You may throw that at his face all you want, but I have a feeling it will not change his mind, so let's not make this any harder than it needs to be."

"And what does she want?" Tom asks.

"Seeing as the judge was willing to offer half of Mr. Moore's yearly salary, she would like five hundred thousand dollars to rebuild her life, the keys and title to her Dodge Challenger, and for Kyle to have zero contact with her."

"Yeah-fucking-right," Kyle scoffs. "She's not getting the car."

"Kyle," Tom hisses.

"That is *my* car!" Kyle hisses. "I paid for it with *my* hard-earned money, just like everything else!"

"Yes, but that was out of your free will," Jasinda notes. "Gabrielle would like the title switched to her name, as well as the keys to the car. All effective immediately. You must agree to that today. If not, she will not come to any other agreement, and you will have to turn over half of your yearly income, which is slightly more than $500,000, Mr. Moore. With that kind of money, she can easily purchase another vehicle. She's cutting you a break here."

"You can't be serious! After everything I've done for you, you really have the nerve to sit there and request *more* money from me!" Kyle barks in my face.

"Yes, I have the nerve to request more money from the man who fucking *traumatized* me!" I bark back. "You choked me, and kicked me so hard it left a bruise on my face for weeks, Kyle! You *raped* me. I lived in fear because of you! You're not walking out of this with everything you had, when you've taken things from me I'll never get back!"

Kyle shakes his head, his fists clenching on top of the

table. "You are un-fucking-believable. I have no idea why I married a bitch like you."

"And you are a sad, worthless excuse for a man. In fact, you aren't a man. You're a spoiled little boy who hates when he can't have his way."

Kyle's jaw steels.

I stick my middle finger up at him.

Jasinda places a hand on my shoulder, a silent plea for me to relax.

"This is the only offer we will make. If you don't agree, Kyle, you will have to deal with what the judge hands you. You will lose money every single year, for the rest of your life. Do you really want that?" Jasinda asks.

"No, he doesn't want that," Tom answers rapidly, giving Kyle a stern look. "Give me a moment to talk to my client."

"Sure." Jasinda collects her papers and stands.

I go with her, heading to the bar. "Gah! I hate him so much!" I growl when we're by the bar.

"I know, but this is almost over," she says, rubbing my shoulder. "It happened much faster than I anticipated. I'm glad we were appointed to Judge Walker. He's a good man. Very old-fashioned. I heard he was a total mama's boy growing up."

"That's good," I sigh. "I'm glad we had him."

We look over at the table Tom and Kyle are at. Kyle is fuming, slamming his fist on the tabletop, arguing with Tom.

He finally pushes out of his chair and storms out of the restaurant. Tom comes our way, fixing his tie.

"My client has agreed to the settlement. The title for the car will be signed over to Gabrielle as soon as possible, and she will have the $500,000 by tomorrow. After the case is over, she will never see or hear from Kyle again, and he will adhere to the restraining order."

"I'm pleased to hear that. We will have this agreement in writing and signed by the end of today." Jasinda extends her arm, and Tom shakes the hand she offers.

Tom then shakes my hand, nods once at me, and leaves the restaurant.

Jasinda grins. "I would ask you if you want a drink, but we have to get back. We'll celebrate afterward, though, yes?"

I laugh. "Yes, yes. Let's go."

## CHAPTER THIRTY

### GABBY

I DIDN'T GET off easy about my affair. Like Jasinda said, Judge Walker is an old-fashioned man, which means he doesn't believe adultery is okay either but, despite the scolding he still got me through the case $500,00o richer and with the dream car that I missed so, so much.

I think I'm shocked, more than anything. It's all so surreal.

Jasinda announced the agreement, and though Kyle's family was upset, Kyle was the angriest. He wasn't going to live this down for the rest of his life, and that's all I wanted. I wanted him to have no choice but to swallow his pride and deal with it.

The funny thing about Kyle is he doesn't know when to give up. He believes that he is always right, and that he is untouchable. He figured, because he had money, that he could walk out of the courtroom without so much as a dent.

I made sure I had enough evidence that he couldn't. He didn't exactly lose the case, but he didn't win either.

Mrs. Moore made one little mistake when she found me at the mall though, and Judge Walker made a point in bringing it up before the case was dismissed.

When Mrs. Moore told me about Kyle having an ex-girlfriend he hit and paid off, I told Ricky, and he, being a huge tech-guy and all, found out exactly who the woman was.

Her name is Emery Tundra. I contacted her myself on Facebook several weeks before the trial, and she agreed to write up a statement giving her name, age, the year she and Kyle dated, and her address and number in case she needed to be contacted. Her statement, I believe, was the icing on the cake. It made Kyle look like a man with a pattern of domestic abuse, not just situational, and for that, the affair became a back-burner issue.

Judge Walker no longer assumed my affair was the reason for Kyle's lashing out. He realized it was much deeper than that and required Kyle to have a full year with a well-known psychiatric therapist in New York.

To top it all off, as we left the courthouse, my dad was at my side one moment and gone the next. Before I even realized what was happening, he was standing in front of Kyle, as Kyle pouted to his parents about the money he had to send.

When Kyle saw my dad, he snapped at him. "What the hell do you want, Will? I have no more money for you!"

"Oh, I'm not here for money," Dad said. "I just want to let you know that I haven't forgotten about the bruise you left on my daughter's face, or the things you did to her."

Then my dad's fist slammed into Kyle's face, and I gasped as Ricky yelled out, "Oh, shit!" with a laugh.

Kyle stumbled backward and landed on the ground with blood gushing from his nose. He looked dazed, like he had no idea what was going on.

"Why would you do that!" Mrs. Moore screamed as she and Mr. Moore rushed to help Kyle up.

"What would you have done if you had a daughter and it happened to her?" Dad flung his hand out, shaking off the pain as Mamá ran toward him.

"I can sue you for this!" Mrs. Moore spat at him.

Dad shrugged, walking away. "Go ahead! I don't give a damn! You and I both know your son needed to be taught a lesson."

Damn.

Even I felt those words.

Mrs. Moore looked from my dad to me. I pressed my lips and lightly shook my head. She knew he was right, but she'd never admit it.

Fortunately, they didn't press charges. I'm certain, once Kyle shook it off, they decided to cut their losses. No judge would have cared about him being punched in the face after he'd kicked me.

It would have dragged into another case for Kyle, and for the sake of his company, he needed to avoid the scandal.

After catching lunch with my parents, Teagan, and Ricky, Marcel and I went back to the hotel, showered together, and had a victory fuck on the bed.

He kissed me everywhere, sucking my bottom lip, teasing me with his cock, before pushing inside of me and making me his.

We owned that night, and I couldn't have been happier.

I didn't think I would be able to escape Kyle so easily. I thought, surely, he would haunt me for the rest of my life, make me suffer for what I'd done.

I suppose that's what living in fear feels like. You never know what to expect, so you're always looking over your shoulder, waiting for the attack. Waiting for the other shoe to drop.

But not anymore.

No. I am free now.

It's all over. I can breathe again.

I'm behind the wheel of Lady Monster with the sunroof open and my windows down. I picked her up from Tom last week, and I've been riding around Hilton for days, listening to this beautiful car's engine rumble.

In the passenger seat is Marcel, who is smiling at me, calling me a wild woman. I don't care. I am a little wild, but he loves that about me. He appreciates me for who I am, and I'm glad he's stuck by my side during all of this.

I feel empowered, victorious.

I didn't know what it was really like to be in love until I met Marcel, but now that I know, I intend on keeping it that way for a very, very long time.

Hell, maybe even for life.

# CHAPTER THIRTY-ONE

## GABBY

"Here's to Gabby, for finally divorcing the son of a bitch who made her life a living hell!" Teagan has a shot glass full of silver tequila in the air as she cheers.

I laugh and everyone at the bar cheers with her, holding their shot glasses up too.

"As a matter of fact, let's get her another shot!" Ricky taps on the bar counter, getting the bartender's attention.

"Cheers to that!" Meredith says after downing her shot.

We're at a modern bar in Hilton. Of course, Teagan found the place, seeing as she loves to look into reviews for clubs and bars to make sure her money will be worth it.

She wanted to celebrate the divorce formally, so the weekend after the trial, she contacted Ricky, Mamá, Dad, and even Meredith, asking them to join us. My parents couldn't make it. Dad had a meeting to attend for a loan, and Mamá had her citizenship test this morning. She passed it, thank goodness.

I can thank Marcel for helping me handle the remainder of her lawyer and immigration fees. He's been so good and accepting about all of this.

Speaking of, Marcel wraps his arms around my shoulders and reels me back. He kisses my cheek, and I laugh then spin around to hook my arms around the back of his neck.

"Rumor has it I'm a free woman now," I say with a smile.

"Well that rumor is a lie, 'cause you're not free. You're all mine."

I giggle while he smirks. "Yeah." I kiss his lips. "I'm so yours."

"Look, I know it's too soon, but when do you two plan on getting married?" Teagan asks, holding a margarita in her hand. She's looking right at Marcel and me with a grin.

I pull away from Marcel and turn toward her with narrowed eyes. "I think we can both agree that it is *way* too soon to discuss marriage, T," I laugh.

"Yeah, just a little bit," Marcel chuckles, then he says something that catches me completely off guard. "Not that I would mind makin' her my wife or anything, though."

"Aww!" Teagan chimes as I look back at Marcel.

Marcel gives me a small shrug.

I fight a blush. I can't pretend I haven't thought about what it would be like to be with Marcel forever. I don't think it would be wrong, but for the sake of my sanity—and his patience—and a little more time is best.

But…in the meantime, a girl can always dream, right?

## CHAPTER THIRTY-TWO

**MARCEL**

**ONE YEAR LATER**

I FIGURED I'd surprise Gabby with a trip to Clearwater Beach.

We've been working hard this past year, and it's about time we have another one of our getaways.

With the money she got from Kyle, she started fresh and opened up her own paint, sculpt, and sip studio in Hilton Head. In the studio, she teaches people how to paint a certain painting she's created, or mold a sculpture, all while they get to sip on wine and eat cheese and crackers. She gets a lot of business, and I'm damn proud of my girl, but it's time for us to escape reality for a little while.

She's been looking so tired lately, and I feel like I haven't been doing enough for her because my schedule has been full too. Don't get me wrong, it's a good thing to be thriving, but we need the escape.

She doesn't know where we're going, but I'm driving Lady Monster. We left Callie with Meredith, who was happy to spend some time with our girl. Even though she's much bigger now, Callie's still such a sweet thing.

When we make it to Clearwater, the sun has just set.

I check into the hotel I booked online several weeks ago, unbeknownst to Gabby, and then go for our bags in the trunk when I reach the car again.

"I think I need a nap after that ride," Gabby says after a yawn.

I smile over the trunk. "You should have slept in the car."

"How could I? I was too excited!"

When we make it to the room, Gabby changes clothes and crashes in the bed. She was up late packing last night and getting Callie's things ready.

I told her to get some sleep last night, but she swore she'd sleep during the ride. She didn't sleep a wink because she was too concerned about where we were going. She just couldn't let it be a surprise, and I had a good laugh about that.

By the time she figured it out, it was too late for her to catch some shut-eye.

~

Around two in the morning, Gabby pulls me out of a deep sleep, sliding her hand down my chest and then going beneath my boxers.

"Someone's awake, huh?" I rumble.

She laughs softly, her nimble fingers wrapping around my dick. "Just thought I'd thank you for bringing me here. Surprising me."

"Yeah? And how are you gonna do that?"

"You'll see." She makes her way between my legs, pulling my boxers down and revealing my semi-hard cock. In an instant, her lips are sealed around the head of my dick and I groan.

"Shit, Gabby."

She moans around me then takes me deeper into her mouth.

A hiss spills through my teeth. I bring a hand to the back of her head and thrust upward. She gags around my dick, and I love the sound of it, so I do it again.

She pulls back up, sliding her tongue up and down the length of me. When her tongue slides over my balls, I clutch a handful of her curly hair. Damn, it feels so good.

I can't take the teasing anymore. I release her hair and sit up, flipping her onto her stomach. She positions herself on her knees, her ass tilted in the air, and I yank her cotton shorts down, as well as her panties.

Running a finger through the slit of her pussy, I sigh, kissing the arch of her back.

"Already so fuckin' wet," I rasp.

She moans, spreading her hips wider. She's ready.

I position my dick at her entrance, sliding into her with ease. She moans even louder with every inch she takes from me, and when I'm all in, she throws her head back.

I grab a fistful of her hair and draw my hips back before slamming them forward again.

"Fuck me harder," she begs, and I do, but I wish she hadn't begged me because I already feel myself about to come. Still, I don't stop.

She gasps when I thrust my hips forward several times while letting out guttural noises. I love the sticky sound her pussy makes when I'm inside it.

With one more deep stroke, she groans, and I pull out, squirting my hot cum all over her ass in thick, white ropes.

"Stay on your knees, just like that," I command.

She lets out a small noise while I grab my shirt to clean the cum off her gorgeous skin. I climb back on the bed but turn onto my back, placing my head right between her legs.

"Sit on my face," I demand, and she lowers her hips. Her pussy is right on my lips and I open my mouth, sliding my tongue through her damp slit and making my way up to her clit.

"Oh my gosh," she breathes raggedly, lifting her hips.

"Nah-uh. Don't pull away. Fuck my face, baby. I'm all yours."

My words clearly set her on fire. She lowers her body again as I grip her waist and rolls her pussy all over my tongue while in a deep squat. Her hand comes down to my hair, and she clutches a handful of it, looking down at my eyes.

"Fuck, I love you so much." Her voice is shaky, breaths ragged as she grinds her pussy back and forth on my tongue. I can't do anything but groan in response. It's all I want to do. I love the taste of her pussy.

"Oh, babe! I'm about to come," she cries softly, and then she stills on top of me, but I lift my head, circling her clit repeatedly with my tongue to finish her off.

Her legs quake and she tosses her head back, yelling my name even louder. I don't let up until her body goes limp.

She collapses beside me, chest heaving, a lazy grin on her face.

"What are you smilin' about?" I ask with a laugh.

"Because I'll never get tired of that," she pants.

I let out a belly-deep chuckle. "Shit, I hope you don't."

She turns onto her side, caressing my cheek for a second. When she pulls away, she flops onto her back again and closes her eyes.

"Do you ever think about how we got here?" she mumbles.

"What do you mean?"

"I mean, like...just us, being in this place right now? If I hadn't taken that risk with you, I wouldn't be here. I'd still be miserable. Lonely. Hell, I might be dead."

"Oh." I bring her over to my chest and run my fingers through her hair. "Yeah, I do think about it sometimes. Still shocks me that you want my crazy ass."

"Well, to be fair, the things I wanted to do with you were just fantasies at one point."

I bust out laughing. "Oh, really? And what did you fantasize about, exactly?"

"A lot of stuff," she giggles. "I remember one night I actually masturbated on my couch because I was picturing you doing exactly what you just did to me a minute ago."

"What? Eatin' your pussy?"

She laughs softly. "Yes. That."

"I assume what you got in real life exceeded the fantasies?"

"Oh, for sure, but don't get cocky."

I laugh, and several seconds later, silence rains down on us. From where we are, I can hear the ocean roaring, the waves crashing.

I notice a moment later her breathing has evened out.

"Gabby?" I whisper, but she doesn't respond. "How the hell did you fall asleep that fast?" I mumble, more so to myself than to her.

I slide her up to the pillows and cover her with the comforter.

Tomorrow will be a long day, shopping for some food and hitting the beach, so I decide to go to sleep too, but not without having her in my arms.

## CHAPTER THIRTY-THREE

### GABBY

"Are you serious right now? *Jet skiing*?" I shriek.

Marcel looks me in the eyes with a wicked smirk. "Serious as a heart attack."

"I've never done that before! Sounds kind of intimidating!" And it really does. Jet skiing has never even crossed my mind as an activity I'd like to do.

"I haven't either, but we won't know what it's like until we try, will we?"

I shake my head as I collect the pieces of my bathing suit. "Okay, but if I end up falling off and bitten by a shark, I'll be blaming you."

He lets out a deep laugh as I enter the bathroom. "That's funny. I'll keep that in mind if I see any shark fins."

∽

In less than two hours, we're standing on the beach,

listening to the instructor tell us about our life vests and other jet-skiing information. Once we've strapped on our vests, we're taken to two sit-down jet skis. I choose the red one while Marcel takes the blue.

"Make sure you keep your hands on the handle bars at all times," the instructor, a young woman with a razor haircut named Yolanda, says. "And keep your feet on the foot rests. You can now start up your jet ski." She reaches forward to turn the ignition of mine on, and when it comes to life and vibrates beneath me, I let out a small yelp.

Marcel smiles way too hard about it as he starts his up.

I give him a playful stink-eye.

"All right, now we're going to *very slowly* push the throttle. I say very slowly because some people will press down on it and fall right off," Yolanda laughs. I push on the throttle, and the jet ski propels forward just a bit.

"Oh my gosh! Look! I'm doing it!" I scream.

"Good! Once you feel comfortable, you can increase your speed!" Yolanda yells after me.

After Yolanda assists Marcel, she goes back to get a jet ski for herself. Marcel meets up to me, grinning like a child who just scored a bucket of candy.

"What'd I tell you? You have nothing to worry about!" he yells.

I laugh then press on the throttle, giving the jet ski a little more speed. I don't give it too much, still warming up to the idea of this machine, but once I feel like I have the hang of it, I press on it a bit more.

Marcel has clearly gotten the hang of it, because he races past me, belting out a laugh as he does. I'm pretty sure he's done this before. He's too good at it.

If I weren't so afraid to fall off and get eaten by a sea creature, I would race him. Instead, I laugh and keep going. It's a lovely experience: the sun on my skin, the wind breezing by, droplets of the blue ocean water kissing my warm skin as I ride in circles.

I don't think I ever would have done something like this in my old life.

Yes, I say my old life, because that is over now. Kyle is in the past, and what I thought was a life with him was merely a prison.

But this—this is joy.

I watch the man I love riding on his jet ski, his grin stretching from ear to ear.

He's so damn handsome.

So full of life.

When our time is up, we head back to shore with Yolanda and unstrap our life vests. As I hit the shore, though, a slight wave of seasickness hits me. I cover my mouth and steady myself.

"Oh, yeah. If you need to throw up, just go right ahead. I've had many people do it after a jet ski ride," Yolanda announces with a little laugh.

I shake my head and hold it back as Marcel walks up to me, placing a hand on the small of my back.

"I'm okay," I assure him.

"You sure?"

"Yeah. I think I went a little too fast on that thing." I huff a laugh, and he wraps an arm around my shoulders, leading the way to the towels we laid down prior to jet skiing. He helps me sit, and I sigh as I lie down, glad my sunglasses are blocking most of the sunlight.

Marcel takes the spot beside me on his towel, his hands planted behind him as he watches the ocean. From where I lay, the roaring sound of the ocean is soothing. I close my eyes, hoping the seasickness will pass.

"That was fun though, huh?" he asks, and I hear the smile in his voice.

"Yeah, it was. I loved it."

"I'm gonna go in the water for a little bit." I look over, and Marcel is standing now. He drops a kiss on my forehead then walks toward the ocean. I watch him enter the water, showing off that chiseled body of his before dropping the back of my head on the towel again.

When twenty minutes have passed and the nausea doesn't let up, I stand up and walk to the ocean, where Marcel is standing with his hands on his waist at the shore.

"Hey, I think I'm gonna go back to the room. I'm still feeling sick."

He looks me over, concern swimming in his blue eyes. "Okay. I'll go with you."

After packing up, we make our way back to the hotel. I hit the shower first thing and lie down after changing clothes, feeling a little better.

"Take a nap. You'll probably feel better after." Marcel tugs a shirt over his head after his shower. "My sister used to get really sick from too much sun, believe it or not."

"Really? I've never heard of that. Hopefully I can sleep this off."

"Okay. I'm going to grab somethin' to eat. Want me to bring anything back? Somethin' to drink, maybe?"

"No, I'm good."

"Okay. Just checkin'." He grabs his hotel key card and heads to the door. "Rest up. I'll be back."

When he's gone, I sigh and close my eyes. But they pop right open again when another wave of nausea hits me. I push out of bed, running to the toilet, throwing up the delicious breakfast that I shared with Marcel this morning, only hours ago.

"Oh, God. What is going on?" I groan.

I stand, wiping my mouth with a towel. As I curl in bed again, though, a thought occurs to me, and that thought alone makes my heart drop to my damn stomach.

I reach for my phone, snatching it up and checking one of my apps.

"Holy shit," I breathe, sitting up straight. "Holy shit. No, no, no."

I scramble out of bed, sliding into a pair of flip flops and grabbing the spare hotel key and my wallet.

Marcel won't be back for a while, so I take the elevator down and rush through the lobby, going to the pharmacy across the street.

I grab a box of what I need, check out, then scurry back to my hotel, riding up to my room. Marcel isn't back yet and I'm relieved, but only for now.

I tear the box open before even getting to the bathroom, read the instructions, and do as told.

I wait several minutes, biting my thumbnail anxiously as I sit on the edge of the bathroom counter. When the timer goes off, I hop down and snatch up the pregnancy test.

I cannot believe my eyes.

## CHAPTER THIRTY-FOUR

### GABBY

*I'M PREGNANT?*

That's what the test says, but it has yet to register.

How? This can't be right.

*But your period is late*, my mind chants.

"Oh my God." I cup my mouth, staring at the test. As I gawk at it, I hear the door of our hotel open and close.

"Gabby?" Marcel calls.

"In the bathroom," I call back.

His voice is closer as he asks, "Everything okay?"

"Yeah." I try to keep my voice chipper, but it wavers and as if he senses it, he becomes quiet.

"Need me to get you anything? Maybe run to the pharmacy for some medicine?"

*Oh, I've already run to the pharmacy. Everything I need to know about what's going on with me is right in my damn hands.*

"No, I'm okay."

I throw the box away in the trash, making sure to cover

it with heaps of tissue. I wrap the pregnancy test up in a wad of tissue too, then tuck it in my sports bra.

I know I have to tell him. I can't continue this trip with him with something so heavy on my mind. He'll want to drink, and I'll turn the drinks down. He'll wonder why.

I open the door of the bathroom, and Marcel is sitting on the edge of the bed. He looks worried, or like he's thinking about something. He peers up at me when the door is open, and that worry vanishes as he stands.

"Everything okay in there?" he asks, stepping closer.

I twist my fingers, sighing. "Not really. Can we, um…can we take a walk?"

"Yeah, sure." He looks at me oddly. "We can walk somewhere. You sure everything's okay?"

I nod, but don't say much more. I change out of my shorts and into a pair of yoga capris, and Marcel leads the way out of the room.

We go to the beach, taking our flip flops off and carrying them. We walk in silence for a while, until Marcel sighs and caves. He hates when there's tension between us.

"Tell me what's goin' on, Gabby." My eyes shift up to his, and deep in them I see the worry again. "Are you not havin' a good time? Was the jet ski thing too much? I knew I shouldn't have booked it without askin'—"

"No—it's not that, I promise! I had fun doing that with you!"

"Then what is it? I can always tell when somethin's botherin' you."

"Okay. Look." I stop walking and reach for his hand so he can turn toward me. He's terribly confused, so I reach into my bra with the other hand, pulling out the wrapped pregnancy test.

He watches me unravel it, and when I reveal the stick, his eyes grow even wider.

"I have a period tracker app on my phone, and I checked it today. My period is late by a week and a few days. I ran to the pharmacy, grabbed this, and used it." I study his face, unable to gauge his reaction. Other than shock and confusion, I don't know if he's upset about this or what.

"I'm pregnant, Marcel."

## CHAPTER THIRTY-FIVE

**MARCEL**

"*Pregnant?*" The word comes out of me like I've been punched right in the gut. How the hell is that even possible? She's been on birth control for months now, way before she ever even met me. I remember the times she told me she needed to pick up her prescription.

"How is that possible?" I ask in utter disbelief. "I mean—I know how it happened, but…*how*? I thought you were protectin' yourself?"

She shrugs, her eyes glistening. "I don't know! I was taking the pill every single day!" She twists her fingers in her lap. "But now that I've had time to think about it, there were a few days I was a little late taking it. I got caught up at the art shop one week because things were crazy-busy and kept taking the pills late, but as soon as I realized, though, I took them. It was only a few hours after I was supposed to, so I didn't think it would be that bad."

"Damn." I plant a hand on my hip, still in shock.

"Are you mad?"

"What?" I focus on her gloomy eyes. "No, why would I be mad?"

"Are you sure?"

"I'm not mad, Gabby, I promise you. Just shocked, is all."

"I'm so sorry—I know it's too soon for all of this to happen! I didn't mean for it to, so I get it if you don't want it—"

"What?" I face her full on. "Are you kiddin' me? It's *my* baby, Gabby."

Her eyes grow wider. "But it's only been a year and a few months since we've met..."

"And I feel like I know enough about you to know you'd make a great mother, and we'd make great parents." I grab her hands, holding them tight. "Gabby, this kind of stuff doesn't happen for no reason. We did this, and we'll take care of it. I'm not mad. Honestly, I think I'm kind of glad about it. Don't know what that says about me, but I am."

She presses her lips and nods. "Are you sure? I just don't want to ruin your life. After everything we've been through, this will change so much." Her voice breaks.

I shake my head with a short laugh. "When will you get it, little thing? Not once have you ruined my life since you walked into it. You have *bettered* me in so many ways." Tears line the rims of her eyes. I bend down to kiss her belly. "I'm going to take care of my baby. I'm going to take care of *you*. The question is, are you ready for that?"

She chokes on a sob and a laugh. "I don't know, but as

long as you're with me, I know I'll be okay." She cradles my face in her hands. "I love you so much."

"I love you too, girl. To death."

It's true. I love Gabby so much more than I ever could have imagined. I have never fallen for a woman like this before, so hard and so fast. She is my world, and to know she's about to carry *my* baby changes *everything*.

This woman will become my true queen. She will have everything…which leads me to thinking that maybe it's not too soon for what I was originally planning to do today.

I dig in my pocket, pulling out the velvety black box that has been burning a hole in there ever since I left to grab some lunch.

The truth is, I didn't just go out to grab something to eat. I went because I had to figure out when and how to ask her. I wasn't sure if I should even ask so soon, but now that she's told me this, I can't pass the opportunity up.

She's confused at first, but when I bring the box up, she gasps. Soft gusts of wind whip at her hair and twist through mine as I open the box.

"I was thinkin' maybe it was too soon to ask you to marry me, but now that I know you're carryin' my baby, that means you'll have to deal with me for at least the next eighteen years of your life. Might as well make 'em count, right?" I smile up at her, and her brimming tears have fallen to her cheeks.

She pushes a hand through her hair. "Marcel? Are you serious?"

"As a heart attack."

She bubbles out a laugh then drops to her knees with me, cupping my face in her hands. "It's not too soon! It's not. This is just right," she promises, then kisses me wholly. "I can't believe this! How long have you had this?" she squeals.

"Well over two months now. Was waiting for the perfect time to ask." I take the diamond ring out of the box, sliding it onto her ring finger. "Hope you don't mind. I took one of your rings to the jeweler to make sure I had the right size."

"I can't believe this," she gasps, studying the ring.

"I told you from the beginning that I'm not goin' anywhere, Gabby, and I mean that. You stormed into my life like a hurricane and turned my whole world upside down, but only for the better. You're smart, beautiful, kind, and everything I never knew I wanted. I promise to devote the rest of my life to you, if you'll have me for that long."

"Yes," she cries out, smiling hard. "Yes! I'll have you for that long! I'll marry you!"

"Good, 'cause that ring wasn't cheap, and I'm pretty sure I can't return it."

We both break out in a loud laugh and then we kiss.

This kiss is powerful.

It's a kiss that binds and ignites us, our knees in the sand and our fingers in each other's hair, not giving a damn about who may be watching.

I just asked my dream girl to marry me, and she said yes. If anyone feels some type of way about that, then that's on them, but right now, this is how I show my appreciation.

I'm celebrating by having her in my arms.

I love this girl, and I truly do want her for the rest of my life.

She'll be carrying my child, and maybe another man

wouldn't want it to play out this way, but this news makes me happy as hell.

I've always wanted a family of my own, even more so after losing Shay. Knowing that I'll get to have that and more with Gabby completes me in ways that I can't even begin to describe.

# CHAPTER THIRTY-SIX

**GABBY**

**NINE MONTHS LATER**

I THOUGHT when Marcel asked me to marry him, that it would be the happiest day of my life.

But no.

The happiest day of my life is now, as I hold my sweet baby girl in my arms. She's so beautiful that I cried before the nurse even placed her in my arms.

After being in labor for twenty-six hours, I thought I wouldn't make it, but she came out screaming and letting the whole hospital know she was here.

Tears of joy slip down my cheeks as I study her button nose and bright eyes. They're green, like mine. Her cheeks are rosy, and she has a head full of beautiful brown hair, like her dad.

I am filled to the brim with unconditional love.

"Damn. Would you look at that?" Marcel steps beside me, looking down at her. "She's gorgeous." He looks at me, and I smile up at him. He plants a kiss on my lips then drops one on our daughter's forehead.

"You wanna hold her?" I ask softly.

He freezes a moment, studying the baby before looking up at me. He hasn't held her yet. I know he's nervous.

He nods, standing up straight. I offer him to her, and he takes her, cradling her to his chest. His eyes glisten as he stares at her with so much love. Seeing him like this makes my heart do crazy things.

"Wow." I know he's trying not to cry. He's avoiding my eyes, but when he looks up, I notice the sparkle in them. "I never thought this would happen for me."

"What?"

"Havin' my own kid," he says with a light huff.

I swear, he says some of the most innocent, swoonworthy things, and doesn't even realize it.

"Well, she's all yours. You've started a family now."

"Yeah," he says, voice breaking as he laughs.

He rocks the baby in his arms as the nurses clean me up and help me get situated. When they've left the room, he asks, "Still haven't come up with a name?"

I think on it. "I have that list of names, but after thinking about it, there is only one I want to go with."

"Which one?"

"Shay."

Marcel picks his head up, locking on my eyes, then a smile graces his lips and he lowers his gaze to the baby. "I love that," he murmurs. "Shay it is."

I can't even begin to tell anyone how great Marcel is

with Shay. He treats her like a princess. After we've left the hospital and are at home, he makes sure to come home early every day just so he can spend time with her and so I can get some rest.

My mom and dad visit the following week and stay for a whole week. Mamá helps me out a lot, and Dad is great when it comes to watching Shay while Mamá and I run our errands. Of course, Má is happy to have her first grandbaby. When she held Shay, she didn't know how to react, so instead she just cried for way too long.

Shay grows into a beautiful, bubbly baby. She's adorable and catching onto things way too quickly.

By the tenth month, I finally feel like I've got a handle on things. We have a routine, and I know her eating times and sleep schedule like the back of my hand now.

I guess it is true when they say—mothers know best. There are things I know about Shay that no one else would, like how I can tell she's going to be feisty, just like me.

When she can't have her way, she'll frown at me or her daddy and maybe even throw a cup. Marcel calls her a feisty little thing, and it only makes me laugh.

This motherhood thing is all so new, but I wouldn't trade it for anything in this world. In a way, Shay completes us. She completes Marcel the most, though.

After losing his mother, sister, and father at such a young age, he's always wanted to be surrounded by the love of family again.

I'm glad I am the woman who gave him that chance.

"So, guess what?" Marcel asks one night, after we've put Shay to sleep.

"What?"

"I booked us flights to Hawaii." He grins at me, and I sit up in the bed, looking him in the eyes.

"You're kidding!"

"Shh," he chuckles, looking sideways at Shay, who is in a crib in our room. "Yes, I booked flights and a nice little Airbnb cottage," he answers in a low voice. "I talked to your mother, and she said she'd be happy to watch the baby while we take a getaway. I told the guys I'm takin' off of work already and everything."

"Wow." I look at Shay's crib. "I'm a little nervous to leave her. How long will we be there?"

"About five days, give or take."

"That sounds amazing…but why Hawaii? Not that I mind—I've always wanted to go there, but it makes me nervous to go so far away."

"Well, I was thinkin' we could get married there…"

My eyes expand. I push up on my knees, climbing on his lap. "Wait…you're serious right now?"

"Dead serious."

I can't help the laugh that pours out of me. "Okay." I nod, capping his shoulders. "If you've already planned everything, let's do it."

"Okay." He leans forward, kissing me on the lips. "But I didn't tell your mom we'd be gettin' married. I want it to just be you and me. We can elope, spend time together. You don't want another big wedding, so we'll keep it simple."

Warmth coats me, my heart skipping a beat. "I love that." And I'm glad he kept that in mind. Marcel isn't the kind of man who'd want a big wedding either. He's a simple man, only needs the basics, and I appreciate that about him so much.

∽

Before I know it, Monday has arrived.

My parents have flown down, along with Ricky. They'll be watching Shay. She's absolutely spoiled by them, especially by her Uncle Ricky.

"Give me that baby," Ricky insists, collecting Shay in his arms as soon as he's walked through the door. "How's my pretty girl?" he coos to her. I smile as I watch her bite on her chubby little fingers while Ricky holds her in the air.

I'm pleased to say that Ricky has separated from Violetta. I guess he garnered the courage after my divorce with Kyle.

And speaking of Kyle—he lost the company. It is no longer Moore Investment Banking, but Rio Investment Banking.

Apparently, his colleague, and one of his dad's good friends, Taylor Rio, found false accounting reports and turned Kyle over to the board. Kyle resigned four months ago. I have no idea what he's doing now, and frankly, I don't give a damn. His mother had lots of money saved, and Dan still owns part of the company, so I'm sure he's mooching off of them, but deep down, it makes me happy to know that Karma came back and bit him right in his sorry ass.

"You guys all set?" my dad asks as we bring the last of our suitcases down.

"Yeah. So, make sure you feed Callie and take her for long walks. She loves walking," I tell my dad.

"Got it."

"And make sure Shay gets at least two naps in during the day. Don't let her get overtired, or she'll get fussy. And if she gets gassy, her gas drop are in—"

"*Ay dios mío*, Gabby! You've given me the rundown many times before! Don't worry! I've got this! You see I raised you two clowns, and you turned out to be just fine!" Mamá cackles, looking between me and Ricky.

"Yeah, I wouldn't necessarily brag about us, but okay." Ricky fights a laugh, still holding Shay, as Mamá slaps him on the shoulder.

"All right. Let's head out then." Dad has his car keys in hand and opens the door.

"Thank you guys for watchin' her," Marcel says gratefully. He goes over to Ricky, who still has Shay, and gives Shay a kiss on her forehead. "We really appreciate it."

"Yeah, thank you, guys." I take Shay from Ricky and hug her little body before kissing her cheek. "I love you!" I sigh, and she grunts, pressing a hand on my cheek and gently shoving. She's always trying to fight my hugs. Marcel swears I'm too affectionate, but it runs in my family. I can't help it.

I hand Shay back to Ricky and turn for the door.

"Enjoy your trip, and don't worry. We've got this," Ricky assures me.

I smile on the way out the door. Marcel presses a hand to the small of my back when I look over my shoulder again at Shay, ushering me outside.

"She'll be fine," he murmurs on the shell of my ear when we're outside.

"I know she will be, but it's my first time leaving her and it feels so weird."

"I know. It's weird for me too."

But we let the weirdness pass for now.

We're going to get married, and making our family official. Dad drops us off at the airport with hugs and farewells, and in an hour, we are boarding our flight, on the way to our destination.

## CHAPTER THIRTY-SEVEN

### GABBY

Hawaii is absolutely incredible, and even more gorgeous than any of the photos I've seen on the internet.

We're lodged in a beautiful Airbnb cottage on Poipu Beach. The cottage is colorful and cozy and only steps away from the beach.

From the master bedroom and even the kitchen, we have an ocean view, and waking up to it every morning never gets old.

For the better part of our trip, we are true beach bums. We lay around lazily on our towels, soaking up the rays. It does rain every so often, but the rain is peaceful as it taps on the roof of the cottage, especially during the moments when I need a much-needed nap.

On the second night, I drag Marcel with me to the pool behind the house. It's a small pool, perfect for a couple.

"If I get in this pool, you owe me," Marcel says, pulling his shirt over his head and revealing chiseled abs.

I smile then jump into the pool in my two-piece, doing a cannonball. Shay gave me so many stretch marks, but Marcel loves them, and I wear them with pride. Tiger stripes, I like to call them. I am pretty fucking fierce. No point in hiding them.

The cool water rushes over my head as I resurface, and Marcel is laughing, walking into the pool from the steps. "You're an animal."

I swim his way with a grin, lacing my arms around the back of his neck. Wrapping my legs around his torso, I drop a wet kiss on his lips. He deepens the kiss, cupping my ass in his hands with a savage groan.

The thing I love most about this cottage is that it is surrounded by so many bushes and tall trees. No one can see us unless we're on the beach, and of course, we take advantage of that.

Marcel moves to the pool wall, slipping my bottoms down effortlessly in the water.

He sucks on my neck as he lowers his swimming trunks enough to pull himself out. Then he's inside me, and a heavy, wet gasp rushes out of me.

"You'd think you'd be used to that by now," he says, vibrating with laughter.

"I don't think I will ever get used to it," I breathe on his lips.

"Good, 'cause I love taking your breath away."

Our lips connect again, and he fills me up steadily. Slowly. My fingers slide over his hair, dampening some of the strands. Our bodies are pressed so close together, I feel like it'll be impossible for anyone to separate us right now.

He makes sweet, tender love to me in this pool. I sigh

and pant, whispering his name in his ear. He clearly loves the sound of my voice, because I feel him grow harder inside me.

"Shit, baby. I'm about to come."

*So am I.*

He bounces me up and down the length of his cock. In the water, the movements are slow, but I still feel him in this angle. So big. So satisfying. He holds my ass even tighter, gripping like his life depends on it.

Then he sucks on my bottom lip, and I unravel.

I continue holding onto him as I release, and his body jerks and then stills as he moans, coming inside me.

"Oh, fuck, Gabby." He strokes my hair back with wet hands. "Love you. So much."

"I love you, too," I whisper, and we kiss again, this one the most powerful kiss of the entire night.

∼

Our third day in, Marcel surprises me.

He requested that I dress nicely, preferably in *white*. I already know what he's up too, but not quite sure what all he has planned. I take out the off-the-shoulder maxi dress I bought from a store I found online. It has lace trimming on the arms and the hem of the dress, and is amazingly comfortable.

After I style my hair, apply my makeup, and get dressed, Marcel says, "Come with me." He takes my hand, closing it in his, and leads the way out of the cottage. The sun is still setting, and the rain has cleared for the night.

"Where are you taking me?" I ask with a giggle as he

walks hand-in-hand with me through the path that leads to the beach.

He smirks over his shoulder. "You'll see."

I can't help smiling as we walk between a line of palm trees and sand covered in red and white rose petals that weren't there before. I can't fight my smile when I spot them.

*What is this man up to?*

When our feet hit the sand, Marcel turns to the left, and when I pick my head up after watching where I was stepping, I can't believe my eyes.

A trail of lanterns leads to the most romantic setup I have ever seen in my life. A white sheet is spread out on the beach at the end of the trail of lanterns. Red pillows top the sheets, placed in front of a long rectangular table. On top of the table are tall glass vases with candles flickering inside them, as well as plates and wine glasses set up for two. The romantic set up is surrounded by many lit candles in varying sizes of containers.

Marcel releases my hand as we near it, and I cup my mouth, my eyes automatically glistening.

Two servers appear with trays in hand, and they take what I assume is food to the table, covered with silver domes. They bob their heads at us and then walk away to a station nearby.

A Hawaiian man walks toward the setup with a Bible tucked beneath his arm and a smile on his face. He stands by an arch that is swathed in billowing, sheer white fabric, that I totally missed before. It's closer to the water, but there are candles by the arch too.

"Oh my God, Marcel," I gasp. "You did all this?"

Marcel shrugs and smiles. "It's just a little somethin'."

"Are you kidding me! It's perfect!" I rush to him, jumping in his arms. He catches me, and I crush his lips with mine. "I love it so much! Oh my God, it's so perfect!"

"This is a night I don't ever want you to forget." Marcel places me on my feet, holding my hand and walking to the man standing beneath the arch.

He greets us when we meet him then tells us to hold hands. As we do, I notice one of the men who brought the food has a camera in hand and is snapping pictures.

I can't stop smiling. I can't believe he set all of this up. He's definitely a hopeless romantic.

The candlelight shows the sparkle in Marcel's eyes. He has a sure smile on his lips as the man with the Bible speaks. Neither of us prepared vows, seeing as this was supposed to be a simple marriage, so he tells us what to say. Each line is a promise, my devotion to him. Marcel even has the rings we picked out, and we slide them onto each other's fingers.

And when he tells us to kiss, you better believe we kiss. Marcel holds me tight as I throw my arms around the back of his neck. I kiss my new husband so passionately and for so long. I kiss him like my life depends on it, because I do depend on him.

If it weren't for Marcel, I never would have walked away—never would have known this was out there, waiting for me.

If it hadn't been for this gorgeous man in my arms, I'm not sure I'd have found myself. But I did, and I found myself in him.

He wasn't just a man that scratched an itch. Since the moment our eyes connected, I was drawn to him.

Back then he was off limits. Back then, I was clueless. He wasn't a person I should have wanted, but none of that matters now, because he is here, and he is what I need.

Never have I felt a love so fierce. Never have I fallen so hard for someone whom I was never supposed to have, but I have him now, right here in my arms.

He's all mine, and I swear, I am never letting him go.

## CHAPTER THIRTY-EIGHT

**MARCEL**

I HAVE BEEN through so much shit in my life.

I lost everything at one point, and thought I'd never find happiness or even a family again....

Then I met Gabrielle Lewis, a woman whom I didn't even realize was going to change my life at the time."

She ended up getting under my skin, something not many people can do. I was the kind of man who could easily shrug off flirtations, or a faint feeling of lust, but with Gabby, it was a completely different ball game.

She stormed into my life and swept me right off my feet. Sounds cheesy as hell, but it's true, and it's the only way I can describe what she did to me. This woman changed my life for the better.

After getting married and sharing a delicious dinner, we went back to the cottage and made love several times. To be honest, I lost count. We have today and tomorrow left in

Hawaii, and I plan on cherishing these last two days and making her mine in every way imaginable.

I'm now lying on my back on a towel the day after our elopement, looking over at her.

She's resting with a hand behind her head, the other hand splayed on her belly, the gold wedding band shining on her finger. She is mine, no doubt about it. She's the mother of my child. I trust her with my life.

"Are you staring at me, Mr. Ward?" Gabby asks. Her eyes are still closed beneath her sunglasses, her lips curving upward.

"Damn right I am, Mrs. Ward."

Her eyes pop open, and she turns onto her side with a laugh. "Is there something I can help you with?"

I turn over too, smiling. "I think there is. How about we head back to the cottage and find out?"

Her eyebrows shift up in surprise. *"Again?"*

I laugh and push to a stand, then rush for her, scooping her up in my arms and dashing through the sand.

She squeals, holding onto me tightly as I run along the trail that leads to the cottage. I burst right through the door, kicking it shut behind me and tossing her on the bed in the room.

She wastes no time sitting up on her knees and pulling her top off. A low, hungry growl forms in my throat as I unlatch my swim trunks and step out of them.

My mouth lands on hers as I loop my fingers under the straps on the bottoms of her bathing suit. As soon as she's out of them and her bathing suit top, I pick her up off the bed, and guide her pussy down on my cock.

Her mouth parts wider, and for a moment I have to still inside her because she feels so damn good.

"I love you," she moans on my lips.

"I love *you*," I say through a ragged breath, then lift her up and back down again, clutching her ass tight in my hands.

She holds onto my shoulders, shifting her pussy up and down on my swollen cock.

"Let me," she breathes, and I spin around, landing on the bed with her on top of me. She plants her hands on my chest, and I swear she rides the fuck out of me. With her curly hair covering half of her face, and her beautiful tits right on display, I know I won't be able to fight my orgasm for much longer.

Lowering her upper body, she kisses my mouth, but doesn't stop lifting those hips to ride my dick. Her lips trail down to the crook of my neck, then up to my ear, her hair running feathery light over my cheek. I pulse inside her with each kiss.

"I'm close, Gabby," I groan, and I expect her to slow down, but she doesn't let up.

She continues, rolling her hips, grinding her pussy all over my dick. I swear, I never used to come so fast, but there is something about Gabby's pussy that drives me crazy.

Maybe because I know she's all mine, and I'm the only man who can come inside her. I'm the only man who can stake a claim.

Knowing that, I grip her ass, squeeze my eyes shut, and cum, right inside her slick, tight pussy.

"Oh, fuck, baby," I moan. The pleasure is indescribable.

She moans just as loud as she sits back up, planting her hands on my chest and finishing herself off.

Sighing, she slowly lifts off my cock and then rests her head on my chest.

"Your cock is magical," she breathes out.

"I could say the same about your pussy," I pant.

She rubs my chest as she catches her breath.

"Do you think we'll always be this happy?" she asks softly.

I stroke her hair back, sighing. "If we stay committed and keep the spark alive, I'm sure we can always find ways to be happy."

"What about when times are hard?"

I think on that a moment before answering. "Then times will just be hard. We've been through hard times before and got through it. I'm sure we can again." I tip her chin, putting her green eyes on mine. "We have to communicate, Gabby. You understand? That's the only way this marriage will survive."

"I know. And yeah, I understand."

"I know we started on a different path. We weren't supposed to want each other, but apparently we needed each other much more than we thought."

"Yeah," she murmurs. "I used to feel bad about it, but I guess I see it more as the universe aligning for us." She rests her chin on my chest, studying my eyes. "Since we're talking about communication, there is something I should probably tell you."

"What's that?"

"I...forgot my birth control at home."

I sit up with wide eyes. "You're serious?"

"Yes, but it wasn't on purpose, I swear!" she declares, sitting up too. "And I'm sorry I didn't tell you sooner—I just didn't want to ruin this trip for you. I was packing my stuff and getting Shay's things ready for my parents at the same time. I must have forgotten to grab them."

"And you're just now tellin' me on our fourth day?" I ask, laughing. "Gabby, what if you end up pregnant again?"

She shrugs and climbs on top of me again. "I guess I'll just be pregnant then, huh?"

"Lord, you must be tryin' to kill me. Shay's already a handful, you know that, right?"

"Yeah, she is, but we can handle her, and I hear the second kid is always easier."

"Holy shit!" I look her over and can't help grinning like a damn fool. "You've been thinkin' about this, haven't you?"

"Well, I mean, it wouldn't be bad if Shay had a sibling to grow up with, you know? Plus, you told me you've always wanted a family! What's one more?"

I break out in a laugh, grabbing her by the waist and bringing her closer. "Well, I gotta tell you, I don't even know how many times I've come inside you since we got here, especially last night. That pussy was mine for the takin'."

She bats her eyelashes, trying to give me an innocent, doe-eyed look. "Maybe it's meant to be?"

I grab her chin, bringing her mouth to mine. "Well, if that's the case, then I may as well let nature take its course, huh?"

"Mm-hmm," she says behind the next kiss. "I think you should."

I flip her onto her back, give her a passionate kiss, and thrust inside her again.

I don't give a damn about the birth control. Her pussy is *mine*. She's right about me wanting a big family. I do want one. Having another kid doesn't bother me one bit.

So, I fuck my wife in the cottage again, and yes, I cum inside her another time, this one feeling even more powerful than the last.

I make her mine many, many more times during our romantic getaway, because we're in this thing for life.

We might as well get used to the surprises.

# EPILOGUE

**Marcel**

*Three Years Later*

Becoming a father to one child took a lot of energy, but becoming a dad of *two* drains me completely.

I ask myself constantly, *what in the hell was I thinking, wantin' two of them?* Yet here they are, running around my backyard and climbing on the fence like wild little monkeys.

I guess I can't blame them. They haven't had the chance to get crazy all day because I've been cleaning and getting things ready for Gabby's party. It's August 20th. My wife's birthday. Mine just so happens to be a month from hers, on September 19th.

Eventually, we'll have to move to another house. The kids share a room right now, but they'll get older and need more space. This home of mine has been good to me, though.

My kids have filled the void in me. Before, I was so desperate to get to know the kid that didn't know me. I longed to meet him—and still do—but things are different now. These kids are everything to me. They've filled my heart with so many things. I can't even begin to describe the feelings.

Maybe one day I'll get the chance to meet Wylie Briar. Maybe not. All I know is I'm grateful for what I've got right now in this very moment.

"All right, kids, come inside! Your Auntie Teagan just called, said she's on the way back!"

Shay groans loudly as she slides down the curvy yellow slide of the playset I installed. Forrest, my two-year-old son, pushes off the fence, running my way.

"Daddy? Cake?" Forrest asks, his dark curls flopping as I pick him up. Shay runs right past me, straight into the kitchen, with Callie right behind her. Callie wasn't a fan of Shay at first, but as Shay grew, they became the best of friends.

"No cake yet. Come on, let's wash those dirty lil' hands." I carry Forrest to the bathroom, pumping some soap in his hands and washing the dirt off.

Shay bumps into me at the hip, yelling, "I need to wash my hands too!" as she sticks her hands under the stream of water. Forrest starts yelling, telling Shay to move and that it's his turn, and of course Shay, being the little spitfire she is (just like her mother), snaps back.

"Look—both of you better be quiet before I put you in

# THE MAN I NEED

your rooms. Then none of you will get cake," I warn, drying their hands off with a towel.

"No, Daddy! Please! I want cake! You promised I could have some!" Shay whines.

"Cake, Daddy!" Forrest whines after her, his eyes desperate and swirling with innocence.

I shake my head and fight a laugh. These kids, man. They're stubborn little things, but they're adorable, and don't even realize it. They look just alike with their tan skin and dark-brown hair. Shay has Gabby's green eyes and Forrest has my blue ones.

Forrest is our honeymoon baby. I guess nature did take its course because two weeks after the trip, she took a test and was pregnant. When I found out it was a boy, I wanted to do cartwheels. I've always wanted a son.

Now we have two little monsters running around the house, coloring on my walls, or falling off of shit and needing bandages. And don't even get me started on the fact that there are cartoons constantly playing on my living room TV now. Our lives are chaotic at best, but I wouldn't trade any of this, not even for all the money in the world.

I pick them both up with a grunt. "All right, let's go. I'm sure everyone will be here soon."

I place them down in the living room, where there are yellow and pink balloons scattered on the floor. I was only supposed to blow up five of them. Shay insisted I blow up the whole pack this morning. I'm surprised I'm not lightheaded right now.

A banner that says "Happy Birthday" is tacked to the wall in the living room and the table is set up with fruit and cake.

A knock sounds on the door and I go to it, checking the peep hole before opening it. Mr. and Mrs. Lewis are on the other side of it, charging in with big smiles.

"Hey, guys. How's it goin'?" I ask, greeting them.

"Good!" they chime in unison.

"Where are my babies?" Mrs. Lewis squeals, and Shay and Forrest start screaming their heads off. They love their abuela. That's what they call her, though they only say "Buela" instead of the full Spanish name. Gabby finds it so adorable.

"I was just about to put some hot dogs on the grill. Think you can keep an eye on these two rascals 'til I'm done?" I ask Mrs. Lewis.

"Of course!" She shoos me off playfully. "Go. I've got this."

"I'll come out and help you," Mr. Lewis insists.

He picks the package of hot dogs up and brings them outside.

"Everything goin' okay at the dock?" I ask as I turn the gas up on the grill.

"Oh, yeah. Never better. You know, Ricky created an Instagram account, and one of his posts got a lot of attention. He claims it almost went viral."

"Really?" I ask with a laugh.

"Yeah. There have been a lot of teenagers coming out to rent boats, picnic nearby, and so on. Business is great."

"I'm glad business is doin' good. Gabby tells me all about how proud she is of you guys."

"Hell, I'm proud of her." Mr. Lewis smiles, handing me the second pack of hotdogs.

After the hotdogs are grilled and placed on a platter, we head back inside, where we hear a car door shut.

"Oh! She's here!" Mrs. Lewis whisper-hisses.

"Just in time!" I clap my hands together. "I'll shut the lights off! Kids, go hide!"

The kids giggle as they run with their abuela to crouch behind the couch. Will stands behind the corner, and I move behind the door, hitting the switch for the lights.

The lock clinks, and as soon as the door swings open, everyone yells, "Surprise!"

Gabby gasps loudly, her hand on the heart of her chest. "Oh my goodness! You guys are insane! You almost gave me a heart attack!"

I can't help laughing. The look on her face is priceless. I start to reel her in for a hug, but she slaps me on the chest before giving in.

"I told you no party!" she laughs over my shoulder.

"I know, but I couldn't help myself. Plus, it's just a small one."

Gabby swings around to look at Teagan, giving her narrowed eyes. "You were in on this the whole time, weren't you?"

Teagan breaks out in a grin. "Oh, yeah. He gave me the rundown as soon as I landed, girl. Not only that, but I wasn't about to pass on a free spa day!"

"Mommy! Look!" Shay yells, running to Gabby with a wrapped gold package in hand. "I went with Daddy and got you a present!"

"Yeah, present!" Forrest yells, chasing after his sister.

"Oh, really? And what will I find inside? Let's go over

here and see." Gabby walks with the kids to the sofa and takes a seat.

It's no surprise that the kids tear the gift open before she can even get to it. We all laugh as they pull out the gift.

"It's a boring gift," Shay says with a shrug. "But Daddy said it's for Mommy to like, not me."

Gabby laughs at Shay's comment then cups her mouth when she flips the gift over.

I smile.

It's a painting I had one of her instructors at her studio make. It's a photo of all five of us—Gabby, the kids, Callie, and me.

"Wow." Her eyes glisten.

"You like it?" I ask.

She shoots to a stand, rushing my way and opening one arm to wrap it around the back of my neck.

"Are you kidding me? I love it! It's so thoughtful! And beautiful! Aliyah did such a great job on this!"

"She did. I paid her to do it. She knew you'd love it. She wanted me to tell you she's sorry she couldn't make it."

"Oh, that's okay. I can thank her later. I love it so much!"

She stands on her toes and kisses me. I return a kiss just as passionate. When she pulls away, her green eyes are glistening even more.

"I love you so much. Thank you for all of this—for everything."

"I love you too, little thing. More than you know."

And you know what? I do. This woman has given me her heart. She has given me my two beautiful children, whom I love unconditionally. My love for my kids is strong, and of a fierceness I thought was behind me when I lost my sister.

Her family has become mine too. She has completed me in ways I only ever dreamed of.

Happiness was once a useless word to me. It seemed unattainable, out of reach, but I realize *this is* happiness. Yes, there are misunderstandings, and a whole lot of chaos at times, but there isn't a day that goes by where I don't smile.

Without any of this, I am only half a man.

I love my kids.

I love my wife.

I love my *life*.

And I'm going to cherish every second of it for as long as I have left on this earth.

That is my promise.

This love story, although bumpy at first, is my truth, and I don't regret a damn thing.

## SPOILER GROUP

If you feel the need to vent, rage, scream or chat with other readers who have read *The Ward Duet*, please search Facebook for **The Man I Need Spoiler Group** to join.

# ACKNOWLEDGMENTS

These are always so hard for me to write. As you can see, I waited until the end of book two to pop this part of the writing process in there. There are so many people I am thankful for!

First of all, I am so grateful for my husband for supporting me through my publishing journey. Every year gets harder, and every year he is there for me every step of the way. I love you so much, baby!

Thank you Dani Fuselier for enduring all of my crazy messages and for sending me amazing critique for this duet. You are such an amazing friend and I am so, so thankful to have you in my life!

To MJ Fryer, thank you for being so great. I appreciate you taking time out of your schedule to help me better my craft. You are an incredible woman with a great heart and I hope I get to meet you one day and squeeze you so hard!

To Danielle Huffman, you know I love you dearly! You're such a good person and you've been with me every single step of the way! Thank you for always being a shoulder to lean on and one of my hardcore cheerleaders!

To my lovely PA, Autumn Gantz. I cannot express how much you mean to me. I am so unbelievably grateful for everything you have done for me and for taking so much stress off my shoulders. I'm not sure how I survived so long without you. Thank you for everything you do for me…but just so you know, you're stuck with me for life!

To Lucia Franco…you already know what you mean to me. Thank you for listening to my endless rants about life and books and writing. You are my girl, and I love you, OKURRR!

To Michelle Clay and Annette Brignac, thank you for all your hustle, hard work, and organization! You ladies are so amazing!

To my awesome Sweetheart ARC Team, Sweetheart Street Team, and Bookstaqueen Team, I am so grateful for all of you! They say it takes a village and y'all definitely showed up and made some noise for this duet! I love you all so much!

To my Naughty Sweethearts. Gah! You laides mean the world to me! Thank you for getting me pumped to share this story—and every story—and for loving it as much as you do! I know what I write isn't traditional romance, but you take it in stride anyway and you always seem to enjoy it! If you're willing to keep reading, I'll just keep on writing.

Lastly to every blogger, reader, author, and friend who took time to help me share this book with the world and to those who read the Ward Duet, thank you! Thank you for giving this taboo book a chance! Thank you for going on this wild ride with Marcel and Gabby and seeing it through to the end. I love you all so much and am so damn happy to have all of you in my life!

## FOLLOW SHANORA

**Feel free to follow me on Instagram under the username @reallyshanora! I am always eager to chat with my readers there!**

Join my Facebook Fan group! Just search for **Shanora's Naughty Sweethearts** on Facebook to interact with me and fellow Shanora lovers!

Join My Newsletter for exclusive updates and to know what I'm working on next by typing in this link: http://eepurl.com/dKXt-Y

Visit www.shanorawilliams.com for more book information and details.

# WHAT TO READ NEXT?

I have lots of books that I could share with you, but to make your life easier, I'm going to give you a few books of mine that are reader favorites and books that I loved writing. These should definitely hold you over until my next book!

If you love forbidden romances with age gaps, check out *Wanting Mr. Cane*, a juicy love story about a girl who falls for her dad's best friend.

Another juicy one is Dear Mr. Black, where a girl falls for her best friend's dad! Both are reader favorites and favorites of mine.

Trust me, the plots may seem scandalous, but I can guarantee you my forbidden romances are always full of emotion and angst.

If you love dark romances with a thriller edge, then my *Venom Trilogy* will cure any dark lover's craving!

Need something quick and hot to bide your time? Check out my *Nora Heat Collection!* All of the Nora Heat stories are quick, easy, blazing hot reads!

**WHAT TO READ NEXT?**

The rest of my standalones are filled with angst and lots of emotions and you can find them on my website here or flip to the next page and take your pick. Enjoy!

# MORE BOOKS BY SHANORA

### WARD DUET
THE MAN I CAN'T HAVE
THE MAN I NEED

### CANE SERIES
WANTING MR. CANE
BREAKING MR. CANE
LOVING MR. CANE
BEING MRS. CANE

### NORA HEAT COLLECTION
CARESS
CRAVE
DIRTY LITTLE SECRET

### STANDALONES
TEMPORARY BOYFRIEND
MY FIANCE'S BROTHER
DOOMSDAY LOVE

SHANORA WILLIAMS

<u>DEAR MR BLACK</u>
<u>FOREVER MR. BLACK</u>
<u>INFINITY</u>

**SERIES**
<u>FIRENINE SERIES</u>
<u>THE BEWARE DUET</u>
<u>VENOM TRILOGY</u>

*Most of these titles are available in Kindle Unlimited.*
*Visit www.shanorawilliams.com for more information.*

Printed in Great Britain
by Amazon